THE SUBSEQUENT WIFE

THE SUBSEQUENT WIFE

Priscilla Masters

**SEVERN
HOUSE**

First world edition published in Great Britain and the USA in 2021
by Severn House, an imprint of Canongate Books Ltd,
14 High Street, Edinburgh EH1 1TE.

Trade paperback edition first published in Great Britain and the USA in 2022
by Severn House, an imprint of Canongate Books Ltd.

severnhouse.com

British Library Cataloguing-in-Publication Data
A CIP catalogue record for this title is available from the British Library.

ISBN-13: 978-0-7278-5059-1 (cased)
ISBN-13: 978-1-78029-798-9 (trade paper)
ISBN-13: 978-1-4483-0537-7 (e-book)

All Severn House titles are printed on acid-free paper.

Typeset by Palimpsest Book Production Ltd.,
Falkirk, Stirlingshire, Scotland.
Printed and bound in Great Britain by
TJ Books, Padstow, Cornwall.

ONE

I blame Stella, to some extent. She drew attention to my single state, encouraged me to take this course. She was supposed to be my best friend but her bird's-eye view on *my life so far* was making me seethe.

We were on our fourth glass of red wine when she started. 'If only you could meet a decent man, Jenny,' she said in that irritatingly reedy voice. She took another sip while I waited for the next dart. 'I mean, so far your romances have been a disaster, haven't they?'

I scanned the wine bar and didn't fancy my chances tonight.

'Let's face it, Jen,' she continued. 'There's no talent around Stoke. They're all married and on the cheat or else a load of wankers, or they wouldn't notice you unless you were an actual football.'

I followed her scan of the wine bar. Carefully and slowly, 360 degrees, all the way around the wine bar. The lights were dim with strobes flashing around the room like lightning strikes, illuminating for seconds at a time even the darkest, dingiest little corner (which looked full of suspicious creeps and/or surreptitious snoggers), so a proper detailed survey was a bit tricky. But I could vaguely make out a couple of porkers, bellies on knees, thick thighs manspread wide on high bar stools, slurping down pints with all the manners of pigs at the trough who haven't seen food for a couple of months, banging their glasses on the bar to get the barman's attention. A definite no-no. Nothing there.

I moved on. There were a couple of gays holed up in the corner, looking lovey-dovey. I smirked. No chance there either. Another movement brought into focus numerous couples so absorbed in each other they could have been anywhere – from the sinking *Titanic* to the Costa del Sol to here, in the seediest wine bar imaginable in downtown Hanley. *Get a room*, I was tempted to shout over. But they wouldn't have heard me anyway. Not above the thump-thump of the music and the racket of everyone bellowing at each other as though we were in a home for the deaf.

I scoured the other corner.

That held a clump of marauding males, all muscles and tattoos, red-and-white-striped Stoke City shirts, and I could smell their aftershave from across the room. They looked a bit hot and ready for me. I'd had my fill of hot and ready men. Women are on the lookout for them just as they are on the lookout for fresh meat. Hot men get nicked from right under your nose. It's happened to me a time or two, going to a party as half of a couple and wandering home alone, sobbing and without a lift. I turned away from them.

I've tried the internet too and that turned out to be a waste of time.

3 × Boring

10 × Waste of time

and 2 × Bloody Scary.

If I was to change my life, I needed to do something drastic.

I'd finished searching the wine bar for talent and was back to Stella knowing she was right. The answer wasn't here. So where was it? The life I wanted. Home, husband, baby – in that order. Maybe it was more precious to me because I idealized something I'd never really had.

I leaned in a bit closer so she could actually hear what I was saying over the thumpety-thump of the base, which vibrated the entire floor as though we were having an earthquake. Stoke has had a couple of minor earthquakes. Caused by the extensive coal mining, so they said. But maybe it was more to do with the bass thumping out of places like this.

'To tell you the truth, Stell,' I confided, 'I'm having serious doubts there even *is* a Mr Right for me.'

'Nonsense,' she said. 'There's a Mr Right for everyone. You're not looking hard enough, Jen. And you're not looking in the right places.'

'Where are the right places?'

She looked put out. 'I don't know,' she said, slightly irritated. 'You just bump into them.'

I persisted. I was not about to let her off the hook. 'Where?' I said again.

'Work?' she tried.

I almost guffawed at that. 'Work? At The Stephanie Wright Home for the Bewildered? That's how I met David Ganger. And look what happened there.'

Flushed with my job and – sort of – home, I'd had a certain confidence. I was eighteen years old then and a size eight. My hair was striped like a tiger on heat, straightened, down to my shoulders, little flicks at the side, and the night I met him I'd got my make-up just right. What I'm saying is: I was hot. And I knew it.

I'd met David at the same place where Stella and I had worked. Just after I'd left school with my 'disappointing' GCSE results, she and I had started work at The Stephanie Wright Care Home for the elderly infirm. We called it The Home for the Bewildered because that's what they were. It was full of sweet, middle-class old biddies and retired army blokes. David's granny was a patient there. She had dementia but you could tell she'd been a lady. Once. She had a refined way of talking and nice manners – most of the time.

Only recently she'd developed a habit of resorting to bad language if she didn't get her own way. Like, 'Where's my fucking cup of tea?'

It sounded funny in her posh accent, but I resented being called, 'You ridiculous little slut.' However, I grinned and bore it – for David's sake. But even I found it hard not to react when she had a real nasty temper tantrum and actually reached out with her bony hands, smacking and pinching anyone in the firing line. Maybe that should have warned me that her grandson could carry the same nasty gene.

But . . .

David was a gorgeous-looking guy. Tall, well built, *very* good looking. A few tattoos here and there but nothing excessive. No *Cut Here* or *Love* and *Hate*. He had nice brown eyes, very smooth skin for a bloke and a cheeky, challenging grin. He worked as a mechanic at his father's garage and drove a really cool sports car. Postbox red. He was a catch. Unfortunately, I wasn't the only girl who thought so. There was a whole string of them, like pearls on a particularly long and decorative necklace, and he liked to spread himself around a bit. But the worst thing about David was that he was a really good liar. Even when I caught him out, chatting away to someone on the phone, responding to texts with *that look* in his eye, he could look right back, square on, and swear it was a mate from work. It didn't sound like that to me. But because his lovely brown eyes looked into mine with such 'sincerity', I believed him – at first.

He was smart too. His girlfriends. Correction. His *other* girlfriends were all listed in his phonebook under fella's names – I was 'Dean', I found out later. There were always a lot of unanswered calls and wrong numbers on his phone. It was only when a girl called Whitney called me one day and asked me what the hell I was doing with her guy that the penny finally dropped. Whitney came round while he was at the gym and she and I sat down on the sofa with his phone that I'd nicked earlier when he'd been in the shower. 'Brian' turned out to be Amanda, Whitney was 'William', a girl called Fallon was listed as 'Fred', and so on.

I didn't want to dump him, and when he assured me that he was done with playing around I really wanted to believe him. But in my heart of hearts I suppose I knew. He was a cheat and always would be.

He had his grandmother's nasty temper too and that night, for the first time, he blacked my eye and thumped me in the tummy. It hurt for days and I plotted my revenge. I didn't have to actually do it myself. All I had to do was ring round and explain just what David's little tricks were. I'd sensed Whitney had a bad streak in her (she'd cursed and threatened vengeance with a degree of heat), and I was right. She took a knife to him and poor old David had to have a colostomy because she'd sliced through his bowel. That was all I'd had to do. Make the right call. Sometimes it's that easy to get even.

I didn't go to see him in hospital. In fact, I never saw him again.

'I don't think The Stephanie Wright Care Home is going to supply Prince Charming,' I said.

'Well, change jobs then,' she said crossly, and slammed her wine glass back on the table. 'Go somewhere where you will meet men. Decent men.'

I leaned back on my bar stool, sensing hostility now, watching her through my extended and thickened, rather heavy false eyelashes. I wasn't sure I wanted this lecture.

I was going to hear it anyway. She sniffed but patted my hand. I was forgiven. 'You're only twenty-one, Jen. I know you desperately want your own family but there's plenty of time to find a good man.' But then, just to spoil it, she couldn't resist spending the next fifteen minutes expanding on the subject of my past failures which compared so unfavourably with her smug married state.

I went home despondent.

TWO

All the way home I sat on the bus, staring out through the window, reflecting on my life so far. Stella's words had raked up the past as though it was a muck heap on a farm, harbouring flies and rats and unholy diseases.

I had been on my own for eight months after David and I had 'split up'. It was a turbulent time for me. Actually, the past six years had been a turbulent time for me. When I was fifteen my Dad had moved out, planting the seed of destruction and abandonment deep in my perception of the male sex. He'd been cheating on my mum. Actually she'd been cheating on him too. I'd suffered years of shouting and bitter arguments ever since I was born. I used to stuff cotton wool in my ears, but I could still hear it all the time. I tried to bury my head in fairy tales, focusing on the Prince Charmings and blissful Happy-Ever-After creations of fiction writers. Things at home got particularly bad, erupting into noisy slaps, screams and punches while I was trying to scrape a couple of GCSEs. God knows where they were going to lead but there you are. The atmosphere at home was toxic, erupting into homelessness when I was fifteen, which is why I fluffed my exams, leaving Miss McCormick, my English teacher 'very disappointed'. 'You were my big hope,' she'd said sadly, 'one of the reasons I teach. To help children from deprived backgrounds climb out of the bearpit. You have the *ability* to study at university but you've made a mess of things, Jenny.' After that I couldn't ever face her again; neither could I face school. I was recast from victim to disappointment.

There had never been a realistic chance of my passing A levels and I certainly couldn't go to university. I blamed both my parents for this. Selfish mother. Selfish father. They got divorced soon after and both got involved with their paramours. They didn't find much happiness there either. And they forgot about me.

So back to that rainy evening and the Four Seasons Wine Bar. You see I was a ripe apple, ready to drop from the tree, lie on the grass, and be attacked and assaulted by slugs and wasps until I rotted.

I decided I would change jobs.

THREE

Two months after the night at the wine bar, I left the nursing home where I'd worked since leaving school. An old lady had aimed a particularly smelly fart in my face when I was wiping her bottom after a large bowel movement before pulling up her drawers. And that was that. I'm not a proud sort of person but even I don't think I was put on this earth to have old ladies blow off right in my face. So I pinched the offending anatomy hard and before I could change my mind marched to the matron's office and gave in my notice. Which left me with an obvious problem.

I'd been there almost five years. I didn't have a job to go to, no savings (you're having a laugh, right?); as I'd walked out I would not be entitled to unemployment benefit. And to top it all I had no references. Neither did I have a bank of mum and dad. They had gone their separate, selfish ways.

I lived in a flat – all right then, I lived in a rented room in a two-bedroomed terraced house in a lovely little village called Brown Edge. It might not sound much, but Brown Edge looks over one of the most beautiful valleys in the world and if you climb out of it you are instantly in the Staffordshire Moorlands. Aka heaven. High, exposed moorland, Staffordshire's response to the Brontës. I shared the house with a young couple called Jason and Jodi who were struggling to manage their mortgage so had advertised a room to rent. My £300 a month kept their heads just floating above water. I started off happy there. They were a nice couple. Quiet. No rows, tantrums or breaking glass. But I had a horrible feeling they were thinking of starting a family, which would lose me a very nice room of my own with a view across heaven's valley, a view at one time threatened by a Mr Budge, who'd wanted to churn the whole valley up for open-cast mining. He failed in his bid. So it was still a green and pleasant land. My room wasn't big but it was square, had a wardrobe, dressing table and chest of drawers and, best of all? That view, better than any picture! And it was only a short downhill walk across fields to the Greenway Bank Country Park: two pools and the source of the River Trent. On hot days an ice-cream van parked on the bridge.

But having made the snap decision to walk out of The Stephanie Wright Care Home, I had a problem. No job, no money and imminently no home, because Jodi and Jason would soon be wanting the next month's rent. They were tight for money and would easily be able to rent my room to someone who could afford to pay. Who hadn't walked out of their job.

So my new priority was to find work. But I had another problem. Or more truthfully, a whole collection of problems. I had no qualifications and now I had no references either. As I trudged back along the streets and through the rain to the terraced house, I wondered what my future was, how I was going to manage. Mr Micawber's belief was that 'something will turn up'. Yeah. I had that belief too, except in my case whatever came along would be all bad. Even the things that started off good turned sour. The apple falls off the tree only to rot on the ground.

I fretted and worried for two days, sitting in my room and staring out across the valley. As though I was going to find inspiration there. Then I went to the Job Centre in Hanley. The ginger-haired woman, shapeless and somewhere in her forties, looked me up and down. 'So you just walked out of your job as a healthcare assistant?'

I nodded and wasn't going to confide in her the reason why.

She sniffed. 'So what sort of work are you looking for?'

'I don't want to work in an old folks' home,' I said and looked at the floor. There were scuff marks where people must have sat, wanting a job and kicking the floor when one wasn't forthcoming. At least nothing that anyone who had a choice would want.

But, of course, I didn't have a choice, did I? It was a job or back living on the streets.

'What skills do you have?'

I could have answered honestly or dishonestly. I chose the middle road. 'I'm hard-working and honest.'

She waited.

'Do you have basic maths and English?'

I was insulted. I wanted to say, *my English teacher wanted me to go to university*. But what did that mean? Nothing.

I just nodded.

After filling in lots of forms online, I left feeling even more dejected.

And then for once in my life, Mr Micawber was right. Something did turn up.

And the nicest thing of all? It resulted from an almost single, certainly isolated instance of my kind heart. Hah! Actually, more to do with the boredom of sitting in a small, cold (no heating in the day) room, watching my life trickle down the plughole. I didn't want to go back on the streets and neither did I want to return to The Stephanie Wright Home for the Bewildered, even if they would have me. But unless I paid my rent in two weeks' time, I would be out on my ear. I hadn't told Jason and Jodi I didn't have a job any more. When I hadn't headed off for work I'd just said I was owed some holiday.

So . . . back to the 'good turn'.

One of my mates, Bethan Standish, was pregnant and feeling sick all the time. Not just in the morning but all day long. And, to be honest, far from 'blooming', she looked bloody awful. White, peaky, depressed. Her kid's dad wasn't bothered. So long as he had a few pints inside him he wasn't bothered about anything. So I took her to see her GP who was in the health centre in Tunstall. There was a bit of a wait as she didn't have an appointment and I got bored and fidgety just hanging around. Besides, it wasn't *me* wanting to see the doctor, so I went for a little wander round the shops then walked around the corner. And what did I spy but a huge fibreglass model – something tall, long and green. Very green, almost iridescent.

The Green Banana Storage Facility. The banana fibreglass model was six feet high at least. There was no mistaking its logo. Huge metal gates stood open to a yard, an office to the left and some roller shutter doors at the front and both sides. It looked industrial and somehow exciting. Different from a care home. A couple of vans and lorries were parked up, cars too, and people, mainly men, were loading and unloading stuff. It looked busy and interesting and industrial. I watched for a while, intrigued and curious. What, I wondered, did people store in here? As I stood in the entrance, a skinny woman came out to have a fag and she grinned at me. Simple as that. Instead of someone telling me to fuck off or farting in my face or asking me, with a sour face, what skills or qualifications I had, she actually smiled at me. A proper, warm, welcoming smile. And I don't see many of those. She even raised her free hand in greeting and looked friendly, which made me very bold. I also admired the fact that she was dressed in a red leather biker jacket, skintight black leather trousers, high-heeled black leather boots and gold chandelier earrings. Her hair was a tumble of black curls. She was a stunning picture.

I smiled back and held up my hand in a vague returning wave then spoke. 'Hi.' I walked up to her. Now I don't smoke myself but I can manage a few drags when offered one. And that's what happened then. Friendly as anything, she offered me a fag. And I accepted. We'd bonded. She looked round the place with the sort of pride mums extend to their firstborn. 'Not a bad set-up, is it?'

'No,' I said, disliking the taste of the tobacco but reluctant to chuck away this sign of friendship. 'It looks good to me.'

'Thanks.'

I looked carefully at her. She was about . . . I'm not good at ages. Maybe forty? She was one of those women who look much older than their age. Smoked a lot. She had really bad teeth, chipped and irregular, nicotine stained with plenty of fillings. It was her one main flaw. She was also quite wrinkled. Very suntanned with her long black hair, which I now realized was dyed. It was too dull, too black. I decided then that she could be a Traveller, which gave her a sort of romance – in my eyes at least.

'Me and my old man,' she said then, flicking her ash into the raised flower bed. 'We set it all up between us, you know. Saw a gap in the market. Nothing else like this round here.'

'Gosh,' I said, acting more impressed than I really was and dragging up a word I hadn't used for a while. 'Quite the entrepreneurs.' I glanced at the tall green object.

She nodded proudly, then drew out another fag. 'We are that,' she said. 'It was a patch of derelict land. Long time ago it was an old potbank. We cleaned up the site and . . .' she waved her hand around, wanting me to take it all in, 'this is the result.'

She sucked in a welcome and necessary lungful of smoke. 'Making quite a bit of money, we are,' she said. 'Never realized there was so much dosh in . . .' She waved long red vampire's fingernails, 'storage facilities.'

'Really?' I tried to sound well impressed. And interested. 'What sort of stuff—' I never got to finish.

'Oh. Anything people just don't want to get rid of. Hang on to their stuff, you know.' She puffed out her scrawny chest. 'Dead relatives' house contents, businesses that haven't got room, stuff while houses are being done up or when people are decorating or have sold up.' She gave me what I would soon learn was one of her 'little philosophies'. 'Our business,' she said, waving her fag in my direction, 'depends on people not liking to chuck stuff away. Worried that at some later date they'll regret it. Course we've had to work twenty-four seven.' She looked at me then, black eyes suddenly sharp and shrewd. 'Six days a week.' She took another hard drag on her cigarette. 'It's been tough. But now – well the money rolls in. Month on month.' I liked the sound of that. Money rolling in, month on month.

She stubbed her cigarette out between two purple pansies and burst out laughing. 'Reminds me of our holiday in the Caribbean. We were going to call it The Pink Banana,' she said, rocking with the joke. 'But we thought the logo might cause offence.'

I laughed with her, looking at the huge model, its colour a lurid shade of lime. 'I prefer The Green Banana,' I said, and she looked pleased, scrutinizing me with a stare.

Which was replaced by a grimace. 'Never realized it was so much work though. Long hours. A real tie. Always here, you know. Forget I've got a home sometimes.'

Which gave me an idea. I imitated her action with my cigarette. I figured if it was OK for her to chuck her fag into the pansies then it was OK for me too. Then I jumped in with both feet.

'I bet you'd like some time off. A holiday, maybe. The Costa del Sol?'

She looked at me hard then. Stared right through me. It felt like she was stripping me back to the bone like an X-ray machine. She said nothing for a moment but I could tell she was thinking this one through quite carefully. Then, 'Are you after a job?'

'Could be,' I said carelessly. It doesn't do to sound too desperate.

She scrutinized me a bit more then: 'Can you work a computer?'

'Yeah,' I answered casually. 'Course I can.' I drew my smartphone out of my jeans back pocket and wafted it in front of her eyes.

She skewered me with her stare then. 'Are you honest?'

I answered that question by giving her my warmest smile and simply nodding – slowly – to give it gravitas. Another half-forgotten word dragged into service.

'We–ell,' she started. 'It can be quite boring here.'

I lifted my eyebrows indicating, *And I care?* Truth was, I can cope with boredom better than most. I have books. And a smartphone.

She frowned. 'It's very variable. Some days people are coming and going all the time. Others – well – nothing.'

Out of the corner of my eye I could see strong, muscled, working men shifting heavy stuff, shouting to one another.

I looked back at her. It would do. At least it was better than The Stephanie Wright Care Home. I wanted to know what the wages were but she hadn't got there yet.

'Are you happy to work here alone, in the dark, Saturdays too? It can be quite lonely. And you'll have to lock up after you. It's quite a responsibility.'

I nodded, still tucking the question away: *How much?*

She drew in a deep breath. 'I'll have to ask Andrew, my partner, see if he's happy for me to take you on.'

I nodded my agreement and mentally crossed my fingers that she didn't ask for references.

She held out her hand and her face cracked into another wide smile, sending her wrinkles folding into her face. 'I'm Scarlet.' I didn't dare risk, *O'Hara?* She'd probably heard it before. 'Come back,' she said, 'this evening at six o'clock, and we'll have a chat.'

I liked the sound of this.

She paused before reiterating. 'We work long hours. Weekends too. And it can be quite spooky here.' She giggled. 'Even I find that.'

'I don't mind spooky.' *What do you pay?*

'There's usually the two of us here but if Andrew has to work away and I need a day off you could be here on your own.' She was still sounding dubious. 'A lot.'

'I'm OK with that.'

She still wasn't convinced. 'We'll have to have a trial period.'

'Yeah. Course.' I was a bit concerned she seemed to be back-pedalling.

And then the sweetener came. 'But if you suit we can afford to pay you well over the minimum wage. And if you're reliable there's bonuses too. We're not mean,' she said. 'And there's just the two of us.'

I tried another smile that was meant to say, companionably, *Just the three of us now.*

I came out of there walking on air. This was surely better than working for minimum wage at The Stephanie Wright Care Home – even if it was for 'gentlefolk'. Their farts smell the same as anyone else's.

I went back to the doctor's surgery to find Bethan looking a bit happier. The doctor had given her advice but no tablets.

'Stop smoking, eat dry toast in the morning and don't touch alcohol,' she recited like a catechism. Then added, 'He said it would wear off in a couple of weeks.'

'Oh, that's good,' I said, summoning up every available ounce of cheerfulness.

Her good mood didn't last. Her face darkened. 'And that was all he said,' she related angrily, practically steaming with indignation. 'Warned me that Thalidomide used to be given for pregnancy sickness and did I want to give my child bud limbs. Course I bloody well don't.' She stamped on ahead.

Wisely I didn't comment further, instead piping up with my own bit of news. 'I have an interview for a job this evening so you'll have to go back to Stockton Brook on your own.'

'Charming,' she said, really fed up now 'Thanks a bunch. Some people are soooo selfish.' And she stalked off. But don't worry. I have seen her since. We've made up and seven months later she had a gorgeous little girl called Charlotte.

With no bud limbs but perfect, chubby little legs and arms.

Her partner, Neil, left her just after the birth.

I had a few hours to kill before my interview so I went for a coffee in the town then wandered around the clothes shops, knowing I couldn't afford any of it – even the stuff in the charity shops looked out of my price range. I was tempted to nick a smart blue dress but resisted. Even Scarlet wasn't going to tolerate me with a court case hanging over my head. I wanted to get a job, get out there, into what I saw as the real world, the business community. I wanted to meet people, do something else with my life. I returned to The Green Banana Storage Facility.

Andrew turned out to be a slight guy, a bit weedy, younger-looking than Scarlet and with none of her fiery character. He was dressed in scruffy, loose-fitting jeans with a rip through the knees and a grey sweatshirt with a paint stain on. His trainers had seen better days too. I felt my face drop. He didn't exactly look prosperous. But, on the plus side, he had nice brown eyes and a quiet, polite voice with hardly a trace of an accent. When he spoke he reminded me of Helen McCormick, my lovely English teacher. There was something – not posh, but refined – in the way he spoke. He had a nice face too. Kind. Gentle. He shook my hand and invited me through the double doors into a light square office, painted white, sparsely furnished with a desk, a phone and a computer, overlooked by a bank of CCTV screens. No colour, just black and white or rather grey.

We sat down around the desk and Andrew got straight down to business. 'Scarlet said you were after a job,' he began, watching me carefully for my reaction. I felt there would be no pulling the wool over his eyes.

I nodded.

'So what work have you done before?'

I said I'd 'filled in time' working in a care home, but at school I'd studied IT and English. Then, for some reason, I told him something I'd told no one. Not even Miss McCormick. 'I was hoping to be a journalist,' I said.

He looked interested, *almost* impressed, but certainly not dismissive of my ridiculously lofty ambition. 'Really?'

I nodded, feeling pretty stupid now and wishing I hadn't shared that. I had as much chance of fulfilling this dream as being selected to be the next woman on the moon. But Andrew was someone I instinctively felt I could trust. And I sensed sympathy.

But he wasn't going to leave it there. He half smiled and pinned me with a gaze. 'If that's your ambition, why haven't you pursued your dream?'

I find this sort of talk makes me uncomfortable. I have a stack of becauses . . .

I have no money
I flunked out of school
I wouldn't fit into a posh uni
I'd stick out like a sore thumb
And the real reason?

Apart from that fact that I wouldn't fit in with the really clever geeky sorts, the ones who speak with plums and greengages in their mouths and don't come from damaged broken homes. Haven't lived on the street for a while, washing and donning school uniform in public toilets. Cold and frightened at night, searching for somewhere warm, somewhere safe. And tired. Always tired.

Truth? I was afraid. Some dreams are better left as dreams. Because then they can never disappoint.

Scarlet was watching me with wide-open eyes and mouth, as though she could log into my thoughts. Andrew was still waiting for my response. I knew this job depended on my answer. And what I sensed was this. I needed to be honest. Not too honest. But they needed to be able to trust me.

'I couldn't afford it,' I said simply. 'What with tuition fees and—'

Scarlet chipped in. 'What about your mum and dad? Wouldn't they have helped you out?'

I closed my eyes against the memory of my parents. When I thought of them I heard screaming and anguish, broken glass and china, furniture breaking, material tearing, hiding, being frightened, believing it was somehow my fault though I never worked out how.

Substituting. 'Things weren't great at home.' Meaning Mum off with her new guy and dad – who knew where? Last I heard, Thailand. 'There was no chance of them funding me.'

I wished I could leave it at that. I could have kicked myself.

Why did I always feel ashamed saying this when it wasn't *my* fault? It was *theirs*. Getting so bogged down in their own messy problems meant neither could help me with mine. They didn't even notice me. And my younger brother, Josh, had been delighted to see me fall. He'd always been jealous of me because I had a brain and he didn't. He was three years younger than me and he'd never got over the fact of having a clever big sister.

I just shook my head.

'Couldn't you have been a . . .' Scarlet looked at Andrew for inspiration.

'Cub reporter,' he supplied. Again, I shook my head. 'I wouldn't have got near a job on a paper.' I looked at the floor and omitted to mention my period of homelessness. Or the fact that I'd failed most my exams. That I was a disappointment.

Scarlet and Andy did some of that silent eyebrow communication that couples do, tilting their heads to the side. I thought they'd send me out while they discussed me but they both nodded. And finally grinned, and Andrew put a friendly hand on my shoulder. He had a chip in one of his front teeth which gave him a vaguely roguish look and his hair, dark brown, was a little long and looked amateurishly cut with a fringe that flopped wonkily over one eye. 'You can work the computers, Jennifer?'

I nodded.

'*And* the cash machine?'

Again I nodded, hoping it wasn't too complicated and thinking what I didn't already know I'd soon learn.

'Plus keep an eye on all these?' He waved a hand in front of the bank of screens.

'Yes,' I said, watching a couple of fit blokes lifting a table in through the shutter doors as though it was an old Laurel and Hardy film, black and white, with no sound.

Andrew glanced at Scarlet and nodded. Then they both smiled.

'You don't mind working Saturdays?'

'No.'

'Your boyfriend won't mind when you're busy on a Saturday?'

'I haven't got a boyfriend.' I would have liked to make a little joke out of this sad statement, say that I'd given them up for Lent or some other witticism, but for once I held my tongue. I wanted this job. I wanted to be in this world I saw as exciting and different, something earthy and business-like. Meeting people other than 'The Bewildered' or the spiteful staff at The Stephanie Wright 'Care' Home. I liked Scarlet with her Traveller air and casual attitude. And Andy seemed like a decent sort of guy.

I held my breath, waiting for them to ask for references, which could have been a bit of a problem, but they didn't.

'OK,' they said simultaneously. 'We'll take you on a month's trial. If all goes well and you settle into the job and like it, we'll put you on a proper contract.'

And even before I'd said anything more they finished with, 'Twelve pounds an hour OK?'

I tried hard not to gape.

More than I'd earned at the nursing home. Much more than minimum wage. The wonderful thing about earning more than minimum wage is that if you work the same number of hours you actually have disposable income. As in capital. As in spending money. I felt like doing a jig. Maybe I did have a future. Was it even possible I could save enough to study for A levels, even, and this was a very big stretch of imagination, put myself through university?

Step one of my life plan.

FOUR

I started the following day and quickly realized two things. The first was that I'd been right about Scarlet. She was from the Travelling community and wasn't in the slightest bit interested in references. When I mentioned it tentatively she looked almost cross. 'I can make my own mind up about someone,' she said. 'I don't need other people's opinion.'

And the second thing? I could do this job easily, with one hand tied behind my back and a library book propped in front of me on the desk. The machines and computers were easy to work. The job description was simple. I had to keep an eye on the bank of monitors.

I had to keep the database up to date, so I knew which units were empty and which were available, make sure customers signed in when they arrived and signed out when they left. A Health and Safety requirement, in case there was a fire and a fireman rushed in to 'save' someone who had actually left an hour before, or in case a client was accidentally locked in when I left, which was possible as none of the cameras was situated inside the individual stores. All kept an eye on the access corridors. Each individual store was secured with a roller shutter, padlocked on the outside, and the roller shutter doors that led to the outside were opened with a key code, which was switched off when I left the building. Mobile phones didn't work behind the shield of metal. If someone was accidentally locked in, they would have a very uncomfortable night's sleep. Two if it happened to be late on a Saturday as we were closed on Sunday. More if no one missed them. And God help them if it was Christmas or New Year. So signing in and signing out was vitally important.

I had to check contracts and warn people about 'forbidden substances': livestock, firearms, drugs. I worked out the VAT. Lastly, if I left the office to inspect the storage areas, I had to lock the office door behind me, even though there was never any real money there. Everything was done with plastic contactless. Apart from the office work, I swept the corridors and generally kept the place clean. And that was about it.

After slaving away in the SW Care Home, it seemed like money for much less work.

Andy and Scarlet spent the first week teaching me all this: how to work the computer, how to work out which units were empty and which ones full, how to keep the database up to date, how to take credit and debit cards and how to open and close the key-padded steel shutters and close the big gates when I left the site. I started work proper the following Monday, and by Thursday I was there on my own for a couple of hours at a time, with both their mobile numbers pinned up in front of me. For the first time in my life I felt in charge. Powerful.

As the weeks passed I saw little of Andrew. I suspected he had another job, but Scarlet never said and I never asked. On Friday Scarlet went out shopping for four hours. I had her mobile phone number but I'd already got the hang of the place and didn't need to ring, even though two potential new clients asked for prices and availability. I just gave them a leaflet and a nice smile. My pay at the end of the week was enough to pay for my room, bus fares into work, food and a little bit left over for me to buy two smart outfits from the Donna Louise Charity shop, Donna Louise being the name of a little girl who had died, I think, of leukaemia, poor little mite, and the charity had subsequently been set up in her name. With the result that here, in Stoke-on-Trent, children with incurable diseases benefit from the money that pours in, raised by friends and relatives. Money can buy a room for their parents when they are admitted, toys and trips. It can't, however, buy the one thing they want more than anything, life.

One of the outfits I bought from the Donna Louise was a trouser suit from Next – hardly worn, dark blue and a perfect fit apart from the trousers which were an inch too long. I'm not handy with needle and thread, but if I asked Jodi really nicely I thought she might take them up for me. The other outfit I was particularly pleased with was a skirt suit in black and white. Someone must have worn it to a wedding just the once. It was a bit posh but it looked brand new. When I turned up wearing that on that first morning I felt distinctly overdressed. Like going to the local pub wearing a sparkly dress and wedding hat. Scarlet looked me up and down and burst out laughing. 'Darling,' she said, unlit fag dangling out of her mouth, arms draped around me. 'Jeans and T-shirt'll do.'

I felt my face burn. Nothing shows you up more than overdressing. You look like the cleaner out for the annual works trip.

The next day both outfits stayed in the wardrobe and I went to work more suitably dressed in the suggested jeans and T-shirt. Still, better than the crappy white nylon overalls I used to wear at the SW home.

I soon realized the hours were long and customers sporadic. Scarlet and Andrew left me more and more to my own devices. Sometimes, particularly in the week, no one would come in for a whole day and I did grow bored – even with the latest set of novels from the library, social media on my phone and a couple of chats with Bethan and Stella. (Stella with Geraint howling in the background, and Bethan still moaning about being pregnant.) So I'd lock up the office and prowl the premises, checking everything was working OK, alarms, roller shutters, test the doors, make sure they were all padlocked and secure. But after a month or so of doing this the day would still drag – even with a stock of good books. I'd find my gaze wandering up to the bank of CCTV screens and searching for some sign of life, some movement, something interesting. But there was nothing. Just the roller shutters, static for ninety per cent of the time, immobile vehicles, and always silence because the monitors displayed pictures but transmitted no sound. In spite of having more than two hundred units, the place had an abandoned air about it. The folk who hired these storage units were, it seemed, quite happy to pay a weekly fee only to abandon their possessions. Once or twice, as the evenings lengthened, my imagination would take over, my mind playing naughty tricks. I would see shadows hovering in the darker areas, imagine movement when the wind caught an odd scrap of paper, and occasionally I thought I saw someone standing just outside the tall wire gates, peering into the compound.

All in the mind, I said to myself, and tried to ignore the rather sad atmosphere. The Green Banana, it seemed, could not escape its air of clinging to a shoddy past – of failed businesses, abandoned goods, unwanted furnishings belonging to dead people, chairs they had once sat on, tables they had once eaten at, pictures they must once have loved, ornaments they had once treasured. Now all unwanted, like the people, a by-product of a life that the living could not quite discard. They paid their monthly dues by direct debit, paying for their guilt in not taking these unwanted pieces into their own home. Perhaps, like the folk in The Stephanie Wright Care Home, the same had applied to their dead relatives. Abandoned to their fate.

Sometimes it did spook me, watching those silent grey monitors with silent people going about their business. It could feel as though they too inhabited a dead, grey world. It was OK when I left. Once outside the gates I rejoined the living, emerged into the present and left behind all those unwanted possessions. After a while I stopped asking myself the question: why did people pay to hang on to all these possessions?

As I grew in competence, Scarlet often wouldn't come in for days at a time and I was largely left in charge of The Green Banana alone. Andy would wander in, usually at around six o'clock, when I was about to lock up. I wasn't quite sure whether he was checking up that I hadn't left early or whether it was to help me make sure the premises were empty overnight. Maybe it was to check that I was safe. The storage facility was that sort of place, the sealed units oddly threatening. One never knew quite what was inside them, and even though I always pointed out our list of banned substances, one could never be quite sure.

There were various sizes of units, some hardly bigger than a large suitcase, others the size of a shipping container. And all the sizes in between. To one side of the yard there was a large open area, protected only by the wide roller shutter at its entrance. Here people stored classic cars, camper vans and caravans out of season.

Outside, The Green Banana had ample car parking for all vehicles, and was encircled with razor wire, which should have helped me to feel safe. But it didn't. It emphasized the feeling of living in a war zone or a prison, furthered the feeling that something beyond the razor wire threatened me. Which was fanciful, I know. But as I locked the tall wire gates behind me in the evenings and stepped outside I felt vulnerable, exposed. And when the nights darkened and I sat in the office, illuminated as if on a stage, I felt frightened.

You can ask why did I stay? For money, because I was not qualified to do another job, because I would have no references and because Scarlet and Andrew paid well. Also I had the opportunity to sit and read. The work was hardly arduous. Just boring. One day, I planned, I would leave. I would realize my future. And I would know when the time was right for the next step.

Some of the clients were a bit odd, but I had dealt with odd people almost all my life. Starting with my parents and my obnoxious little brother, Josh.

My life is potholed with odd people.

And all my boyfriends, without exception, have been odd. Some scary. Like Tyrone. I guess the name Tyrone should have warned me.

How *do* mothers know what to call their kids before they're born or when they're just hours or days old? And get it so right? One of life's little puzzles. What comes first? Do the names actually influence the child's choice of character? Tyrone becomes a thug while Justin is gay, Wayne works in a car showroom and Stefan is . . . a plumber. It's the way it works. I mean Justin *can't* be a thug. And Wayne can't work for the BBC, can he? Do we grow into our names or is there divine intervention handing them out?

I met Tyrone when I was seventeen through an internet dating site that I visited every now and again. I was registered with a couple of matching websites but so far had only ever been offered the pits. But Tyrone looked fit. And he sort of half smirked into the camera, which intrigued me.

Fit? He was that.

The trouble was that his idea of keeping fit was pumping anabolic steroids into his system. Look up the side effects. They have a nasty effect on your volatility, your temper . . . and your manhood. It can shrink your willy, give you gynaecomastia (man boobs), and so on. (Not many people know that, do they? All they see is the bulging muscles.)

Probably neither knowing nor understanding any of this, Tyrone would spend hours at the gym pumping iron. He was narcissistic. Yes, I do know words like that. I'm not a moron. I would have passed my A level English with flying colours – or so the teachers told me. If I'd not run into problems at home and been living on the streets at the time, I would have studied for them. I might even have gone to university if I'd had any help (financial) or encouragement from either of my parents. If they hadn't been so drowning in their acrimony and their divorce . . . Miss McCormick had tried to make up for my parents' distraction by being extra encouraging. 'If you do well in your A levels you could even try for Oxford,' she said, flapping her hands around. Not knowing my mind was baulking at the very thought. *And how the hell am I going to get on there, Miss McCormick, mixing with all the toffs and academics as well as having the impossible task of financing myself all the way through?* I wanted to say. I just about managed, 'Women like me don't belong there.'

Oh yes, Martin Luther. I had a dream all right. Me in cap and gown, hurrying along the ancient corridors of academia, loving husband waiting to whisk me back home? I would get there, somehow. When I shook my head at my year ten job discussion, they didn't see the fuller picture. Miss McCormick just looked disappointed. 'Oh dear,' she said, eyes heavy with sadness. 'Such a dreadful waste.'

I was too choked up to respond.

But I would make it happen.

FIVE

A s 2016 turned into 2017 I settled into life at The Green Banana. I got to know some of the clients individually. They were a varied lot and I began to speculate about them. In spite of the no-drugs rule, I think a couple of them might have stored illegal substances, particularly my favourite, Tommy Farraday.

Tommy Farraday was part of a rock band, The Oracles, who stored some of their equipment with us and were, according to them at least, about to 'make it big'. Tommy was a tall, skinny guy, about six feet tall with a mop of yellow-blond hair. Not sure if it was dyed. I never noticed dark roots so if he did dye it he kept it up. He was gorgeous, with a bright white grin, a flirtatious manner and a habit of groping bums and breasts when he thought he could get away with it. And he usually did. Tommy was one of those guys born with an easy charm, and he could get away with blue murder with the opposite sex, me in particular. He'd come waltzing in, spin me around, put his arms around me and apologize for being late with the rent. I tried to be severe with him but it just rolled off his back like water down a goose's feathers. That was Tommy.

The band kept their stuff in one of the medium-sized containers, dropping the instruments off on a Monday or Tuesday, depending on how hungover and stoned they'd been on the Saturday, and picking it back up on a Thursday or Friday – depending on how far away the gig was. Tommy was the one who usually collected the gear, although the others helped when they could. But it was Tommy I watched out for. Those long, skinny legs emerging from the pink van they'd painted with black psychedelic letters. He had tattoos all the way up his arms and I'd dream that my name would one day be added to his collection of girlfriends – Sharnee, Fiona, Mirabelle . . . They went all the way up his delicious arms to his shoulder blades. It was a vain hope. Tommy was a born flirt. But still, I dreamed when he signed in – winking at me and puckering up his lips as though he would kiss me like they do in the movies – that one day he would look at me properly and the violins would play.

You want the real truth? If you weren't a set of drums or a bass guitar, he wasn't really that interested. Girls to him were simply arm candy. In spite of the almost obligatory grope, I wondered whether he was a closet gay. I sensed there was no serious intent behind his hand-wandering.

But . . . One can dream.

The winter was quieter and the customers scuttled in and out, like beetles, carrying their wares and anxious to return to the warmth of their cars. I'd watch them on the monitors, sometimes struggling with the larger pieces, reversing their cars or vans right up to the roller shutters. Daylight melted away by four o'clock and tall street lights beamed down like the lights from the watchtowers in concentration camps.

Apart from the bona-fide customers, there was an entire substratum, who would arrive after dark, back right up to the shutters, unload by a waiting car's headlights, faces covered against the CCTV, the contents of their van covered with grey removal blankets. They scurried around like rats in a grain store, signing the book with a swift check to see who else was there and a nervous glance at my bank of monitors. The items they stored, I reasoned, must be secret. They certainly didn't want prying cameras and they kept their backs to the surveillance. They made me uneasy and edgy.

Which, in turn, made me even more sensitive to the isolation of my job. And home life wasn't much better. Josh and Jodi weren't as friendly as they had been when I had first moved in. They wanted my money but they sure as hell didn't want me, certainly not hanging around the house. And I couldn't blame them. If I had had a house of my own, I wouldn't have wanted to share it either, with anyone except with my gorgeous, loving husband and a child or two. So, knowing Jodi and Josh didn't really want to share their home at all, I stayed marooned in my room and scurried downstairs only when I had to eat, opening a tin of soup or sticking a pizza in the oven.

Because both my home life and the job were so lonely, if a customer or potential customer turned up I would engage them in conversation, chatting about anything – from politics, which I have zero interest in, to fashion, to rock music (with Tommy), to the weather, which I've also always found pretty boring. The weather will continue whether you like it or not. Rain, snow, heat or cold. No moaning about it has any influence whatever. It just makes you feel hard done by. The rain in Tunstall has a particularly dreary quality about it anyway.

I saw less and less of Scarlet and Andrew and began to reflect that now they had set the place up and had me to (wo)man it, they were earning money for nothing.

Left in isolation, over that winter, the days appeared longer and longer, and working every Saturday meant what little social life I might have had suffered. My friends, particularly Stella and Bethan, had been into Saturday shopping trips or afternoons spent in wine bars. But now it was all about family. Their little babies consumed them. And Sundays always had been a 'family day'. Except for me who had no family. Mother, father, brother – none of them counted. So my Sundays were mainly about keeping out of Jodi and Jason's way and traipsing the country park alone, whatever the weather.

It didn't take a degree in arithmetic for me to work out that the business was very profitable. Scarlet and Andrew were making money hand over fist. Most of the storage areas were full. There was even a waiting list for some of the larger spaces. I got to know one or two of the regulars and the general pattern of comings and goings. There was usually a flurry on Saturdays at around five p.m., just as we were about to close. Half an hour later I'd swing the gates to, with their metallic scream, wishing with all my heart that I was about to head off somewhere exciting, preferably with an adoring and adorable boyfriend instead of me and the TV in that small, square room. I seemed to be one of the unlucky ones, sitting on the bank of the river while everyone else swam downstream, the girl who sits watching the dance floor while all her friends waltz and dance around her with their beaux. I was twenty-two. If I didn't do something about it, my life would slip away into nothing.

The CCTV screens reflected the sheer emptiness of my existence. I was detaching from reality and growing desperate for change. My breaks were bolting down sandwiches or scooting to the loo. And even that had to be done in a hurry, listening out for the doorbell.

The rule was that if I wasn't actually at the front desk I had to lock the front door. Scarlet, and in particular Andrew, were almost paranoid that we would be broken into, though I couldn't see the fuss myself. All the stores were padlocked and there was rarely any cash on the premises. Ninety per cent of the transactions were done by card or direct debit. And there wasn't much worth nicking in my office – nothing but flimsy padlocks, cardboard boxes galore, rolls of 'Fragile' tape. And what were they going to nick from the stores anyway if they forced the padlock? Serena, the hairdresser's, curlers? Old people's furniture? *'It was Gran's. There when I was growing up. I couldn't sell it. She'd turn over in her grave.'* Tommy Farraday's guitar, which I suspected wasn't quite as valuable as he claimed? Tatty house contents people couldn't bear to part with? Stuff they couldn't even sell on a market stall or through eBay, Gumtree or Amazon? Outgrown kids' stuff: prams, pushchairs, cots, Moses baskets and toys, retained just in case they had 'another one'. The list was endless. In the dull weather even the antiques, which I'd thought looked immensely valuable, were starting to look a bit tatty and seedy when they were being carried in and out of the store week on week for yet another antiques fair, protected from the weather by the ubiquitous grey blankets I was beginning to hate.

But when I got my pay packet I forgot about the rules, the boredom, the sheer emptiness of the job, the loneliness of being in solitary confinement on an industrial island, stranded from the bustling, lively, noisy town full of people, the hours spent staring into those grey screens where nothing moved except the ghosts inside my head. Perhaps understanding the downside of the job, Scarlet and Andrew had raised my pay by almost a hundred pounds a month. For the first time in my life I had disposable income. Just a little.

'Well,' I said, grinning at the pair of them. 'Thanks. Thanks very much.'

I lectured myself, trying to fend off the loneliness. What did I have to grumble about? I could read all day. The job was hardly arduous. I had a life. I had a job. I might even manage a foreign holiday. Maybe there I would finally meet the man who existed inside my head. My Prince Charming. It didn't look as though I was going to find him in the wine bars and night clubs of The Potteries, or here either. I'd tried the internet and that had turned out to be a disaster.

All that had dragged in initially had been Scary I.

SIX

The thing that finally nailed it with Tyrone was that he had the worst case of road rage I've ever witnessed. He drove a souped-up Subaru, decked out in silver metallic paint and with twin exhausts so it looked and sounded like a rocket. I'd actually seen people startle when he came up behind them, lights flashing, horn sounding, exhausts blasting, two fingers stuck out the window. It usually did the trick; they scurried back into the slow lane, particularly when they looked in their rear-view mirror and saw his face – square, determined – and his biceps as big as a baby's head, always exposed in a sleeveless vest with IRON PUMPER on it in big black letters. He wore that vest – or its twin – right the way through the year, summer, winter, spring and autumn. Heatwaves, snow. It was Tyrone's uniform.

Anyway, on that day, when I was witness to his excesses in the road-rage department, we were driving, as the police say, in a northerly direction along the A34 towards Talke Pits, once a mining village but now a collection of retail outlets. There was a favourite shop of his there that sold weights. Tyrone must have had an extra dose of his stuff that morning because he was flying on a broomstick. Mad as a hatter and aggressive as a randy bull. The guy in front was driving a navy Skoda Yeti and, either he wasn't looking in his rear-view mirror, or else he was one of those stupid stubborn guys who think they can stand up to Tyrone, and not give way.

Stupid, stupid, stupid.

So Skoda man, smile on his face, doing the legal forty mph, oblivious to what was steaming up behind him, sits in the outside lane. And on the inside there's a coach full of schoolkids on a trip, maybe. So Tyrone couldn't do his usual undertaking, middle finger poking the air, with all the sound effects his Subaru could muster, *fortissimo*. But instead of pulling ahead or slotting behind the coach, Skoda man sits there, still smiling as though he was listening to Classic FM.

Big mistake. And that irritating smile into his rear-view mirror just made things worse. Besides, some of the schoolkids, as we drew level, were sticking their tongues out and machined rude gestures back which fired Tyrone up even more.

Tyrone does his usual, flashes his lights, sounds his horn, revs up the engine, pretends to ram the Skoda, gets within an inch of the Yeti's back bumper.

Skoda man does . . . nothing. I can still see his stupid face in the mirror, unaware of the homicidal maniac revving up behind him. Maybe he did have Classic FM on, or whale music or something from the rainforest. He seemed so relaxed, the smile so fixed and abstracted, hardly noticing anything around him. Skoda man was in a happy little world of his own: meadow flowers, exotic birdsong, buttercups, violins, waves, while Tyrone is thinking of only one thing. And it involves a hefty punch in the rear bumper. I want to warn Skoda man. Pull over. Let him pass and it'll all be over in a minute. No harm done.

Otherwise . . .

But Skoda man wasn't in a noticing mood.

Tyrone starts effing and b-ing while I sit rigid in my seat, Skoda man still blissfully unaware. Tyrone starts to hyperventilate and I'm getting a nasty feeling. School bus having pulled away, Tyrone buzzes up behind Skoda man, flashes, sounds his horn and, with a bang, shunts him into the verge.

Which forces Skoda man to pull over and get out of the car to take Tyrone's insurance details. I watch with dread as both men get out of their cars, Skoda man little and skinny, Adam's apple bobbing up and down in a collar too big for his scrawny neck, and Tyrone stepping towards him like a bloody great earthquake: *thump thump thump*. And still Skoda man doesn't realize what's coming. Tyrone greets him by headbutting him on his nose (I heard the crunch from inside the car) before knocking him out flat. Then he rolls back towards me, gets in as though nothing has happened and off we drive, leaving Skoda man bleeding in the layby, his car with a dirty great dent in the back, still slewed in the position Tyrone had shunted it. I'm not sure whether Skoda man is dead or alive and I'm hardly going to ask Tyrone. I could guess what the answer will be. If he is alive Skoda man is the loser. He's got no insurance details and I very much doubt, after that greeting, that he's copped Tyrone's car number plate. Even if he had he'll have forgotten it in the excitement of what had followed.

When we reached the fitness and weights shop at Talke Pits, Tyrone was still snorting down his nostrils, puffing and panting from anger and the exertion of knocking down a guy half his size with about a thousandth of his testosterone level. Violence always overexcited him, and that day it was taking him a while to simmer down. I left him to his weights selection and started walking down the A34 back towards Newcastle-under-Lyme. I was not getting back in Tyrone's noisy Subaru. Not ever. I'd managed to filch his keys from his back pocket and dropped them down a drain hole. I swear I heard his bellow of rage all the way into Newcastle-under-Lyme.

Looking back, you could say I was ripe for the plucking – a solitary apple waiting to fall off the tree into someone's arms. You could accuse me of being gullible, naive, lonely, desperate. Yes. I was all of those things. But, luckily for me, I was also an optimist. I always had the conviction that romance was just around the corner, that something momentous was about to happen to me. Until it did, I was treading water.

And then I met Steven.

SEVEN

I t was a fine day in mid-March, a bright spring day when everyone's step was quick and energetic and happy. The daffodils and other spring flowers were everywhere. Even in Tunstall, in planters and pots, outside shops and in the park flower beds. I'd been working at The Green Banana for almost four months when he walked in.

Watching the grey screens, I'd seen a white Ford Focus pull on to the forecourt and park neatly in the bay, reversing and pulling forward twice to get it exactly between the parking lines. He got out, looked around and headed for the office. The door swung open and he walked in.

He was slim, about forty, attractive, height medium, hair brown streaked with grey and rather pretty eyes, hazel with tiny gold flecks and long lashes. He walked right up to the desk and waited shyly for me to speak first. 'Can I help you?'

'I'm not sure,' he said doubtfully, looking around, at the stacks of boxes, rolls of tape, CCTV monitors and finally back at me. I studied him further. He was wearing a navy jacket zipped up to the chin over beige trousers with a crease in them. Tramlines, actually. Careless ironing in a middle-aged man's uniform. And I noticed quite quickly that he was wearing a gold wedding ring. I met his eyes and his mouth tightened. I was only too familiar with Mr Married Man masquerading as Mr Bachelor. As though I wouldn't notice the dent or the tan line on their third finger left hand. But at least he wasn't hiding behind that fiasco.

I asked him again, changing the words slightly. 'How can I help you?'

His turn.

His eyes flickered. He still looked doubtful, as though coming here had been a whim he was now regretting. He looked around, doubt in the dropping of his shoulders, his gaze focusing on the floor. He licked his lips. 'I don't really know.'

My instinct was to tell him to come back when he did, or some other dismissive, rude remark, but his voice was soft and quiet and polite, his manner hesitant. I waited, thinking perhaps I should change the name I'd given him, Mr Middle-Aged Average Married Man, to Mr Doubtful.

He cleared his throat in an awkward little cough and I tried to help him by speaking in a voice gentler than usual.

'Do you have some items you wish to store?'

He spent enough time thinking about this for me to try to prompt him. 'Did you want to rent a container?'

He gave his head a vague, dismissive shake and looked at me helplessly.

I hadn't quite lost my patience but I was getting near. Still, I did try. 'We have lots of different sizes of storage facilities.'

He still looked uncertain, but he was thinking about it.

'From not much bigger than a shoebox to a full-sized shipping container,' I finished. We had a few that were empty that we needed to fill. Besides, I got a bonus when I found a new customer who signed on for a minimum of six months. I tried an encouraging smile.

He flapped his hands. 'I don't know how big a space I might need. Not much.'

Well, I don't fucking well know. I was losing it.

He hardly looked at me but seemed to find the floor more interesting – or else his shoes, which were brown leather. Quite good-quality brogues. I waited and searched his face for a clue, something. His eyes sidled away from a direct gaze. He looked pale, as though he spent all his life indoors and never saw the sun. There was a tiny bead of sweat on his upper lip and he was breathing quickly. I hoped he wasn't about to have a heart attack. I glanced at the poster on the wall, The Green Banana's nod to first-aid precautions. I'd never tried CPR but I reckoned I could have a go. Someone had told me you just thump the chest in time to the Bee Gees' 'Stayin' Alive' (very appropriate) and blow into their mouth every now and then.

He seemed to be recovering without all that.

Again, I tried to be helpful with a 'professional' smile. 'Well, what is it you want to store?'

'My wife's . . .' He stumbled over the word which already had me wondering about her. Divorce? Death? Estrangement? A shopaholic? He still wore his wedding ring, which in my personal experience is one of the first casualties of marital disharmony. Chucked at the about-to-be-ex-spouse.

So, divorce unlikely. But he didn't look quite sad enough for a widower, though the tramlines on his trousers were a hint that he was having to do his own laundry. But neither did he look well off enough to support a kleptomaniac spouse. Having failed to arrive at the right solution, I tried to mix helpfulness with sympathy and produced the list of sizes and prices printed out on A4, laying it gently on the counter, following that with a questioning look. He frowned over it, reading it through slowly before looking across at me, helpless as a kitten and indecisive as a child in a sweet shop and finally repeated, 'I don't know how big a space I'll need.'

I gave him my most confident, most 'winning' smile.

'Tell me what you want to store.' I tried again.

He flapped his hands again; the simple question had thrown him into another panic.

He still looked worried, so I followed that with a more practical suggestion. 'Would you like to look at a couple of our storage areas?'

His frown wasn't at all relieved by my offer. He just looked even more confused. 'I don't know. I'm not sure.' Following that up with, 'Perhaps I should.'

'Yeah.' And then I waited.

Before taking over. 'As it happens,' I said, 'we do have a couple of medium-sized storage areas vacant. Some of the six-by-fours. And one or two of the smaller sizes.' I knew now how to help new customers, prompt them along the way, help them sign the contract. Andrew and Scarlet had only recently introduced the benefit scheme. I had signed up a new tenant for the minimum six-month period and for that I'd got a thirty-pound bonus.

'And for the first month they're on special offer. Just one hundred pounds for the whole month.' I made my tone deliberately encouraging but he didn't appear to be wavering. I narrowed my eyes and tried to read him while I waited for his response. In my experience there is nothing like a special offer to reel most people in. But this guy was bypassing my experience. He was also inscrutable. I had no idea what little tussles were going on in his mind.

I tried again recalling Scarlet's mantra.

Empty spaces earn no money. But I couldn't work out how to steer him in the right direction – to make a decision. Preferably in my favour. I had my eye on a very sexy dress online and every girl knows a new dress demands new shoes. I could do with that extra money and so I pushed perhaps a little harder than I would normally have done.

I glanced over his shoulder eyeing the white car. A Ford Focus is a good load carrier. 'How many carloads of stuff will you have?'

'I really don't know,' he said, shrugging, but in a friendly and more relaxed way now. He gave me a tentative smile and twisted his wedding ring around his finger. 'Probably the contents of three wardrobes?'

Bloody hell, I thought. Three wardrobes. So my kleptomaniac wife theory was the correct one. A clothes collector. Someone who can't say no to Marks & Spencer's by the look of him. 'In bags? Suitcases?' I prompted. 'We have lovely cardboard and plastic disposable wardrobes that you can hang clothes in. Or hanging rails,' I finished dubiously, losing confidence.

He shuddered. 'Boxes,' he said abruptly, 'a trunk and one or two suitcases.'

I picked something else up. He was uncomfortable about this. His hands, by his sides now, were opening and closing like a jelly-fish. His eyes slid away from mine, but not before I'd read something else in them. Shame? Embarrassment? Guilt? He looked a teeny-weeny bit shifty, took a step back, scooped in a lungful of air and, for one weird second, I wondered if he was about to faint he looked so pale and – well – odd. He gulped.

'A six-by-four should do it,' I said, suddenly decisive and wanting to close the deal, get him signed up before he changed his mind, which I sensed he was about to do. But I knew the ropes, the way these commitments worked. On impulse.

I still hadn't converted him. He still looked a bit uncertain, so I pushed him a little further along the way.

'You can move in right away if you like.' Big smile. 'We're open six days a week. Ten till five.' While he wavered, I studied him further, trying to place him. He was nearer my dad's age than mine. His smile was tentative but no showstopper. No big display of huge white horse-teeth. His voice was as quiet and soft as a pair of bedroom slippers. His hair was slightly thinning on top. He'd made a half-hearted attempt at a combover but they don't work even in the most skilful of hands, though his hands were actually an asset. Long, slim, capable fingers, which looked surprisingly strong, like a pianist's. I looked at them with fascination. They, along with those lovely eyes, were quite beautiful.

He was still hesitating. And I was curious about his backstory. Let's face it, I didn't have a lot to think about all day, so imagining the stories of our customers was one of my pastimes.

I started to guess at it.

The poor man was browbeaten by an extravagant wife. She not only embarrassed him but had landed them in debt? He'd had to clear out her wardrobes so he could have some hanging space for himself, for his cheap, double-creased trousers made of too thin a fabric.

I'd already discarded the theory of divorce because of the wedding ring and the way he twizzled it around his finger, always conscious of it. No grief or fury there. Although maybe he still loved her and hoped she'd come back, even though she'd buggered off with a fancy man. But he couldn't bear coming face to face daily with her belongings, seeing her clothes every time he opened the door, perhaps remembering painfully the occasions when she had last worn them.

Maybe he even clung to the possibility that she would come back – and all would be forgiven. He'd come back to The Green Banana and retrieve her stuff. I sneaked another glance to check while he still ruminated. He looked the forgiving sort – or rather – not the sort to make a fuss. Bereavement was lower down my list, but I tried it out anyway. She'd died tragically. Cancer or an accident. Something really sad – the story that invites the phrase, 'she was taken from me much too soon', with a dab of the eye. He'd simply adored her and couldn't bear to take her stuff down to the charity shop where it would be picked over by strangers, so he had boxed her belongings up lovingly and would preserve them here for ever, maybe visiting periodically to sit and remember. A 'Lest We Forget' pilgrimage. I sneaked another study and discarded this theory too, putting it straight in the trash bin. He didn't strike me as a grieving husband.

So, a couple of boxes, a trunk, one or two suitcases.

Normally I could work out what stuff people were storing and why. Often they told me anyway but this one was defeating me. For now. I'd get there in the end, but he needed further encouragement to earn me my thirty pounds. So I said in my brightest, most encouraging tone, 'Let's take a look at the available units, shall we?'

Then he properly looked at me, a steady, slow, appraising gaze. I worried he was about to confide in me, and almost put my hand up to stop him.

Don't tell me your backstory, I wanted to blurt out. *I'd like to guess it.*

'OK,' he said finally.

EIGHT

I locked the office door behind me and took him across the yard to the storage units, some of them no bigger than cupboards, others as big as a room, and rolled up the shutter to the vacant six-by-four. It should be easily big enough for his stuff. He studied the empty space while I waited, thinking. There's nothing to see in there except steel sides and ceiling, concrete floor and the roller shutter. You can prowl and peer but that's it. It's an empty space waiting to be filled. Maybe he was picturing the contents of his three wardrobes already stashed inside and himself rolling down the shutter on them, padlocking them safely away and eventually forgetting about them. I watched him curiously and realized this was a man who concealed his emotions. His face was as expressionless as a Chinese Immortal while I, waiting for a response, mentally spending the thirty pounds, studied the interior too.

There is something coffin-like about being encased in steel. In these units you are removed from all everyday sensory stimulation. Any sound has a strange metallic echo like the introduction to a sci-fi film. I'd swept this area out only the day before. Part of my job was keeping everywhere clean. But inside, even though the roller shutter was raised, I'd felt claustrophobic, worrying it might drop, I would be unable to lift it from the inside and – encased in this metallic tomb – any shouting, any hope that someone would walk by and rescue me, would be in vain. Most of the time I was the only one here. A figment of your imagination, I'd scolded myself, as I'd swept the dust and debris into a dustpan and tipped it into a black bin liner. You can't afford to be overimaginative.

He still stared around him with an air of sadness. I peered past him. What on earth at? There's nothing to see.

I wanted to say something to urge him into taking the unit. I wanted my thirty pounds. Normally I'd have closed the deal by now, contract signed, thirty pounds safely in my pocket. But my new customer appeared deep in thought, his face troubled.

I waited.

What could I say to tip the balance?

There are no lights inside this small cupboard area. The only light source is from the corridor. Standing at the entrance we threw huge shadows against the metal ribs. Someone, in one of the other corridors, was lifting his roller shutter. I heard the metal clang followed by a rat-tat-tat as the shutter was raised. But it was too far away to know who had arrived. I did, however, feel reassured that we were not alone.

He looked sad. Oh dear, I thought, sorry for him now I'd worked it out. Divorce. She's told him she doesn't love him any more, that she wants (her fingers cruelly scratching the air) 'space' and she's moved out, probably to be with a lover.

His head dropped to his chest while I further expanded on my story.

He's waited for a while, hoping she'll change her mind, but she hasn't and now he needs to come to some kind of decision. He'll store her stuff here for a year or two while he and his ex sort it all out. And then he'll dump it, along with the wedding ring. Some to the charity shop and the rest to the municipal tip. I realized he was lost in the memory, unaware of my presence. Then he gave a little shake, turned to me and more or less confirmed my suspicions. 'What a shame,' he said without any explanation, and I nodded a sort of agreement, not asking the question: *What?* Maybe I was wrong and she had died after all. Or did he mean this empty space?

My mind had shifted from the dress I'd buy to a pair of red stilettos I'd seen in New Look. Hot as a chilli pepper. I didn't address the question: where was I going to wear them?

Something or someone would turn up.

I came to. My client was still standing motionless.

I decided he needed a prod.

'Minimum term six months initially,' I said brightly. 'You pay half upfront and after that you're on a rolling contract. Best if it's direct debit.' I wasn't going to give him a chance to back out so spoke quickly. 'Then, when you want to leave, you just give us a month's notice – after the initial six-month period,' I repeated severely, so there could be no misunderstanding. His face crumpled and I changed my mind again. She's died, I thought, enlightened now. Cancer or a horrible accident. He continues to wear the wedding ring as a tribute. Or . . .?

He faced me. 'Are these *sealed* units?'

I frowned, not sure what he was getting at. 'You mean airtight?'

He simply looked at me and didn't answer, so I had to make it up. 'They're not *quite* airtight,' I said, 'if that's what you mean.' He wasn't helping me out here. 'Do you mean safe? Secure?'

He gave a funny little smile and I decided I needed to improvise.

'They're *practically* airtight. And they are *certainly* secure. Very secure.' Spoken sternly, in my best teacher's voice.

'Does anyone come in here?'

What exactly was he planning? 'Once the units are let, no one enters. The space belongs to the person who's paying for it. We don't come in here. We've no reason to.'

'No one inspects the contents?'

'No.' I lifted my finger to point in the direction of the office. 'There's a list of banned substances.' I smiled. 'No drugs, livestock . . .' That wasn't what he was asking so I repeated. 'It's quite private.'

'I'll take it,' he said abruptly.

I gave a faint smile back. D5 – let. I was thinking. Shoes. New Look here I come. Maybe I could persuade Stella or Bethan to get a babysitter and we could have a night out on the town together.

Sometimes when a client had finally made up his or her mind I'd say, 'Welcome to The Green Banana club,' but it seemed inappropriate with this reserved man. So I led him back to the office and poured him a coffee while I drew up the paperwork. I handed him the sheet with our opening hours and a list of all the things he was not legally allowed to store. He scanned the list and smiled, his eyes warming. 'None of these,' he said, and read through the opening hours while I continued with my spiel.

'You provide your own padlock, though we do have some for sale.' I indicated the rack of goods with a wave of my arm, as though I was an air hostess giving the safety talk. He was still looking dubious, so I added, 'As well as our coat and dress storage bags, cardboard boxes and wardrobes, bubble wrap and "Fragile" tape.'

He looked straight at me then and smiled again, politely. 'No need for any of that, but thank you.'

He produced a Barclays debit card which he fingered awkwardly, reluctant to hand it over, as though he still needed convincing. Perhaps he was reluctant to part with the money. (Mr Mean aka Lee Williams was another of my failed romances.) Perhaps it was more that he felt it was severing the connection with . . . whatever.

'That'll be a hundred and fifty pounds.'

He still did not hand over the card. He was having second thoughts, so I prompted him. 'Are you OK with that?'

Slowly he nodded and slipped the card into the machine. I inserted our code and waited for him to put in his PIN. He was still looking at me when he fed in the four numbers. I did the theatrical, *I'm-not-seeing-your-PIN turnaway*.

Job done. Payment authorized. I had my thirty quid and the shoes.

'And I can move in . . .?'

'Right away,' I said, which seemed to confuse him. He frowned, looked around, and then smiled and left without another word. I stared after him. Strange guy, I thought.

I watched him to his car and read through the form he'd just filled in.

His name, Steven Taverner. His address was in Stanley, a small, pretty and exclusive village only four miles from where I lived, Brown Edge, the Edge being the edge of the Staffordshire Moorlands. The name of his house puzzled me at the time: Yr Arch. Like, The Arch in another language, I assumed. His writing was neat, almost schoolboy-round and childish, and his card had gone through OK. So far so good.

Under contents he'd written, *Varied*.

And under value he'd put < £1,000.

And he was prepared to pay over £100 a month to store this? Maybe he hopes she'll come back.

Boy, I thought, she must be some person. At the time, I was touched. Sentiment, romance, love and a mystery. Don't we all love a bit of intrigue?

NINE

I'd said he could move in straight away, but as it was I didn't see Steven Taverner for almost three weeks. Still wondering about why he needed to rent out a unit, I focused on the people who stored their secrets in those steel sealed units.

A7 contained Stanley Evan's stuff. His mother had died five years ago and he couldn't bear to get rid of her belongings, he'd told me, with a sob. 'It's all I've got left of her, see?'

He was a thin man with a prematurely bent back and rheumy eyes, which he rubbed almost constantly as though that would improve his sight. He appeared in his sixties, though I suspected he'd looked like that almost from birth. His hair was sparse and almost purely white, but there was a hint that once, long ago, it had been ginger. Just a few coloured strands were left. He constantly sniffed – whether through a sinus problem or a sense of grief for the dead mother who had been the mainstay of his life, I couldn't begin to guess. He was sweet, harmless. Outdated. Like the stuff he stored. I'd watched him and a friend move it in. Old people's stuff – chairs upholstered in stained tapestry, a little table of some ugly, varnished dark wood, with a pale ring in the centre where – I imagined – flowers had stood in a vase. There were boxes of crockery and a lace tablecloth. All crap. But he stored it with love, as though waiting to reunite the pieces with his beloved mother: folded old blankets, the shabby three-piece suite, the prints in their thin wooden frames, photographs of people probably long dead and all the kitchen stuff, rusty enamel and well-worn plastic utensils. His mother must have been a heavy smoker. I'd visited his store not long after he'd moved in and caught a waft of cigarettes as I'd passed. The stuff stank. But however tatty it was, he loved it. It was as though he was storing his mother inside A7, paying two hundred and fifty pounds a month to preserve something of her. Perhaps he believed she would some day return to claim it, sit in those old chairs again and light up a fag. He'd have been much better off spending three hundred quid on a skip and chucking the lot in. Job done. But not Stanley. His devotion was touching. His devotion and that of his fellow renters funded our business.

The Green Banana was a tribute to sentiment. People can't bear to get rid of things, can they? Poor old Stanley would come in, usually on a Friday afternoon. I'd see his white Skoda sidle into the yard, hear his footsteps approach the office door, watched by the cameras which swivelled to follow him. He'd swing the door open with surprising vigour and always greet me with the same phrase. 'Another week gone, eh, Jennifer?' And I'd smile and say, 'Yes,' as though it was a surprise to me too. He signed the book with another flourish – probably the only flourishes he ever managed in his life. He'd cross the yard, again watched by the eye. I'd hear the roller shutter rattle as he raised it, watch him on the CCTV, shoulders bowed as he walked inside and disappeared.

Another week gone, Jennifer. It was always the same phrase.

He never brought any more pieces; neither did he ever take anything out, so I didn't know why the weekly pilgrimage. I assumed once inside he just sat there looking at the stuff, imagining his mother sitting on the chair or pulling a plate from one of the cupboards. He'd spend about half an hour inside before he emerged, empty-handed, leaving it all behind. Roller shutter down. Door locked. Then he'd come and sign out in the office, baggy-eyed now,

looking for all the world as though his mother had just this very
minute died. Maybe one day, I thought, I'd suggest he chucked the
lot away and saved himself enough money to go on a Mediterranean
cruise a couple of times a year. Maybe he'd meet another lady to
substitute the one he'd lost.

I began to feel that I was living my life, if at all, through the
customers of The Green Banana.

Who came and went.

There were a couple of failed businesses, miserable-looking
guys who practically hurled the stuff into the back of the store,
muttering snippets about receivers, auditors, bailiffs and bank-
ruptcy. They were the worried ones, generally followed closely by
the bailiffs who jemmied the padlocks, threw their stuff into the
back of their vans and drove away, the skid of rubber their final
disdainful action.

There were young couples who stored prams and pushchairs,
saying 'when they had another one . . .'

Sometimes they came back. Sometimes they didn't and months
or even years later returned, tight-lipped, taking the stuff out more
carelessly than when they had put it in. When you walked past their
open shutters you could still smell baby powder.

There were the divorced, who paid their bills with twisted lips
and a scowl, muttering dark threats against the cow or the bitch,
the ram or the bastard – the 'animals' who'd ruined their lives.

There were sad couples whose homes had been repossessed
because they'd fallen into debt. They were the haunted ones.

The Green Banana was a microcosm reflecting the world outside.

And so a couple of weeks rolled by. And there was no further
sign of Steven Taverner. The store was his but it remained empty.
I wondered if he'd had second thoughts.

We had to turn some people away because the size of store they
wanted was unavailable. As I passed D5, still empty, I wondered.

We had another police raid in late March – very dramatic, with
lots of shouting and orders to me to stay inside. So I watched through
the window. Battering rams (I could have told them I could probably pick the lock and save them the bother). The vans sped into
the courtyard at breakneck speed, men jumping out with shots and
shields – they suspected a couple of jihadists were storing explosives.
Turned out it was nothing more than banned books and some dirty
magazines. But that day went very quickly and provided me with

some much needed excitement. In general life was humdrum, though, a bit boring. Until . . .

It was early in April that the white Ford Focus appeared again, sliding in through the gates.

I watched him back the car right up to the roller shutter doors. I needed to remind him about signing in and out, so I locked the office and crossed the yard.

'Mr Taverner,' I said. 'You need to sign in.'

He looked startled then guilty.

I glanced at the contents of his car. Two cardboard boxes taped up with a name inscribed in thick, permanent felt-tipped pen. *Margaret.*

He followed the direction of my gaze. 'Sorry,' he said quickly. 'Sorry. I forgot.'

'No worries. I'll do it for you this time.'

'I won't forget again.'

I smiled my forgiveness. 'And another thing,' I said. 'Be sure you prop the roller shutters up. Sometimes they spontaneously fall down. There's no way of lifting them from the inside unless you're Hercules, so just be careful.'

He looked alarmed. 'I will. I will. I'm a bit claustrophobic, you see. I'd panic in there and panic sets off my asthma.'

I felt bad then. Maybe I'd overstated it. 'Just be careful,' I said.

'I will.' He turned around and tried to lift one of the boxes but it seemed too heavy for him. I showed him the trolleys that released for a deposit of one pound, like a supermarket trolley, and he thanked me. Always polite, I noticed, and he spoke in a pleasant, soft voice, hardly accented.

I returned to the office and watched him on the CCTV screen. So now I knew his wife's name. Margaret: divorcée, dead wife, extravagant hussy? If she was still around, why wasn't *she* giving him a hand? It was her stuff after all. Why was it *his* responsibility? And if this was her stuff, surely *she* should have been the one to consider the storage space? And pay the bill?

My curiosity was piqued.

Most of our customers give you a clue as to why they need a store and what they intended to keep there. It gave them a chance to offload their life stories. Have a moan about circumstances or crow about their success. Not Mr Taverner who was, by nature, I guessed, secretive. It would take a lot to winkle his secret out of him.

And then the day grew busier. Scarlet and Andrew came in and I didn't give my new client any more thought. There were more interesting clients then him. I didn't see his car slide away because Ruby Ngoma had arrived.

Ruby was seventy and, well, she looked . . . seventy. Skinny as they come, addicted to cigarettes and gin. A native of Tunstall, Ruby was currently 'staying with a friend'. Sofa-surfing, which was why her meagre possessions were with us. Eight years ago, she'd been on a holiday to The Gambia. And there she'd met Number One Charmer Solomon Ngoma. Only he wasn't so much a charmer as a conman. And Ruby, desperate for love – and sex – fell in 'leerv'. Solomon followed her back to the UK, professing undying leerv also, and Ruby made the biggest mistake of her life. Reader, she married him. They lived in her house, a modest ex-council semi, but a palace to Solomon Ngoma, who quickly adapted to the ways of a love rat/man on the make. Before long he'd realized how much the house was worth – £120,000 – which was a lifetime's earnings for him as a beach bum. And so he'd worked it all out and married Ruby, who had quickly remortgaged the property in order to lotus-eat on cruise ships and luxury hotels with her leervver.

'I was a bit of a fool,' Ruby said when she brought her stuff to the store and signed the contract. 'I fell for it.' She had given me the benefit of her experience. 'Listen to me, my girl. Men – don't trust them. When you're young they want to get inside your knickers. When you're old . . .' Her faded eyes fixed on mine. 'When you're old,' she continued in her deep, wheezy voice, 'all they want is your bank account.'

Having married Solomon – big mistake that – though she said with a wink that it had been a darned sight better than her first wedding (Stoke registry office, pissing down with rain, wearing a borrowed blue evening dress). 'No,' she said, 'I pushed the boat out. Had a bloody lovely Victorian-style wedding dress, long massive skirt and a veil and took our vows on the beach.' Cough, cough, cough. 'All the trimmings.' She rasped out another few coughs and winked at me. 'Gorgeous, I was. You should have seen me.'

And I wished I had. I really wished I had. But the official photographs had been a casualty of her marital break-up. 'Smashed them all. Ripped them to pieces . . .' Her face had saddened.

'Regretted it later but there you are.' Said bravely, with the spirit of the Blitz.

You could almost see it coming. Ruby had been made a fool of, in spite of her seventy years. Within three, Solomon had hopped it back to The Gambia, having forced the sale of her remortgaged house. 'Lovely it was too. You should have seen it. Proper posh. I'd got it lovely. With an en suite off the main bedroom.' She pronounced it N suite. Solomon had taken his share and scarpered.

'I wasn't so much heartbroken,' she said, 'as I felt a bloody fool. Bloody lawyers,' she grumbled. 'How the heck do they expect me to buy a house with less than thirty grand left?'

I shrugged and she fixed me with a glare. 'You be careful, my girl. Don't make the mistake I made.' Too late, Ruby realized she had been made a monkey of, fallen into a trap set by a clever young man who had only his youth as a bargaining chip.

But at least she'd had a man, been married – twice. (Widowed then divorced.)

I'm old fashioned, I know. I wanted to be married. I wanted some family of my own. Not my mum or dad, who were busily, selfishly, proceeding with their lives separately, and as though I didn't exist. I didn't even get birthday or Christmas cards from them any more. I wasn't even sure they knew my address. And certainly not my evil brat of a brother, Josh. I wanted a husband who adored me as Sonny did Stella. An adorable fat baby like Geraint. I wanted love. But where was I to look?

I'd tried the internet.

With Scaries I & II, and half a dozen other experiences, I wasn't going to chance it again.

Which left me exactly where?

You guessed it. No Woman's Land.

TEN

My newest client turned up again two weeks later in late April, this time lumping one heavy suitcase, the size you take on a two-week holiday. I watched him struggle to lift it out of the car before wheeling it into the store. He remembered to sign in this time, but scribbled hurriedly, without looking at me, shuffling in, eyes on the ground, steps quick. He couldn't wait to get out of the office. I would have offered to help him with the keypad or open the shutters but I didn't have the chance.

He was the one real enigma in The Green Banana. Which left me very curious. When I am curious, I spin stories. The current one was he'd murdered his wife, chopped her up and put her in the boxes and the suitcase. So I watched for clues. I kept my eye glued on the screens and watched him emerge into the corridor ten minutes later. He looked shell-shocked and pale, kept glancing back nervously inside the store before rolling down the shutter and fixing the padlock. Even then he didn't leave, but stood with his hands on the roller shutter, face pressed against the steel. I watched, fascinated, already giving a statement to a tabloid (for a massive cheque) about how I'd suspected him from the first. He stood at the locked shutter for a while, not even moving when one of the other clients walked past him and seemed to speak. I could guess what it would be.

'*You all right there, mate?*'

I caught sight of his face, lit by the strip light in the corridor. He looked ill. Distracted. Whatever was in there, I thought, this was not just the clothes from three wardrobes. Maybe my theory about him being a wife killer was the right one.

But that was as far as I got in my Sherlock Holmes deductions that day, because Tommy Farraday arrived, jaunty as ever, grinning from ear to ear. 'We,' he announced importantly, leaning across the desk to give me a sloppy kiss on the cheek, 'have a recording contract, Jenny Wren.' Apparently not just a song by none other than Paul McCartney but Jenny was also the old countryside name for a wren, he'd told me when I'd asked him.

'Really?'

He gave a big, stagey nod, blond hair flopping over his face.

Fact is, I was not just impressed. I was overawed. I'd never met anyone who had a recording contract. I felt my eyes widen, my face warm and my jaw drop. I would have fallen at his feet and worshipped except the desk was in the way. My vision of a wife killer was replaced with rock stars and their glamorous girlfriends piling into The Green Banana, all storing their drums and bass guitars, instruments and music here, me signing them in and out. The place would buzz with the rich and famous. Maybe I'd make it into a magazine. (In the background, of course!)

After swanning around and dancing me round the office, Tommy exited with a twirl and got cracking unloading the equipment. Three guitars, a synthesizer, set of drums . . . Some kit. I wondered how the hell he and his band, The Oracles (dreadful name), had afforded such expensive stuff. This contract must be very lucrative. And have paid up front. I'd never actually heard them play but imagined it was some sort of heavy metal stuff, noisy with a bass that would shake the floor.

I watched on the monitor as he and Callum shifted the equipment, struggling a bit. The drum kit, in particular, was heavy. Even from the office I could hear them laughing, handing each other a roll-up, what I imagined was a spliff, and had a quick vision of Tommy swanning back in here and asking me if I'd join them on the next gig as his girl.

I know, pathetic. As likely to happen as the queen requesting a six-by-four to keep her crown in.

I tried to focus on my job. My business was to fill the storage facilities, keep the database up to date, keep the place clean and get the money paid up on time and in full.

I glanced back at the screen. Steven had not left but was lifting a trunk on to the trolley, which had a mind of its own and was twisting around, refusing to move straight, like a wayward child. As I watched, Callum – still laughing – put his synthesizer down and held the trolley for Steven. There was a brief exchange between the two men and Steven patted Callum on the shoulder as though they were friends. I felt both excluded and part of it as I continued to watch the silent movie providing sounds of my own, little huffs of approval, even a giggle or two. Everyone on my screen today looked happy.

I did too. Perhaps the job wasn't all bad.

An hour later they had all left and the yard was empty.

As April melted into May and May into June, the days became long and light. I often sat on the forecourt of The Green Banana, listening out for the phone, sunning myself and, one day, when it was very hot, I turned up in a pair of cut-off denims. There was more coming and going in the summer and the folk were more sociable, not in such a hurry to leave. Steven visited a few times; he didn't bring anything more but he spent time in the store. I didn't know why or what he did in there. When he left his face was set but sad. If he'd murdered her maybe he regretted it now. He'd walk slowly back to his car, feet dragging, like a child being marched to the doctor's. And when he signed out, he looked almost tearful. Sometimes his colour was so bad I thought he might be sick. I longed to try to find out more but I felt sure he would rebuff me. Even so, when he deliberated one day over his signature, almost as though he'd forgotten his name, I did try.

I had the perfect excuse. His three months would soon be up. He needed to pay more dues. He couldn't leave for another three months, having signed up for six. I really didn't want him to leave then, not until I knew his story.

I mentioned it. He looked at me as though he hadn't even realized I was there.

'Now your three months are up you need to pay. In another three months you can go on a rolling contract,' I repeated, parrot-fashion. 'A month at a time. And you only need to give us a month's notice.' It was the perfect opportunity. 'Do you think you'll want to retain the store beyond that, Mr Taverner?'

He didn't respond, instead saying, without smiling, 'You have very nice hair.'

To say I was taken aback is an understatement. I gaped and blurted out, 'Thanks.' And I stroked it self-consciously.

It was true, I do have nice hair. Long, shiny, brown, with a natural bounce in it. No tiger stripes these days.

He was still staring, and I didn't know how to follow this up, so I stood, like a teenager, biting my lip and smiling stupidly.

Then he reached out and touched it. Not smiling now. There was nothing intimate or even friendly in the action. He was looking not at my face but at the hair that was now draped across his hand.

While I just stood and felt awkward and chilled.

Today he was dressed in a royal blue polo shirt, rather baggy jeans and still those brown leather brogues.

He gave a little shake and dropped my hair. Gave a little nod and shuffled off, the doors left swinging behind him. I watched him on the CCTV then. He was walking very slowly, as if he was in a funeral procession. Each step he took seemed even, measured, deliberate. His shoulders were bowed, his focus on the floor. He looked up once, straight into the camera, as though he knew I was watching, and I felt embarrassed, found out. Then he climbed into his car and was gone.

I locked the office door behind me, crossed the yard and stood outside D5, sniffing the air. If his wife's remains were in there, as the weather was so warm, she would smell, I'd reasoned. Even if wrapped in plastic, she would still smell. But my nose picked up nothing but a faint scent of a perfume I would later identify as Dolce & Gabbana's Light Blue.

Two weeks later, on another blazing hot day, he arrived, again with an empty car, and I realized he hadn't signed in. It gave me the perfect excuse to leave the office, walk softly up to his store and spy on him if the roller shutters were raised. But when I reached the corridor I heard the roller shutter being dropped and he came out. I felt caught. Trapped. He looked enquiringly at me but neither of us spoke. Until I gathered my wits.

'You didn't sign in,' I said, trying to make the statement friendlier, less accusatory. 'Fire regs, you know?'

'I'm so sorry, Jennifer,' he said politely. I was startled for a moment until I realized. It was on the badge pinned to my T-shirt. *Jennifer Lomax.*

'I'm sorry,' he said again. 'I apologize. I just forgot.' And then he gave me a blast of a smile. The first time I'd ever seen him smile and it changed him. He had nice teeth and his eyes were warm and attractive. 'Will you forgive me?'

I returned the smile with interest, laughing. 'Of course.' I risked a joke and tried out his name. 'It's not a hanging offence, Steven. It's just regulations.'

If he could call me Jennifer, I'd reasoned, then I could call him Steven.

'I could do it for you.' Another lame joke. 'I'm good at forgery.'

His eyes rested on me for a longer moment and I felt a small quiver. Isn't it funny? Someone uses a name that's pinned to your breast for all the world to see and it feels . . . intimate. Personal. A step into your inner space.

I returned to the office in a bit of a daze. As I was letting myself in, Scarlet arrived, in a skimpy top, skintight leather-look shorts and flip-flops. Seeing my pink face, she glanced up at the screen. 'That the new guy?'

'Yeah.'

'Looks quite cute,' she said, soon losing interest and focusing more on her newly gelled blood-red fingernails than Steven.

'Yeah?'

For some unfathomable reason I was anxious to defend him, or at least paint him in nice colours.

She wasn't really interested. 'Failed business?' It was a throwaway, disinterested remark.

'No.' My eyes drifted across. 'I think it's his wife's stuff. The stuff had her name on it.'

Her mind followed the same track mine had done. 'Divorced, is he? Separated?' She screwed her eyes up to study the images. 'Looks a bit young to be a widower. But tragedies happen.' She was still focusing on her nails while I watched him cross the yard.

'Yeah. Maybe.'

She gave a sudden snort of laughter. 'And you haven't found out, Spinning Jenny?'

I'd acquired the name when she'd caught me dancing round the office to an old Abba song. I'd had my ear buds in and hadn't heard her arrive.

'No,' I said shortly. I wasn't going to share my musings about him.

At last her attention abandoned her fingernails. 'Spinning Jenny,' she scolded, then looking over my shoulder added, 'He's not bad looking, is he? For an old 'un.'

I turned round in shock. 'He's not that old,' I blurted out, not knowing what to say.

She gave me one of her looks that drilled right into me. 'He's old enough to be your dad.'

'You think?' I studied the screen too, searching for a clue. 'He's only about forty, isn't he? He'd have to have fathered me very young.'

'We-ell, it's possible,' she said airily.

She looked at me fondly and tapped my shoulder. ''Bout time we got you fixed up, Spinning Jenny.'

I shrugged.

But she wasn't going to let it go. 'What about doing a bit of digging around?'

I kept my thoughts to myself. They weren't even properly formed. I really liked Scarlet's rough-and-ready ways, but I wasn't about to make her my confidante. I knew she liked what she called my 'innocence'. She used to dig me in the ribs and tease me about my previous disasters which I'd poured out to her in the first week. And she was always on about my not having a boyfriend. She'd laugh even more when I said I'd had enough of men, that there was something wrong with all of them. She always threw back the same retort. 'What about Andy?'

I had my answer ready. 'He's the exception that proves the rule.'

As though we were reading each other's minds, we glanced simultaneously up at the screen. Maybe that was when I reached a turning point. What if he wasn't a wife killer? Or kinky like Scary II? What if he wasn't married? I remembered the wedding ring and shook my head.

This was a no-go area.

I'd had a taster of married men and I was never going to go through that humiliation again.

I should have suspected something when Kris Martin was so particular about my never ringing him at work or at home. 'No worries, love. It's just my mum gets a bit protective. Married? Course not.'

It hadn't taken much detective work to watch his house one afternoon and see a pregnant woman shepherding a toddler out to the shops.

Married? Course not.

I would have accosted her, but she'd looked so worn out and her pregnancy was so far gone I didn't have the heart. So instead I texted him, called him a wanker, and said if I found out he was still on the dating site I'd go round to his house and cut his bollocks off myself.

His response was swift – and predictable – a plea not to tell 'Andrea'.

As if. I'd switched my phone off without reassuring him. Let him simmer.

But the experience was a valuable lesson. These days I could spot a married man a mile off. Or so I believed. Even without a wedding ring I knew the clues. I might be desperate but I wasn't one to crap up somebody else's life.

I screwed my eyes up.

So who was Margaret? What was in the boxes and cases he was paying to store? And why did he roll down the shutter when he emerged from D5? I'd seen him do it, almost furtively, every single time.

But the Ford Focus had gone now and a lorry which I knew was full of packing materials had pulled up, together with its flirtatious and noisy driver and passenger. I signed Steven out myself, imitating his writing as best I could. He'd forgotten again.

Next time I looked back at the screen it was to see Serena, the mobile hairdresser. There were two mobile hairdressers, Esmerelda and Serena, who kept their stuff in containers. Serena was a particular favourite of mine. She drove a pink Ka that I was really jealous of, even though I couldn't drive. She was always perfectly turned out, nails, make-up, hair different colours week on week, different styles. Her scent? I couldn't identify it. Something she wafted around her like an expensive cloud. And her clothes? To me she was like a model, completely beautiful, with teeth so white they looked as though she was sucking pieces of ice. She was friendly to me too, a generous person who seemed to want to make everyone as beautiful as she was, offering to do my hair, nails, give me a facial. But the trouble was she would have had to use the office with its newly laid wooden floor, and there was no way Scarlet and Andy were going to put up with Serena's stilettoes spiking it, her hair dye staining it or bits of hair scattered over it. Scarlet and Andrew were quite particular over the look of The Green Banana, proud of its success, and they wanted to keep it looking pristine. So I had to reject Serena's offer, even though I would have loved to take her up on it.

I watched her in the yard chatting with Esmerelda, Serena having a fag, leaning against her Barbie-Doll-pink Ka. I would kill for that car. Literally. She looked relaxed and was smiling and laughing, tossing her hair around. Today her hair was platinum blonde – not streaked – but a block of bright pale lemon which I also envied like crazy. What I wouldn't give to have her hair. Long, silky, blonde. Not just brown. In skintight jeans with ripped-out knees and an off-the-shoulder silver T-shirt, she was gorgeous. And always immaculately turned out from head to foot. I loved her and hated her at the same time. In a sudden fit of jealousy, I thought if I wouldn't actually kill to look like that I could at least scratch her Ka. If I had looked like that Tommy Farraday would have fallen at my feet. And maybe Steven Taverner would at least have noticed me. But my mum was right. I am just me. Dull, ordinary, plain. I would never attract someone glamorous like Tommy or even decent like Andy. All I'd end up with would be the collection of misfits who had searched me out on the internet, the detritus of the dating world.

Scarlet too was watching the two hairdressers on the CCTV screens. 'Manufactured articles,' she said. 'All paint, false hair, false nails . . .' She giggled. 'False eyelashes. And who knows what else?'

I giggled too. 'Well, I wouldn't mind being manufactured if the finished article looked like that.'

She laughed and tapped my shoulder again. 'Come on, Spinning Jenny, let's get on with the VAT receipts.'

ELEVEN

The day was long and felt heavy and threatening, the skies so dark as to seem like night. I switched the light on in the office and watched black clouds gather over the yard. Any minute now, I thought. Any minute now the summer storm will break. When I left at almost six o'clock it felt more like midnight. As I was locking the gates behind me the heavens opened; there was a great clap of thunder and, seconds after that, a flash of proper forked lightning lit up the yard, the road and beyond, silhouetting the bottle kilns of Burslem. Typical, I thought. I hadn't brought a mac as the day had started fine and warm. It was June, for goodness' sake. So, ignoring the weather warnings, I'd come to work in jeans and a light jacket. So now I was going to pay the price and get bloody well soaked. Out of the gloom I saw the white Ford Focus, dazzling me with lights on full beam. Since he had left more than an hour before, he must have hung around or else come back with more stuff, but he'd missed the boat. The gates were locked.

Through windscreen wipers battling with the cascade of rain he caught my eye, raised his hand in a half-friendly wave and pointed at the locked doors. Surely, I thought, he doesn't expect me to open up for him? In this weather? He pulled parallel as I waited, getting drenched, but already smiling as I anticipated the warm interior of his car, thinking for sure he'll offer me a lift? But he didn't. After another wave he slipped the car into gear and rolled off, soaking me in the process.

Thank you so much, I thought, tempted to stamp my foot at the sight of his retreating car. *You might at least have . . .*

The only response I got was another flash of lightning and the rain got even heavier. Quite cross now, as well as cold and wet, I trudged to the bus stop, rain dripping from my hair and clothes. Down my neck. I felt miserable as I waited almost half an hour for a bus, getting colder and wetter as the shelter had been smashed to pieces. Vandals, I thought viciously, as I boarded. I would like to get my hands on them too.

The route took us through Burslem, passing Port Vale football ground, down the great hill at Smallthorne before rising to Norton and the little coal truck that had been placed on the village green either as an ornament or a reminder of the industrial past. I hardly noticed it. In my frustration at this nadir of my life, everyday objects had become invisible. I felt bitter resentment. Some people have cars. Some people have nice cars. And then there's me, waiting for the bus, getting splashed as they speed past in their *nice* cars, despising me for being on foot. Some people have homes. Lovely, warm, comfortable places where they are welcomed. I have one room in a house where I am treated like an intruder.

At that moment I felt that everyone's life was better than mine. And I hated them for it. Why should my parents have chucked me out when they'd divorced? Why had they spent their last couple of years together arguing and fighting? Why had they both preferred my nasty, smarmy little brother to me? Why had life dealt me a dump of shit? Why did all the boyfriends I ever had turn out to be rotten?

I tried to tell myself not to be so pitiful. Some were worse off than me. They experienced hurricanes, landslides, ethnic cleansing, malaria, starvation. But these were faraway people seen through the TV screen. Not in rainy Staffordshire in what should have been summer. I peered through the bus window, seeing my life stretch ahead of me – bleak, uneventful, one piece of bad luck following another. I would be eighty-something one day and would still be standing at a vandalized bus stop, an old woman, her shopping in a bag or pushing a Sholley, getting splashed by other people's nice cars as they headed for their nice homes. I felt vicious.

I carried on peering out of the bus window at an unrelenting grey urban sprawl. It should have felt more like summer. Blazing June. But here, in Stoke-on-Trent, it seemed that summer was passing us by. When I got off at my stop in Brown Edge, I still had a long walk, trudging for twenty minutes through driving rain, threading along the tangle of lanes, passing church and village hall and climbing the small bank to the row of terraced houses, within which one room was my home. For now. I let myself in.

Jodi was in the kitchen, washing up, hands in yellow Marigolds plunged into soapy water. There was a strong scent of cleaning: bleach and synthetic spring flowers.

She half turned. 'Cup of tea?'

In that one bland movement combined with the question, I had caught a hint of evasion.

Instead of simply accepting the offer and saying, 'thanks', my mind was busy, trying to work out what she was about to say. As she filled and switched on the kettle, I had worked it all out. On top of my dripping clothes and generally shitty projection of my life for the next sixty years, I anticipated the story she was about to relate.

She's missed her period, suspects she's pregnant and wants me out of what will no longer be my room but the baby's.

And then where would I live? I knew I'd been lucky finding here. For £300 a month, all my bills were paid. I had a small but nice bedroom, beautiful views. Jodi and Jason were a quiet, civilized pair and I loved the rural location and feel of the Victorian terrace with its blackened stone walls. It was warm and felt secure. I had a TV in my room. I could use the bathroom more or less when I liked and the place was lovely. Clean, smelling of lavender. Not like some of the grotty, filthy, mouldy places up for rent in Hanley. I had my beautiful view. When I opened my window, I inhaled the scent of that glorious valley, trees and fields, and behind me the Staffordshire Moors. If I had to leave I would lose all this. Even with my increased wages and generous bonuses I would struggle to afford much on my own. I would never be able to buy a house or even a flat. But my two closest friends were in relationships. They didn't want to share a flat with me. I felt a snatch of panic as though on the edge of an abyss. Where would I live? My hand actually shook as I reached out for the proffered mug of tea. I was terrified of going back on the streets.

Jodi was quiet as we drank our tea and I caught a snatch of her guilt. I didn't say anything but I sensed we both felt awkward.

In the end I blurted it out. 'Is something wrong?'

She shook her head, tried to brighten up, but it didn't work. Then, unexpectedly, she reached across the table and touched my hand. 'Doctor says.' Then she bubbled up. 'Apparently I'm going to have a problem getting pregnant. I have some weird chemistry inside me that does something to Jason's sperm and it means . . .' And she burst into tears, leaving me feeling awkward and guilty. But I also felt a rush of relief. Selfish. Selfish. Selfish.

'So you don't mind me staying?'

She jerked her head up then. And there was hostility in her eyes. Too late, I realized she'd expected sympathy – not her lodger looking out for herself. The sense of insecurity flooded back. She looked affronted at my selfishness and something hard and brittle changed her face into a gargoyle. I knew then that I would be given my marching orders one day. There was no longer any pretence at friendship. Her bitterness at not yet being pregnant was going to displace on to me, as though it was all my fault. Well. I was used to taking the blame for things that were nothing to do with me. No change there.

My father and mother's affairs and destroyed marriage, my brother's practical delinquency. Oh yes. Josh's TWOC-ing, substance abuse, and the ABH charge that was still hanging over his head. All my fault obviously. And added to that list of sins now was Jodi's failure to have a baby.

I used my wet clothes as an excuse to take my half-drunk mug of tea upstairs. I stripped off right down to my underwear, towelled my hair dry, sat on the bed and stared out at the view feeling glum. I looked over my pretty valley but this time it was spoilt with Mr Budge's diggers and dust and the dismal moonscape of open-cast mining.

TWELVE

We had a bit of excitement at The Green Banana that week and it finally broke the ice between myself and my newest customer. Three unmarked navy blue vans pulled up simultaneously one afternoon. Some police – not the ordinary sort, but with face masks, bulletproof vests, shields and guns came, demanding to be given entry to E14, Tommy Farraday and The Oracles' store. Apparently they'd had a tip-off that drugs were being stored there. One of the police, a bit younger than the rest, a guy with warm brown eyes and the beginnings of a paunch, gave me that in an excited aside.

'Drugs bust,' he said, speaking like James Cagney through the side of his mouth, hoping, I'm sure, to see me either open my eyes in stark amazement or swoon into his arms, like a Jane Austen heroine.

I did neither. 'Really,' I said. 'Well, fancy that.'

I think their plan was to break in using some boltcutters. But . . . Scarlet winked at me, took a key from around her neck, unlocked the top drawer of her desk and produced an odd-shaped skeleton key before marching to the head of the queue (which included two very excited sniffer dogs) brandishing it and leading the force in the direction of E14.

Though I would loved to have gone along with them and witnessed the drama, someone had to stay in the office! And that someone was bound to be me. Scarlet was far too fond of drama to let me go with the police. Besides, she was the one with the skeleton key. So I sat on the bar stool and watched what I could on the silent screens, following teams of men coming and going, carrying stuff, the dogs straining on the leash. They were there for over four hours. Obviously doing a very thorough search. I thought of ringing Tommy Farraday myself and letting him know what was going on, but I thought I'd probably get charged with obstructing justice or something like that. Anyway, the drama continued. And at three o'clock who should saunter in but Tommy Farraday himself, probably going to pick something up for a gig. Luckily he obeyed the rules for once and called in to the office to sign in. I signalled with my eyes, jerking my head meaningfully towards the screen. He looked at me curiously for a moment, perhaps wondering whether I'd had an epileptic fit, then he said, in his lazy, half-interested voice, 'Jenny, love, either you've got a nasty disease – tetanus or meningitis or else . . .' I jerked my head one last desperate time towards the screens. This time he followed the direction of my gaze, stared for two long minutes and then saw what was happening. 'Shit,' he said. Then he laughed. 'Good job we, umm . . . tidied the place up last week, isn't it, Jenny Wren?'

Why was it that everyone had some silly epithet to add to my name? Spinning Jenny, Jenny Wren. What was that all about?

So I didn't respond apart from a smile, and I avoided casting my baby blues meaningfully on the notice which specifically forbade the storage of drugs.

He frowned a moment longer at the busy little screens and then, while I was still watching the drama, he slipped away. When I looked around the office was empty, the door still swinging, the book unsigned. And there was no white van in the car park either. Just the sound of skidding tyres and a vague smell of exhaust.

I was still watching, open-mouthed, when Steven Taverner walked in.

The rule is you *have* to sign yourself in and sign yourself out. This is a requirement of the fire service so they know who's in the building and who isn't and don't go charging into a burning building, risking life and limb to rescue someone who actually left the place half an hour before. And hopefully it stops people from being accidentally locked in when the outside steel shutters slide down and the unfortunate customer forgets the emergency code. You may smile but it has happened. Once. There is no emergency alarm inside and the stores themselves are hermetically sealed. God help any of our customers if they were locked inside. Another reason why we are so fussy about the signing in and signing out. Of course, *all* our clients don't *always* comply. But Mr Taverner almost always did, except when he forgot. He struck me as an obedient sort. A rule-observer rather than a rule-breaker, unlike Tommy Farraday who would always challenge authority. Serena always signed in too but it was nothing to do with the fire service (she'd have loved to have been subjected to a fireman's lift). Oh no, it was because she was claustrophobic and terrified of being locked in one night. I have to admit it would be a horrible experience, imprisoned by locks and keypads, floors cold concrete, running out of air, trapped with the stuff of dead people and things nobody wanted, unable to escape the steel roller shutters. When no one was watching the CCTV monitors you could shout and scream all you liked. No one would see or hear you. And mobiles didn't work inside the units.

Maybe Mr Taverner was claustrophobic too and, rather than simply observing the rules, his compliance was a symptom of his secret fear.

I suppose that because of the excitement and the obviously dramatic events that were taking place right in front of my eyes, I was a bit more babbly and excitable than usual that day. My defences were down so I didn't even hold it against him that he'd let me get soaked a couple of nights before. 'The police are here,' I said flatly.

'Really?'

'Yeah.' I looked at him and added, 'In the units.'

'Not in mine, I hope,' he said with an unconvincing smile.

I held my breath while he stared up at the activity on the CCTV. I could have prolonged his concern but I didn't. 'No, Mr Taverner, not in yours. E14. Looking for drugs. In the band's.'

'Ah,' he said, scribbling his name very quickly, adding the time and his unit number while I focused back on the screens, though right now the police seemed to be standing around, chatting. When I looked back, Mr Taverner had gone. It seemed he had changed his mind. He had filled in an exit time too.

I looked for him on the CCTV and watched his car easing out of the gates and slide out on to the main road.

The police spent all afternoon coming and going and, judging by their disgruntled faces, it looked as though they hadn't found anything. Which made me a bit more admiring of Tommy Farraday. He'd pulled one over on them because I knew they did keep a great big stash in there, whatever the rules. Maybe someone had tipped him off about the police.

When Scarlet came back she was still giggling. 'Bloody full of drums, guitars, sheets of music, amplifiers. All stuffed in one on top of the other. Falling all over the place. You should have heard the noise.' She made an effort. 'Clunk, Bang, Tweet, tweet. Da-da-da-rah-rah,' she sang before collapsing across the counter. 'Not so much as a spliff in sight. The dogs' tails weren't even wagging.' She put her hands on her skinny hips and roared. Today she was dressed Country & Western in a fringed leather skirt that just about covered her bum and a checked blouse teamed with leather boots. She looked amazing, but I did keep expecting her to burst into some Doris Day 'Whip Crack Away' type of song and smack her sides.

She was chewing gum too, which added to the cowgirl image. 'Nothing like a great big raid, unsuccessful too, to make the police look absolutely friggin' stupid.' She put the gum in her cheek and dragged on the e-cigarette she'd recently switched to, releasing a cloud of scented steam. 'You gotta laugh, haven't you, Jen? They was convinced they'd get a massive haul of cocaine or heroin or something. And all they found was an ancient, dried-up dog turd.' She roared again but I was squirrelling something away. Already sensing the possibilities this knowledge might bring I schooled my voice to sound casual.

'I didn't know you had a skeleton key.'

She gave me a sharp look before replacing it very deliberately in the drawer, locking it, removing that key too, threading it on the chain and tucking it back into her cleavage. Then she tapped her nose. 'Insurance policy,' she said. 'You never know what dirty tricks people play on you. They leave the stuff there when they're fed up with paying. You never see them again. At least I can get some compensation. And sometimes they do put forbidden stuff in so I charge them a little bit extra. Can't have The Green Banana compromised, can we?' She jabbed my chest with a meaningful forefinger, her eyes wide open and very bold. '*We* could get prosecuted for that, even if we didn't even know it was there. So it pays to be vigilant, Spinning Jenny. You keep your eyes open, love, and don't trust anybody. And I mean anybody. Not even Mr Innocent-Looking Steven Taverner. People are not always what they seem. *Some* people only want to take advantage. They put stuff in, pay up for the first three months, give out a false address and stolen credit card details, remove it bit by bit when the fences are buying the hot stuff and that's the last you see of them and their hoard. This business wouldn't survive if it depended on trust.' She tapped the side of her nose. 'You need this. Nous. Instinct.' Then she got sharp and her jabs harder, almost hurting me with her long, pointed nails. 'Don't you go tellin' anyone about that key. OK? I don't want our clients knowing I've a way of checking up on them.'

Next morning, Tommy rang at ten on the dot. 'They still there, Jenny Wren?'

I knew who he meant, and I was not going to play games pretending I didn't.

'No,' I said. 'They left. With nothing except a dried-up dog turd, apparently.'

He exploded with laughter. I had my fingers crossed behind my back because I didn't want him to ask how the police had got in. If I'd said boltcutters he would have noticed that the padlock wasn't broken. I worried about that until he burst out laughing. 'They're a joke,' he said.

'Who?'

'Friggin' police.'

'Will you be in later?'

'Nah. Think me and the boys will lie low for a couple of weeks. Try not to miss us, Jenny Wren.'

'Just so long as you don't forget when your rent is due.'

But his mind was tracking along a different railway line. 'Wonder who tipped them off . . .?'

My heart gave a little skip and a hop. I hoped he didn't think it was me. I changed the subject. 'What happened to your recording contract?'

'Umm . . .' I sensed evasion. 'Didn't prove quite such a good deal as we'd thought. Basically, Jenny Wren, they were exploiting us. Things weren't as good as they seemed.'

'Nothing ever is,' I responded gloomily.

He didn't come around for a few weeks after that. And life settled down and got a bit more boring.

Perhaps because life was so quiet then I became even more curious about Steven Taverner. I couldn't quite categorize him. He was still a mystery. I couldn't even place him geographically. The Potteries accent is quite distinctive, unmistakable. I love listening to regional accents. But Mr Steven Taverner didn't have one. He could have been a Scot or Welsh, Liverpudlian or a Londoner. There was no clue in the way he pronounced words.

I couldn't even work out whether he was currently married, divorced, separated or a widower. He still wore the gold wedding band. But was he a killer, a griever, a devoted husband? I didn't have a clue.

And then I had the chance to find out a little bit more about him.

THIRTEEN

It was a warm day in early August. July had drifted by in the usual mix of sunshine and showers, hot days and cool days, days that were windy and some that were still. On that day the weather was that perfect combination of blue sky and fleecy clouds. The temperature was somewhere in the mid-seventies and there was a holiday air, even in Tunstall, Stoke-on-Trent.

It was mid-morning and I had been witnessing one of life's tragedies.

Teresa Simpson had taken out a large store a couple of months before. And it hadn't taken much detective work to know which category to put her in. A sad, wrecked face and the bitter, angry way she'd signed the book, almost gouging out a hole in the page with the pen, told me. On this particular day Mr Simpson had come with her and they were arguing over some of the contents of A9. Even on my silent grey screens I could sense the heat between those two, while their children cowered in one car or another. I was watching the entire scenario, with appalled fascination, when Steven Taverner walked in to sign in.

He followed my gaze and his mouth hung open.

'Horrible,' I said. 'Divorce is horrible, isn't it?'

'It is,' he said gravely. 'I don't think I could ever get divorced.'

I turned to look at him but he was oblivious, his attention all focused on the screen. 'Particularly,' he said, 'if I had children.'

I squirrelled the facts away and offered him a bit of a taster. 'Remind me of my mum and dad.'

He put his hand on my shoulder. 'Really, Jennifer? Your parents were . . .?'

The row was still going on. If anything, it was becoming even more heated. Even in the office, some of the sound penetrated.

His hand, on my shoulder, felt cold and heavy, the fingers long and strong. I could feel each one pressing into my collarbone.

'Yes,' I said. 'They were this bad.'

'That must have been awful.' His hand slid down to the top of my arm but was gentle now. The grip had melted into a soft touch.

'It was.' I wasn't going to tell him how awful, about my months living on the streets; neither was I going to describe to him my years at The Stephanie Wright Home for the Bewildered, but my parents' acrimony had been the start of it all. That descent into vulnerability.

'I'm sorry, Jennifer,' he said. 'No one as nice as you should have been subjected to . . .' His eyes drifted upwards. 'That.'

Then the hand was gone and so was he. I watched him walk across the yard to the units, shoulders bowed as usual, his steps dragging, slow and hesitant. Almost a stumble. I screwed my eyes up. Was he upset at the spectacle of the warring couple or at my experience?

Miss McCormick, like probably most English teachers, taught us that the word 'nice' is a lazy adjective. 'It doesn't really tell you anything,' she'd said. But to me, on that fine August day, Steven Taverner's kind gesture and words felt nice, as though someone had dropped a pearl into my hand.

I watched the Simpsons as I'd watched them many times before on my screens. Marriage can be hell. They quarrelled with an almost murderous hatred. They quarrelled about everything: the car, the furniture, the piles of CDs, the computer, the TV, the children. Noisily too. Shouting and screaming so everyone could hear. Even

I, in my office, was treated to the sound accompaniment when they argued in the forecourt. Hurling abuse at each other like rocks at a sea monster. When they drew up in their separate cars but in convoy, the entire place would erupt. People would walk the other way, hide in their cars, retreat into their own storeroom. There was something toxic about this pair, as poisonous as a chemical cloud. Scarlet rolled her eyes at the screens. 'I'm going to have to do something about them,' she said. 'Have a word. They're upsetting the other customers.'

'Maybe you should,' I murmured.

It was hard to believe that the Simpsons had ever made wedding vows to one another, to love, honour, cherish, obey.

Scarlet and I watched in appalled paralysis at the escalation in the scenario. They were actually shaking fists at one another now, Teresa Simpson, leaning in to her ex-partner, Philip, jabbing him in the chest. Had Steven Taverner's marriage to Margaret been like this? *'I don't think I could ever get divorced.'*

If he couldn't be divorced but the marriage had turned toxic, how would he have rid himself of her? If he had killed his wife, had this been how it had started? I couldn't imagine him having fierce arguments. He seemed passive, quiet and polite.

But I had learned one solid fact from his next sentence.

'Particularly if I had children.'

'Bloody good job they are divorcing,' Scarlet said. 'Imagine having that pair as your mum and dad.'

And for the second time in a matter of minutes I said, 'Remind me of mine.'

She too put her arm around me. 'Oh, Spinning Jenny,' she said. 'Poor little you.'

The explanation for Mrs Simpson's fury had presented itself one afternoon, about a week before, in the passenger seat of Mr Simpson's car. A redhead who had sat and stared straight ahead of her, detaching herself from Mrs Simpson's hammering on the window, her turning the air blue with swear words. I was on the verge of calling the police. But then Mr Simpson emerged from the store carrying a basket chair (straight out of the sixties), stuffed it in the back of his Honda and sped away with the redhead, leaving Teresa standing, forlorn, in the middle of the yard, not even moving when a lorry swung in and almost knocked her down. The driver didn't bother with his horn. He opened his window and yelled at her. And she still didn't move. In the end I went out, put my arm

around her and led her into the office with the offer of hot, sweet
tea, Scarlet watching, fag drooping from her mouth. (She'd given
up on the e-cigarettes, said they just didn't hit the spot.) She didn't
even remove it when she said to me in a very kind voice, 'You are
such a softie, Spinning Jenny.'

After that exit with the sixties chair, we hadn't seen Mr Simpson
again until the day when Steven had put his hand on my shoulder.
After that Teresa would turn up alone and struggle with the stuff.
She was a pathetic sight. Thin, old before her time, her ten-year-old
boy struggling to help. Maybe it was better to stay single.

I learned something that day and tried to reconstruct the puzzle.
Margaret was either alive and he was still married, or she was still alive
and they were separated, he refusing to grant her divorce; maybe he
or she was a Roman Catholic. Or else Margaret was dead (body stashed
away in D5?) and he was a widower. The trouble was I couldn't know
which was the true version. It was all conjecture and suspicion.

Steven wasn't a flirt. He was no David Ganger, with a devious
talent for balancing a bevy of girls. Neither was he a Kris Martin,
married man ready to cheat. He wasn't Scary I or Scary II. I had
no hint that he was into S&M or had an uncontrollable temper.
Judging by his build he was not on anabolic steroids. So what was
he? Probable answer, a happily married man whose wife had too
many belongings.

But my curiosity refused to abate.

I turned to Scarlet. 'Keep an eye out, will you? It's such a lovely
day I think I'll go for a wander.'

'You do that, Spinning Jenny,' she said, distracted by her mobile
phone, as I'd known she would be.

The sunshine in the yard was bouncing off the tarmac but inside
the stores were cool. I found myself walking very softly until I'd
reached D5. He'd left the roller shutter up this time and I peeped
around. He was kneeling on the floor, his back to me. Draped across
his arms was what looked like a midnight-blue dress. Something
long and silky. He was stroking it, holding it up to his cheek. As I
watched he kissed it, bending his head down, covering his face with
it. I felt embarrassed, as though I'd barged in on a couple having
intercourse. I breathed in the scent of Light Blue. I breathed in again
and caught no smell of a decomposing body.

I watched for a moment, appalled at my latest theory. He was a
transvestite. 'Margaret' was his alter-ego and he was storing the

clothes here, hiding them from his wife. The wedding ring was a hoax. That was his secret. I backed away, anxious he would turn and see me spying on him. I could still feel the pressure of his hand on my shoulder, felt it slipping down my arm. As I've said. As flies are drawn to rotting meat I attract the wrong sort of man.

I had my answer. Or at least an answer.

Once outside I walked very quickly back to the office and holed up behind the desk, head down.

When he came into the office to sign out, I was cool towards him. And he felt it. He had watched me for a moment, followed that with a look of concern, cocked his head on one side. 'Are you all right, Jennifer?'

I looked away, pretending I was searching for something in the desk drawer, rummaging noisily through pens, paper clips, hole punchers and Post-it pads. 'Yes. I'm fine, thank you, Mr Taverner.' Even I could hear the ice in my voice. A hostility. A deliberate distancing which paradoxically seemed to encourage him. When I looked up he was giving me a warm smile. 'You have no idea how pleasant you make it to come here.'

Inwardly, I shuddered.

He paused for a moment, perhaps waiting for me to say something, but I kept rummaging in the drawer. After a brief pause he signed his name, gave me another curious stare, turned on his heel and left.

I know your secret, I thought. *I know who you are now. I know what you are.*

Or least I thought I did.

In the end it could be just another theory.

FOURTEEN

After that day, Steven Taverner started turning up more often. Sometimes twice a week. There was no regular day or time; he would arrive randomly and on each visit he tried to engage me in conversation, about the weather, something from the day's news or simple observations. He volunteered nothing about himself, brought no more boxes or suitcases with him and spent only a few minutes inside the store, as though D5 was simply an excuse for his visit. He never brought anything out. He walked into D5 empty-handed and he left empty-handed. Sometimes he didn't go into his store at all.

And though he engaged me in conversation, he never gave away anything of himself. After that declaration when the Simpsons had argued and he had vehemently spoken against divorce and indicated he had no children, he remained an enigma. He was still wearing his wedding ring and always came alone.

Each time he came I followed his movements on the screens as he passed from one to the other and wondered. While I learned nothing more about him, my curiosity grew.

I sensed that something had changed between us. I was no longer just the girl at the storage facility. I was Jennifer, though what my role was I had no idea. I am not a conceited person but I even wondered whether he was coming to The Green Banana just to see me. Or was I flattering myself? After all, my track record hardly included a quiet middle-aged man who was possibly a transvestite, wore a wedding ring and appeared to have an invisible wife.

I was wondering this one day in late September as I watched him enter the roller shutter outer doors, emerging half an hour later, crossing the yard holding a plastic carrier bag and entering the office. *Have it your way, Mr Steven Taverner*, I was thinking. *Keep your secrets. I don't care. I'm not interested.*

'I–I–I wondered . . .' He was looking at the floor while I watched, open-mouthed. 'I thought you might like . . .' He stopped abruptly and handed me the carrier bag.

'I thought you would look nice in it.' He quickly looked away, obviously embarrassed, touchingly shy. He tilted his head and seemed to concentrate. On what, I couldn't guess.

I peered inside the bag and could see it contained blue silk. The perfume wafted out as I stood awkwardly without a clue what I was supposed to be doing with it.

I looked to him for my cue but he quickly looked away, down at the floor. His cheeks were very faintly pink and I realized, with a smile, that he was shy.

'It's for you for being so nice,' he said.

I pulled out a dress, long, blue, the same one I had seen him caress. For a moment I didn't know what to say. I almost felt his touch in the silky material. Stunned, I fell back on my manners.

'Thank you, Mr Taverner,' I said. He was watching me and I felt I should add something more. 'I don't get many gifts from customers.'

He shrugged. 'That's all right.' And then he bent over the book, filling in the time after glancing at his watch. So precise he even put 15.48 when most customers would just have put four o'clock. Then, without another look at me, he bolted. Minutes later his car inched out through the gates as silently and unobtrusively as a submarine. He was gone, leaving behind hardly a ripple of air while I still had the dress draped over my arms.

It still had the price label attached, well beyond what I would pay: £287.00. I checked the size of the dress. Size twelve. My size. Coincidence? Size twelve is, after all, a pretty average size. But it was new. Margaret had never worn it. Had he bought it for me?

To say I was confused would have been an understatement.

I gaped at it.

Not one of my boyfriends had ever given me a gift – let alone one as expensive and inappropriate as this. Inappropriate because I didn't have a clue why he had given me it or where I would wear it.

I smiled to myself. Dinner at The Ritz? On board a friend's yacht? I folded it up and replaced it in the bag.

The seed of curiosity which had been germinating ever since Steven Taverner had first come to The Green Banana had firmly taken root.

Curiosity, my mum used to say, in the days when she had bothered to speak to me, killed the cat. This was beyond curiosity. Riding on it was suspicion. In my experience, men don't give you presents without expecting something back. So what did he want from me?

My imagination ran through and discarded possibilities.

Sex? Sorry, mate. Not for sale. Sex is a gift not a commodity.

So what was he? Another cheat? He didn't seem it. The alternative could be a lonely widower? Separated, never to be divorced because he was a Catholic? A transvestite who believed I would *understand* him? A wife killer? Had I attracted yet another weirdo? I was, I admit, desperate to learn which.

Business was booming then, many starting up or changing direction. That and a volatile housing market meant that many folk could not find a place to settle and were forced to rent, so some of their possessions ended up in The Green Banana waiting for the new home. We were busier than ever. Andy and Scarlet had bought a piece of adjoining land and constructed two further lock-ups in an extension of The Green Banana Storage Facility. So there were more new customers, people coming and going, VAT receipts, enquiries, and I didn't have the time to chat to or even ponder my enigmatic customer. When Steven Taverner visited weeks later, there was a queue of people at the desk. He took one look and fled.

In B8 there were two solicitors, Nash and Broughton, neatly suited, looking rich as Croesus, or maybe David Beckham, who is, I suppose, richer than even Croesus was. They always wore the same uniform, the uniform of the confident and wealthy, and arrived in their waxed and polished Audis oozing aftershave and leaking confidence. They had too many case files in their poky little offices to store them all, they'd told me with the haughty air of someone deigning to speak to an inferior. Legal documents have to be preserved for ever. So they had to keep them somewhere. And for that they had to pay. Grudgingly. Isn't it funny? They were the rich ones. Out of all the folk who rented our containers, they were the ones who could afford it most easily. But boy, didn't they grumble when they had to pay the bill? And you always had to remind them they were overdue. It's always the rich who grumble about money, isn't it?

Their files and envelopes smelt too. Of musty old money, of manipulation and deceit and enormous bills. I wouldn't trust Nash & Broughton with my nonexistent money. They were too greedy. Too mean. Too money-grabbing. I didn't like them either, with their air of condescension. Often they wouldn't speak to me at all, just stride in, sign the book and walk straight out again without even looking at me.

Well, fuck you, I'd think.

Everyone's belongings have a peculiar scent of their own which seeps out of their unit doors, so when I walked along the corridor – if I had shut my eyes – I could have told you whose store I was passing. D5. The scent that I recognized most easily was the Dolce & Gabbana Light Blue. It must be his wife's perfume. She must spray herself with it every day because I could smell it, albeit faintly, on him.

It was halfway through October before my curiosity burst through and I had the chance to speak to him. The office was, for once, empty.

I started being businesslike. 'Do you think you'll need our storage facility for much longer, Mr Taverner? We do have a waiting list.' I hadn't meant to sound quite so sharp but that was how it came out. I was aware that I hadn't thanked him properly for the dress, just a perfunctory couple of words spoken in front of a couple of browsers studying the cardboard boxes. He'd seemed embarrassed even by that small expression of thanks. He'd received it with a flush, a frown and a nod. While I wondered. Had he bought the dress initially for his wife? Maybe she hadn't liked it. Or maybe it wasn't her size. Or had he bought it specially for me, having guessed at the size – and got it right?

My claim that we had a queue of potential customers was true. In fact, we were so popular we'd recently put up our prices, excluding customers under an existing contract, so we were perfectly happy when people cleared out. The rise in prices had been mirrored by my wage rise. Maybe, I'd thought, if he left and took the stuff away, my dreams and curiosity would fade and I would have peace. But a small, empty space. No one had ever treated me so courteously.

He didn't respond to my question straight away but stared at me until it became almost embarrassing. This was scrutiny. Staring almost through me without saying a word or twitching a facial muscle? Then, instead of answering my question, he said the same thing he had said before. 'You really do have nice hair, Jennifer.'

I gaped at him utterly confused. Was this clumsy flirting? Personally I think my hair is probably my best feature, but David used to say (with a leer) it was my legs, while Tyrone used to like to span my waist with his big, meaty paws. Sometimes he'd span it so hard I could hardly breathe. 'Doll,' he'd have said while I collapsed on the floor, blue as midnight, 'what's youz problem?' Hey ho. That was Tyrone for you. And Scary II?

Scary II was the product of some internet fishing. And somehow my profile had managed to attract him. (I've never worked out what were the fateful phrases or the angle of my selfies that drew him in, and he wasn't insightful enough to tell me.) He had described himself as 'into manly pursuits'.

But while I translated the phrase into boozing with mates and football, Scary II's idea of manly pursuits was something quite different.

His real name was Darren Finnegan, but I called him Scary II because six months previously I'd had the encounter with Scary I, Tyrone.

In Scary II's photograph he'd looked normal enough – almost handsome – apart from a thin scar which puckered his right cheek from the corner of his eye to around an inch before the side of his mouth. So he wasn't quite perfect but then neither was I. At that point in my life I had the beginnings of a rounded tummy and my skin had developed some nasty red patches.

The evening with Scary II had started OK – we'd met outside the pub and the first thing I noticed about him was the way he walked, a rolling gait that reminded me of a sailor. He kissed me on the cheek, got my name right and bought me a drink. A glass of cider, if you must know. He'd started chatting about his job – at a gym in Fenton. He was dressed well – jeans and a clean shirt – and smelt of soap and just a hint of aftershave. Not sweaty feet, stale booze or BO. Tick, tick, tick.

Things were going nicely with Scary II. I was actually just beginning to enjoy the evening, thinking I'd found Normal Man, when all of a sudden, from his man-bag he produces a magazine and lays it flat on the table. It took me a minute or two to realize what the magazine's pictures were telling me. And then I did. Images of women mainly but also a few men, handcuffed, frightened, or more probably acting frightened. They were wearing all sorts of clothes – mainly black, with chains, whips, rubber, studs. Piercings in all sorts of places. One man had a stud that went right through his penis and he was leering down at it as though it was his Christmas dinner. I turned that page over pretty quickly – it was making me feel sick. But the worst picture, the one that stayed with me, was a sort of mask that went over the face, black with tiny slits for the eyes while both nose and mouth were sealed. How was one supposed to breathe? They weren't. I drew in a sharp, reassuring breath and looked away, feeling dizzy. Scary II was watching me curiously and with an intense and meaningful interest. I could read his mind. He was watching for my reaction before suggesting . . . I looked at the pictures for about twenty seconds more and then across at him. He had this gleam in his eye. Determined, measuring me up for one of those outfits, small, medium or large, waiting for my response, inviting me to join him in this dark and ugly place where suffering was erotic and being suffocated pleasurable. Looking at his face and eager eyes I could read his question. *Are you up for this?*

All I knew was I had to get out of there. Fast. I stood up, left my cider on the table (a first for me) and felt his eyes follow me out through the door. I had never been so frightened or felt so ill.

In fact, I was so frightened he'd follow me out of the pub and back to my flat that I took a taxi home and didn't go outside my front door for two whole days. Just lay on my bed, periodically peeping to check he wasn't outside. When a blue Fiat that I didn't recognize pulled up outside the house, my heart rate went up to 300 and stayed there for half an hour.

Scary II was from Congleton, he'd told me, in the moments of normal conversation we'd exchanged before he'd pulled out his magazine. Congleton is only twenty minutes away from Brown Edge across the moors, and I've had a thing about the place ever since. I never go there. Though I know that's a bit unfair. I'm sure some lovely people come from Congleton. Just not him. I was tempted to put something online, add something to the Me Too movement warning other women not to give him an opportunity to test his weird and wonderful tastes out on them. But I was worried I might run into legal trouble for blackening his character, so I didn't. Maybe one day I'll read he's been convicted of a sadistic murder and I'll feel guilty that I didn't shop him. Maybe that will turn out to be yet another mistake I've made.

My life is potholed with them.

When he asked for a second date, I blocked him from my social media. You need social media to have a life. But it does expose you.

One of my nightmares was that one day, when I glanced up at the bank of grey and black monitors, Scary II's face would loom up in front. In many ways I found him more frightening than Scary I. Simple temper and aggression I could understand. Scary II's predilections were deep, dark, invisible. It is like the film where the camera creeps up on an unsuspecting victim. It is the terror you can't see that looms largest.

What was I going to find out about Steven?

We were at a sort of impasse, him staring at me, me regarding him back completely confused. Then he smiled at me. It was a sweet smile, shy and somehow sad. I felt drawn into him, unable to look away. His eyes warmed, the gold flecks shining like tiny stars. He tilted his head as though listening to or for something then, unpredictable as ever, without saying another word, he nodded, turned around and walked out, leaving me dumbfounded. What was going on in this guy's mind?

FIFTEEN

Again, I didn't see him for a couple of weeks. The clocks went back and the evenings lengthened while the days shortened. It was dark when I locked the gates. Steven stayed away and I drew my own conclusion. He was embarrassed. When I opened my wardrobe door I'd stare at the blue dress trying to divine some clue, a meaning, but I was as confused as ever.

Perhaps what I'd interpreted as flirtation was nothing of the sort. Yet again I'd misread the signs. He had paid a simple compliment on my hair and given me a dress his wife probably didn't want and now he was embarrassed. His stuff was still here but he'd soon stop paying. I'd send reminders and, finally, he would come with a hired van and move the lot out. And that would be the last I'd ever see of him. Mr Steven Taverner would vanish back into the ether. And I would never really know why he had given me the dress.

But I had one small clue.

On the price label there was the name of a shop. An upmarket place in Wolstanton. I'd gone past it on the bus and admired the beautiful outfits in the window. The sort of clothes you know instinctively cost megabucks. The sort of clothes you might wear to a society wedding. Beautifully made, no skimping on design or embellishment. But I had never ventured inside. It was not my sort of place.

I asked Scarlet for the afternoon off and took a bus to Parakeet.

I am used to shops where you walk in, browse racks of stuff on hangers, fight your way into the changing rooms and make your choice, queueing up at the till. That or charity shops and supermarkets.

Parakeet was nothing like that. For a start, when I pushed open the door a little bell tinkled – politely. The shop was empty and a woman with lilac hair looked me up and down, sniffed the air and turned up her nose. She knew I didn't belong here.

'Can I help you?'

There I floundered. 'Umm.'

Her mouth squeezed tight as she waited. I could almost see her mentally counting the seconds ticking by, checking the stock for anything that might be 'lifted'.

Her pretend smile was condescending.

I squared my shoulders and tried out a sort of story. 'My dad bought me a dress from here but it's a bit long.'

She had glasses on a chain around her neck. She lifted them on to her nose. Her eyebrows shot up. 'We do carry out alterations,' she said reluctantly, 'for a price. If you would like to bring it in.' Again, she looked me up and down, suspicion creasing her brow, and then she smiled. 'Nice of your dad to buy you a dress.'

I could read her thoughts. I may be a down-and-out but my *dad* might have the readies. I gave her a sweet smile and pressed forward with my investigation in my best Queen's English. 'You might remember him.'

She moved her head, querying.

'Taverner,' I said. 'Mr Taverner.'

Her brow wrinkling was almost a comic act. 'I don't think so,' she said.

I tried a little bit harder. 'About . . . so high. Forties, thinning brown hair. Nice eyes.'

She repeated her get-out clause. 'I don't think so.' She'd tried to make the words sound sweet but it still sounded condescending.

Blind ending, plus I'd embarrassed myself. I left, summoning up every ounce of dignity.

I tried to drag myself into reality. He'd only said I had nice hair. And I was so starved of compliments and affection that I'd grabbed at it with both hands, reading something into it that was never meant. The dress I found harder to explain. The boxes and suitcase in D5? Life's little mysteries. I would never know who or what Margaret was but would have to rely on surmises.

I caught the bus home on Halloween feeling flat, vulnerable and raw. And watching the kids in their costumes tricking and treating – along with the pumpkin faces leering at me – didn't help one little bit.

It was time I stopped seeing ghosts in shadows and moved back into the real world.

That was my resolution.

By November the shops were gearing up for Christmas. They were full of Christmas tat, everything red and sparkly and cheap looking.

I was dreading Christmas. Not only would the store be closed for four whole days but I would be spending those four whole days confined to my room. Jason and Jodi wouldn't want me around. Our relationship had soured and I wasn't sure exactly why. Christmas was my very worst time of year, a parody of what it is supposed to be: family, love, turkey and presents. What was I supposed to do? Sit in my room and have a pretend Christmas dinner? Ring one of my parents (if I could track either of them down) and ask if I was invited for turkey and stuffing? Find out where my shitty little brother was and gatecrash whatever his plans were? Or play the maiden aunt and sit on the sofa while my girlfriends had fabulous presents from their loving husbands and watched their little adorables play with their new toys? My only single friend, Bethan, had recently hooked up with a new Mr Wonderful so that was out. It wasn't much of a choice, was it? In fact, no choice at all.

In the end I decided I would probably try and cancel the festive season altogether. The year before I'd bought myself a bottle of Bailey's Irish Cream but had felt sick halfway through so I wouldn't be repeating that experience. No thank you.

I'd already bought Scarlet and Andy a bottle of prosecco and put it in a festive bag.

Things at home (or more literally in my room, plus scuttles in and out of the kitchen and bathroom) had become increasingly frosty, but neither Jodi nor Jason had said anything more about a baby or, more importantly, about my moving out. They just seemed to silently resent me, never sparking a conversation, watching me if I was around, as if they thought I might steal the silver. I knew they couldn't wait to see the back of me. I could feel their hostility beaming on me in every single corner of the house. There were no overtures of friendliness. I never watched TV in the evenings with them any more; neither did we share takeaways. I would have moved out except I had nowhere to go.

In the middle of December I got a Christmas card from my mother. (So she did know where I lived.) She had remarried a man with the unimaginative name of George. And Dad was currently living in Thailand. He sent a card wishing me a Happy Christmas and mentioning a string of women – a Jasmine, a Meena, a Kachina, which he told me meant dancing spirit. Oh yeah, I thought, I bet she danced all right. Dirty old man gets taken for a ride by beautiful young Thai hooker. Seen it all before, Dad. Anyway, that meant that neither of my parents was in the slightest bit interested whether I lived in Brown Edge or fucking Timbuktu. There is something tacky about being faced with your parents' sexuality – especially when in my early twenties both of them were probably getting more sex than me. And especially when the objects of my father's lust were probably younger than me.

At least 'George' sounded like a proper grown-up man.

I'd kept to my vow about celibacy and not mopping up the wrong guy. But is there a little light that goes out in your head when you're just not interested? Like a dying firefly? There must have been, because on the odd nights I did manage to persuade Stella or Bethan to abandon husband and kids and come out with me, guys didn't seem interested in me either. It really was like something had been switched off. I could see right into my future. I was going to be one of those old ladies, looking years older than they actually were, who'd shuffle on to the bus. Someone everyone would ignore or sidle away from as though she smelt. I might even be homeless – again.

That night when I went to bed I heard Jodi and Jason copulating in a futile effort to *make a baby*. Mutters and moans and that rhythmic bonking that tells you a couple are connected. I shoved my pillow over my head but couldn't shut it out. The entire house was vibrating.

I was beginning to feel terminally sorry for myself. Christmas had dropped me, as usual, right into the Slough of Despond.

SIXTEEN

And then on Friday 15 December, at around four o'clock, I saw the white Ford Focus slide into the forecourt and park neatly. Steven climbed out and walked towards the office. I managed a polite smile. 'Hello, haven't seen you for a while.'

'There's been no need for me to come in. And . . .' He gave me a proper warm smile that lit his eyes. 'It's Christmas.'

I let my gaze drift around the office, at the three-foot-high artificial tree draped with silver tinsel, the cards stuck around the walls with Blu-Tack and the soundtrack of continual Christmas oldies and managed a smile I would have classed as ironic. 'I know.'

What happens to people around Christmas time? Scarlet had been in a jolly mood earlier, twirling around in killer white stilettoes, fishnet tights and a red micro-dress trimmed with fake white fur. Andrew was taking her out for dinner and she was in festive mode, humming Slade's 'Merry Christmas Everybody'. She'd breezed in at a quarter to two and left at two telling me she wouldn't be in again until Monday so I was on my own.

I'm no philosopher but I've worked out that being dissatisfied with your life at this time of year puts you in a particularly vulnerable position. It heightens the emotions, makes you desperate, makes you long for change. The New Year beckons with threats and promises. Your brain flaps around like a skate on the bottom of the ocean, one eye open but seeing nothing, distorting everything. Not even seeing danger ahead, sharks looming.

And so . . .

I dipped my toe in the water and said, quite brightly, 'Nearly done then?'

He gave me his full, puzzled attention before regarding me with that grave, solemn smile that seemed to appraise me. Not in a sexual way but almost trying to decipher what I was saying. 'Sorry?'

I tiptoed a little further into his private life. 'So you've found another house?'

He looked completely confused now. His eyes (hazel with gold flecks, almond-shaped, slightly Oriental-looking) flew open. 'Sorry?'

'Oh,' I said, glancing down deliberately at the gold wedding ring. 'I'm sorry. Didn't mean to pry. I just thought you and your wife might be moving house.' He looked even more puzzled now, while I felt suddenly awkward, so I tried – and failed – to turn the intrusion into something light-hearted. 'None of my business unless you have . . .' Smiling, I pointed to the board which showed (for those who couldn't read) pictures of forbidden substances. 'A gun. Drugs.' I laughed, 'Livestock as in a baaing sheep, any of these.' He still looked confused and frowned at me while I squirmed. What must I sound like? He must think me so friggin' stupid. Then his eyes drifted across to the pictures, graphic enough for a teen magazine *Wham. Pow.* Firearms. Livestock as in rearing horses and snarling dogs, etc., etc.

Then he looked back at me, his head tilted to one side and I felt my face burn. I felt such a fool and tried to back away from his private life. 'I'm so sorry, Mr Taverner,' I said shortly. 'None of my business.'

He gave me just half a smile. 'I'm not moving house, Jennifer,' he said gently. 'I'm staying where I am.'

I felt even more of a fool then. A feeling which was compounded when his statement was followed by an even more awkward and prolonged silence between us.

We seemed to be staring at each other without any words coming out. It was odd. He had an open, honest face and yet I couldn't, for the life of me, work out what he was thinking. And I wasn't going to find out either because, after a couple of seconds which seemed to stretch into minutes, instead of signing in he turned on his heel and without another single word, left, so I simply watched the doors swing to and fro and then I watched him on the CCTV screens.

I was still watching him when Ruby Ngoma came in and followed my gaze. Steven was standing by his car, hesitating. I saw his lips move. He was arguing with himself. What about?

Even Ruby had entered into the Christmas spirit. She was wearing her uniform of skinny jeans (baggy on her), and a shapeless brown anorak. But she was wearing decorated Christmas tree earrings which flashed when she moved her head. She had the usual fag in her hand. For Ruby there was no such thing as a non-smoking area. 'That man,' she said, bony finger stabbing at my chest, 'don't you trust him, my love. He's not all he seems, that one; there's something strange about him. Something secretive.'

And you're such a good judge of character, I thought resentfully, and put it all down to envy. She continued with her mantra. 'When you're young they want to get inside your knickers, my love. When you're old . . .' Her faded eyes fixed on mine and I read the same pre-Christmas sadness that afflicted me. I watched Steven Taverner still arguing with himself by the car door. After a few more minutes of tense argument, he opened the door, climbed in, drove off.

And Ruby sidled off leaving behind an aroma of stale smoke.

I was alone again.

Of all the people I knew, Steven Taverner was the hardest to read. I couldn't work out whether he liked me, disliked me or was indifferent. I couldn't work out why he paid me compliments but never followed it up with anything more. I didn't know whether he was shy or simply reserved. He had no body language but tended to hold himself still. I didn't even have a clue why he needed to store Margaret's belongings or who she was. And the biggest mystery of all? Why had he given me that blue dress?

What did it mean?

I'd thought I knew all the reasons why people used the services of The Green Banana Storage Facility: sentiment, divorce, money, hoping their goods would increase in value, lack of room, business necessities. But I couldn't work out which of my theories was applicable in this case.

I tried a theory to see if it fitted. Maybe Margaret, his wife, was not dead but disabled. That was why she never came here, couldn't wear the blue silk dress he'd bought her. His gentle voice and polite manner would prove a winning combination for a husband nursing a sick or disabled wife. He would be nurturing, patient, kind. He would not shout or be bullying. One could trust a man like Steven Taverner. I smiled to myself, keeping this warm, trusting feeling wrapped up inside myself.

I must have been feeling particularly nosey that day because sniffing at the puzzle was driving me mad. And maybe I wanted something a bit more in my life. Something kind – like . . .

That image of me in the future, an old maid shuffling her way on to the bus, shunned by the other passengers, seemed even more vivid then and even more likely. The blue dress would hang in my wardrobe for ever, the price label still attached and would never be worn.

The frustration was beginning to drive me mad. I searched through his bank details for a clue I could have picked up months earlier. Joint account? Not a bit of it. Just his name. Mr Steven J. Taverner.

John, I decided. Steven *John* Taverner. John is a stolid, traditional name well suited to him.

There was a cold wind blowing in from the northeast that was rattling the shutters that day, heralding ice, whisking leaves and rubbish around the empty courtyard as though ghosts danced and mocked in the dark. In the office I felt illuminated, on stage, exposed.

I continued testing theories.

He'd seemed surprised I'd assumed Margaret was his wife. But he wore a wedding ring. Was it possible then that Margaret was not his wife but his sister?

At which point my imagination ran riot.

Who had died of a tropical disease. After hitting the internet and playing around on the tropical diseases information page, I decided on bilharzia rather than the more common malaria. At that time there were no current reports of an Ebola outbreak. His beloved sister, Margaret, had been in Malawi, working for a foreign food-aid charity. Steven had cleared her flat but couldn't bear to get rid of her clothes but was worried they might harbour the infection. This version took firm root in my brain. I expanded it further. And his wife never came with him because she was . . . agoraphobic.

SEVENTEEN

S carlet had told me we were to close on Friday 22 December and not reopen until the New Year. I dreaded it. Christmas was bad enough when it lasted just two days. A week and a half was far too long. But I rallied enough to buy a pack of Christmas cards, handing them out when anyone turned up, which resulted in more jolly-looking cards to paste around the office and gifts from some of the customers (not Nash & Broughton, needless to say; all they'd done was grumble about us being closed for so long and tried to get a reduction in their rent – fat chance), a few bottles of wine plus a very thoughtful Boots token for ten pounds. Steven arrived on Thursday the twenty-first and I handed him one addressed to Steven and Margaret.

He stared at the envelope, apparently puzzled.

While I watched and held my breath.

But all he did was open the card and read it. Inside I'd written: *Thank you for your custom, Jennifer.* I'd toyed with the idea of adding an X but decided against it.

He looked at me. 'Thank you, Jennifer. It was a nice thought.'

And he gave me a tentative smile followed by the usual avoidance of a direct gaze.

'I'm sorry,' he said, speaking to the floor. 'I don't really go in for cards.'

I swallowed any disappointment I might have felt, masking it with an airy, 'Lots of people don't now, they donate money to a charity instead.'

'Yes.' *He gave nothing away, did he?*

'Besides,' I added, 'you've given me that beautiful dress.'

His face froze, his entire frame stiffening.

'And I haven't had a chance to say thank you.'

He looked anxious. 'Does it fit?' There was real anxiety in the question and still he could not seem to look at me.

'Oh, yes.' I paused before diving into the deep end. 'But doesn't your wife mind you giving expensive gifts?'

He didn't seem to know how to answer. After a brief pause, he shook his head.

And left.

The Christmas period was just as dreadful as I'd anticipated. Mum and Dad had both included ten pounds in their cards with the same message: *Get yourself something nice.*

For twenty pounds? I was going to struggle.

The weather was miserable, my room cold. Jodi and Jason had a blazing row on Christmas Eve and that set the atmosphere in the small house for the entire 'festive' period. I turned my telly up as loud as I dared but I could still hear the bitterness in their voices souring the atmosphere and belying the Christmas tree which winked and blinked 24/7. On Christmas morning I woke to hear them squabbling until Jason did what men do when they've had an argument and disappeared down the pub for several hours. I would have offered my company to Jodi but her sobs sounded hysterical and I thought she might turn her upset on to me. So I opened the present I'd bought with my parents' twenty pounds – a bottle of fake Chanel No. 5. It looked convincing enough but for twenty pounds from a guy who'd parked himself outside The Potteries Centre and scarpered when the police came sniffing around, what do you expect? I splashed enough on me to smell like a Kardashian, watched television, went for horrible walks through muddy fields and was glad to return to work. I wondered what the New Year would bring. Something told me it would be different.

Or was that just blind optimism?

I was back on Tuesday 2 January, a bitterly cold day with an evil wind that tried to cut you in half. Needless to say, there was no sign of Steven. In fact, there was no sign of anyone except Teresa Simpson, who was one of the few who turned up to return her artificial Christmas tree to A9. And surprise, surprise, she'd bought me a bottle of Bailey's. 'I meant to give you this for Christmas,' she said apologetically. 'I hope you like it.'

'I do,' I said. 'I love it though I don't get to drink it much. Thank you. That's very kind of you.'

'You've been very kind to me,' she returned, 'and Darrel and Fay (her children). It's been an awful year.' She gave a brave smile and I noted she'd put some lipstick on and done something with her hair which no longer looked lank and greasy but a bit more like hair. Still streaked with grey but a vast improvement.

I couldn't disagree but put my head on one side and nodded. She touched my hand. 'But this year,' she said, 'will be different. I've got through Christmas and the New Year. I have a job. I've finally accepted the divorce and Darrel, Fay and I have a holiday booked later on in the year. So here's to the New Year. The new me.'

'I'll drink to that,' I said, and felt a further surge of optimism.

On 4 January Melanie and Patrick Randall made their annual pilgrimage to F3 to pick up their skis ready for their holiday. As usual they were bursting with health and vitality. I watched them with envy. I would love to be like that, surrounded by noisy, healthy friends, about to embark on a skiing holiday. It was about as far as one could get from my humdrum life as was possible. The farthest I'd been was to Blackpool with my mum and dad when I was around six. And that was out of season – because it was cheaper. I only remember a biting wind, the sound of the waves splashing against the seafront, seagulls who nicked my chips and the sound of endless slot machines, their lights winking and blinking through the day and the night. I can't remember where we stayed. Probably it would have been in one of the numerous boarding houses or B & Bs. I just remember the scent and sound of bacon frying.

We were busy during January and February. Once Christmas is over many people have a mighty big clear-out and rethink their homes, shifting unwanted stuff into the store. This is what happens. They are busy and enthusiastic for a week or two, expending all their energy moving their stuff in. And then they forget about it. While, thanks to standing orders, and the minimum six months, we keep creaming the money out of their bank accounts and into ours. As a business plan it works.

Another factor that keeps the store filled is it's surprising how many people choose to die over the festive period.

I watched bereaved people unload the contents of Grandma's

house; on another day some gorgeous pieces from an antiques shop in Leek that had recently closed and more stuff arrived from Serena's mobile hair salon. (Did she really use *all* those different dyes and shampoos, mousses and conditioners?) Business must have been good because she'd recently swapped her Ka for a Fiesta. Still pink, of course. I think she must have had it specially sprayed to her own peculiar car colour – Barbie-doll pink. Some people might call it bubble-gum pink. Anyway, to my mind it was striking and sickly. I no longer envied her as I watched her on the CCTV screen, toppling on her six-inch heels with an armful of bags and boxes, hair still immaculate (probably lacquered stiff). Well, I had to have something to bitch about, didn't I, because there was no sign of Steven and I was surprised how much I missed him. I worried that I had driven him away. Maybe, I thought, he took offence at my Christmas card, felt it too personal, an intrusion. Or he was embarrassed when I'd mentioned the dress. Maybe I'd misinterpreted the gesture, thinking it was a romantic overture when it was nothing of the sort. It was a dress he'd bought his wife but she didn't like it and the shop wouldn't take it back. Perhaps. I took heart in the fact that his stuff was still here and hoped I would be able to smooth over any awkwardness when he finally arrived. It was beginning to bother me.

I felt I was tumbling backwards, away from my New Year optimism. My single state was beginning to look too much like a lifestyle. I was so desperate for a relationship – even a bad one – that one warm day, late in March, I even considered internet dating all over again.

Bad idea. I know.

So my life had fallen back into the same rut, which might explain why my curiosity about Mr Taverner didn't go away. Instead it got bigger, my stories even more fanciful. Now I was imagining his wife had done one of those missing persons things – disappeared into thin air and he was grieving yet hoping that one day she'd come back. Poor man. Or else, she'd killed herself and their child but he still loved her and had decided it was due to undiagnosed depression. Cancer was always a possibility. Or . . .

Now I'd built up narratives, each one making him, perhaps, more interesting than he really was, I felt drawn to him. His life had held disappointments and letdowns as mine had. I was watching for him to come again and find the clues. The truth is, in a funny way I missed him. I liked his voice, soft, unaccented, coaxing, his sliding eyes. He was gentle and polite and, I felt, trustworthy.

Trouble was I was merging perfect man with Steven Taverner. (Who might still be a Bluebeard!)

I might collect wankers like pearls on a necklace. Which hung around my neck like the Ancient Mariner's dead bird. But one day, surely, I had to hit lucky? Was this my chance?

As I watched the silent grey screens, white people scurrying in and out with items, I watched for the white Ford Focus and dreamed.

My ideal man had a soft voice. He was polite, mature, someone who'd lived a bit. Travelled a bit. Knew about current affairs, as in politics, wasn't permanently skint. Drove a car that wasn't held together with duct tape and exhausts deliberately wide and noisy for maximum sound pollution. My man was intelligent, polished. Urbane. He dressed well. Smelt of soap and deodorant. Not smelly feet and . . . Perhaps because I worried I would never meet anyone like that, and if I did he wouldn't look twice at me, I started to cast Mr Taverner in that role.

It was Serena who shook me out of my torpor. She marched in one Tuesday afternoon and found me sitting on my office stool staring moodily into the CCTV monitors.

Today, as usual, she looked massively hot in skintight jeans and a pink blouse knotted at her midriff. Her hair was platinum blonde and scraped back into a ponytail. She was wearing pink high-heeled cowboy boots.

She stood and regarded me for a moment, hands on hips. 'What are you doing just staring into those for?'

I came out of my trance and shrugged.

'You know what,' she said, eyeing me from underneath thick black false eyelashes, 'you . . .' pointing a long pink fingernail at me, 'are turning into something quite passive and pathetic. And it all starts with your hair,' she said firmly. 'Lock the office for half an hour. I'll kick my shoes off and give you a shampoo and trim. For nothing,' she said with a grin. 'Jenny Lind.'

'Who the heck's she?'

She smirked. 'The Swedish Nightingale,' she said. 'A singer.' Then explained, 'She came up in a pub quiz.'

So now I had another epithet. Not just Spinning Jenny or Jenny

Wren. I could also be Jenny Lind. Except I couldn't sing. Not like a nightingale, more like a frog.

But whatever she called me she was offering to transform me. I wasn't going to turn down a free hairdo.

I locked the office, keeping an ear and an eye out, of course.

Naturally when someone's trimming your hair the conversation drifts towards boyfriends, and I had to confess that I didn't have one and further that I hadn't had one for almost two years.

'Gosh,' she said, painted eyebrows practically meeting in the middle. 'How sad. How awful.' Then she screwed up her face and looked at me. 'How odd.'

'I attract the wrong sort,' I said gloomily, water trickling down my neck, only partly compensated for by the lovely scent of coconut shampoo. 'They're all disasters for me, Serena.'

She was thoughtful for a minute, holding a strand of hair vertically then giving it a decisive snip.

'I never meet anyone here,' I complained.

'Course you do.' Serena was always bright. Always positive. 'People are coming and going all day. There's always someone here. Loads of blokes too.'

'All married or in the middle of a nasty divorce,' I said, picturing poor old Teresa standing in the middle of the yard looking so small, so sad, so pathetic, her son trying to look big and brave and in control when really his little boy's heart was breaking. I put myself right by her side, mentally toasted her in Bailey's for her transformation.

'You could go on the Net.'

'Tried that. Didn't work any better.' And I told her a little life story about Scaries I & II.

When she'd stopped laughing, she sobered up. 'Hmm,' she said, taking two strands of hair and holding them up to see if they were the same length. Then she brightened. 'I know what you could go for.'

I waited.

'A silver surfer.'

I turned around a bit too sharply, nearly got the scissors in my eye. 'That's *exactly* what I fancy, Serena. Someone older. More mature. Someone at least solvent . . .' My voice trailed away. But Serena, clever girl, had picked up on my train of thinking.

'What about,' she said, 'the guy in D5. He fits the bill, surely?'

'Married, I think. He wears a wedding ring.'

'Is he? I've never seen his wife.'

'Agoraphobic.' I'd said it without thinking; the fantasy narratives had become so real. 'That or he's a Bluebeard.'

'What the Dickens . . .?'

'Not come up in a pub quiz?' I mocked. 'Guy who killed his wives.'

'Oh, surely not.'

I shrugged. 'Who knows?'

'Oh,' she responded, 'shame that. He's so nice and polite. Not like most of the guys round here. Not bad-looking either.' For her it was a throwaway remark. For me it was a game changer – or do I mean life changer? She buzzed around with the hairdryer which was practically burning my neck.

'There.' She finished a minute later and was holding up the mirror for me to study the back of my hair, without realizing just what she'd said.

I admired the neat scissoring while she waited for my comment, the inevitable. 'Gorgeous. Thanks.' It has always seemed odd to me that you make these comments about the back of your head. But you can't not say anything, can you?

'Oh, well,' she finished packing her brushes, combs, scissors and hairdryer into a neat black trolley suitcase, 'hope you find your perfect man.' She sighed, then said, 'Back to the drawing board then, Jenny Lind.'

But I had just realized something. I didn't want to return to the drawing board or the internet. I liked the idea of a silver surfer by my side, keeping me safe. But he hadn't dropped by for months now. I couldn't start something with a man who wasn't even here. Who was probably married.

And then I got my perfect opportunity.

Steven's account was overdue – by one day. (He'd elected to pay monthly, doing it online by direct transfer month by month rather than set up a standing order which we preferred.) One day late? Not much, but it gave me an excuse to ring him. I still wanted to smooth over any embarrassment I'd caused by my clumsy response to his gift of the dress. I didn't want him to think badly of me. I dialled the landline, fingers crossed he picked up rather than Margaret, words lined up in my mind. I'd practised what I was going to say.

Hello, Mr Taverner, it's Jennifer here – from The Green Banana Storage Facility. (I thought that sounded really posh.) *I'm just reminding you that your balance was due yesterday.*

I didn't get to say any of it. His voice kicked in. 'Hi, you have reached Steven. I can't take your call at the moment. Leave a message.'

I said my bit.

Should I try his mobile?

No, Jen. I could almost hear Stella's voice advising me. *Leave it alone. Let it drop. Forget him. He's never been late with his payments before. He'll cough up. Or else he'll come and collect his stuff.*

But never one to take the safe road or listen to advice, I rang his mobile anyway.

It rang for a few minutes. Then he answered, sounding very confused, obviously not recognizing the number. 'Hello?'

'Hi,' I said jauntily. 'It's Jennifer here.'

Silence. As I absorbed the depressing fact that he didn't have a clue who I was.

'Jenny from . . .' and I trotted out my spiel again. There was another long silence before he said, very politely, 'I'm sorry about that, Jennifer. I completely forgot the account was due to be paid yesterday. How about . . .'

I strained to hear what was in the background. Traffic? People talking? But I heard nothing. He picked up the conversation. 'I'll drop by tomorrow, Jennifer. Will that be all right?'

'Yes. Of course. See you tomorrow, Steven.' Even to my ears it sounded daring.

Another silence then, 'Yes. Yes. I'll be over about eleven. OK?'

It was a very precise time. But then he was a very precise man.

EIGHTEEN

I awoke with the delicious feeling that today something momentous would happen, as though my horoscope had predicted a windfall. Ignoring Jodi's slightly frosty look as I munched my cornflakes, my heart continued to skip around in my chest. The delicious feeling was not going to go away, even though Jodi was getting positively hostile these days – as though I was to blame for her infertility. I couldn't really understand my optimism; there was no rationale behind it. I didn't know why I felt pleased at seeing Steven Taverner again.

I felt strangely empowered and decided that I would drop by the estate agent's in my lunch break and buy a copy of the *Sentinel* to see if I could find somewhere else to live. Jason had gone all quiet on me while Jodi was like this, frowning whenever my presence registered. Surely now I was earning more money I could afford something a bit better? I'd even got a bit saved. Sod it if they were struggling with the mortgage; it wasn't my problem. I couldn't give a flying fuck. And it wasn't my fault Jodi wasn't pregnant either. Judging by the sound effects through thin walls in a small house, they'd made up their Christmas row and these days and nights seemed to be at it like a pair of rabbits. Still trying.

Ignoring the dress code of jeans and fleece, I wore my best dress that day. I'd picked it up from the charity shop in the shopping centre by the storage facility. It looked expensive. Felt heavy, always a sign of quality. It was plain grey with a stand-up collar and seriously classy. I wore it with the only pair of leather shoes I possessed (bought in the sales). Black with a T-bar. Very sixties.

I'd washed my hair and brushed it till it shone. All right. I admit it. I wanted to make an impression. I wanted him, wife or not, to at least *like* me.

Bang on eleven I watched his Focus glide into the yard.

Another of my life's philosophies is this:

You can judge a man by his driving. There is Reckless one, who take risks, overtakes on blind bends, drives while drunk, fiddles with his mobile phone and very little attention on the wheel, the road or any road-users.

There is Selfish one. Who hogs the road, gaily tootling along without a thought to the people behind him who want to drive faster. This person is not above manoeuvring, deliberately blocking the way forward for anyone who might want to pass him and accelerates when they try. He hogs both lanes on a dual carriageway, swinging from one to the other, and turns right without first checking his mirror then curses when the car behind, driven by Impatient one, who was driving too close anyway, flashes angrily and almost shunts into the back.

Impatient one revs up at traffic lights and belts off at red and amber. He can't wait for green.

And when Selfish one parks? He slews across two parking places or else in the disabled or mother-and-baby bay, in spite of fulfilling neither criteria. *Sod you* is his mantra. If he even has one.

Then there's Dreamer who doesn't realize he's in charge of half a ton of potentially lethal metal because he's on some little private trip of his own.

Tyrone was the perfect example of Angry Man. Everyone on the road is his enemy, a journey a battle. He joins the motorway accelerating straight into the fast lane, flashing his lights, beaming out the message, *Move over, motherfucker.* And if they don't he erupts into road rage and the lethal dance of who owns which lane.

And then there's Mr Perfectly Polite who remembers his Highway Code, obeys the speed limit, keeps his distance. Thanks anyone with a wave when they allow him out.

Steven Taverner was Mr Perfectly Polite, and his timekeeping was almost obsessive. Eleven o'clock, he'd said. Dead on.

He parked, as usual, in the centre of the marked bay, climbed out and locked the car, checking the handle to make sure. I watched it all on the monitor, smiling. No boxes or suitcases today. I watched him walk towards the doors. And then he was inside wafting in the scent of a meadow.

I gave him my best smile which he returned – with interest.

'Hello, Jennifer,' he said. 'Sorry about that,' and with a mischievous smile and catching my eye, he added, 'I've come to pay my dues before you lock me in my store.'

I held his gaze a fraction longer than was absolutely necessary and he didn't flinch or look away but returned my gaze steadily.

I was the one who looked away first. 'Great,' I said. 'Thanks. I hate to nag but I do have to keep the books in order.'

'Sure.'

'If you think you might be here for a while why don't you set up a direct debit?'

He frowned. 'I–I don't know how long I'll need your facility,' he said carefully. 'It's hard to say.'

My heart sank. He was planning to leave?

He handed me his debit card. I tapped in our code and the amount and slid the machine back across the counter. He typed in his PIN and passed it back to me. Then his eyes wandered up to the bank of monitors. 'Is that all you get to watch all day?' That tentative little smile was back.

'Pretty much.' Two huge guys, using a porter's trolley, were unloading a washing machine from a furniture removal van. Steven Taverner smiled. 'Not very edifying, is it?'

I laughed out loud and agreed. 'No.'

His eyes left the two Hercules and turned right back to me. 'Don't you get bored?'

'Yes,' I admitted.

He nodded as if he was agreeing. Then, 'You look smart today.'

I dipped my head.

He put his head on one side. 'You know, Jennifer, you have the most beautiful smile.'

I was logging them up. Nice hair, a beautiful smile. He'd noticed my effort.

'Thank you.'

There was an awkward silence between us.

A struggle appeared to be going on in his brain. He was doing that thing again, tilting his head as though listening to or for something. I watched, not quite sure what was going on. It seemed to be a struggle. Good versus bad, Ego versus Id. He didn't know whether to take this forward or not. I could almost smell indecision. Something like limes mixed with sharp peppermint.

He looked at me, his eyes flickered. He gave an embarrassed smile, turned on his heel and walked out without saying another word. I watched him take long, firm steps, all the way to his car. I watched him hold the key out and press it to unlock the door. I watched him bend to open the door. And then he must have changed his mind. He stood upright and walked straight back. Pushed the doors open and reached the desk in three long strides.

'Jennifer,' he said. 'Will you have dinner with me?' Then he lost his determination and finished with a weak, 'Some time? One day? I mean one evening?'

I'd never been asked such a thing in my life. Never. *Out for dinner?* A drink maybe, a night at the pub to watch the football. But dinner? Seeing myself as a woman who was taken out for dinner, I was flattered.

He was looking at the floor, not at me.

'Yes,' I said, tucking all my doubts away, 'I would. When?'

He looked flustered at that. I'd called his bluff. 'Tomorrow night?'

'Fine,' I said and wondered what story he would spin to Margaret.

'I'll pick you up from . . .' He waited while I prayed he wasn't already regretting his invitation.

'Umm.' He smiled then but his expression was evasive. 'I'll need your address. Where do you live?'

He didn't need to know that I simply rented a room in a terraced house. I was going to keep some of my secrets. I gave him the address, specifying, 'Brown Edge.'

'We can go to The Plough in Endon,' he said carefully. 'It's near.'

'Yeah.'

'So – eight o'clock? I'll book.'

Another phrase I was unfamiliar with. *I'll book.* I nodded. He turned to go.

'Till then?'

'Yes.'

I watched the doors swing behind him, watched him on the monitor taking silent steps toward his car. This time he climbed in, started the engine and eased the Focus out of the parking space, twisting in his seat to check behind him. I switched to another dumb monitor and watched the car disappear through the gates. And then I stopped to think. What was I playing at? A married man was not on my list of requirements. I recalled the redhead sitting smugly in Philip Simpson's car and Teresa's anger and misery. For the first time in my life I disliked *myself*. Not my parents or my horrible brother. I was worse than all my useless boyfriends rolled into one.

I felt like retreating into myself. I didn't like who I'd become.

I had no one to confide in. Scarlet and Andrew had gone away on a last-minute jaunt to Spain and were soaking up some sunshine, or so the postcard told me. Jodi would not be in the least bit interested. From being my friend, she had turned into an enemy, someone who resented my very breath sharing her air, almost as though I was stealing it from her even though I was paying for it. So, without mentioning why, that evening I asked her if she'd mind if I hogged the bathroom for twenty minutes the following night. Living in such close quarters with only one bathroom between us meant that things like showers and baths had to be prearranged. I tended to draw the short straw. No hot water, baths before seven a.m. or after ten p.m. There was an outside toilet for absolute emergencies but it was pretty grotty, full of spiders and reached along a muddy, uneven path and only used as a last resort. Jodi didn't answer straight away but spun out the tension, then looked at me with venom in her eyes as she rapped out the words. 'What time?'

'Seven?'

She nodded, her chin dropping on to her chest as though she was depressed. And my resentment turned unexpectedly to pity. 'Are you OK?'

She nodded again and said '*Yes,*' though the answer was patently *No.*

I sighed and left the room to return to my own little domain.

My bedroom is tiny, as you would expect from a Victorian terrace. It is painted Shell Pink, my choice, but Jason had wielded the paintbrush in the early days when they were glad of my money and seemed anxious to make me feel welcome. It contains a three-quarters bed, built-in wardrobe, chair and a chest of drawers on which stands a small TV which can also play DVDs. If I am careful I can actually walk all the way round the bed, which is my usual resting place, half watching the telly but really staring out over the valley, imagining another life, another room, another house. A home. A home like I'd never had, a haven, somewhere peaceful where anger and hatred didn't bang against every wall. And I felt sad because this little room in Brown Edge had, once, been a haven. Safer than the street. It was so different now from my early days, when Jodi, Jason and I would sit in the lounge/diner, drinking lager and watching the same TV programmes. Not now. Somehow the distance between us had developed and these days had grown so wide it was now impossible to bridge. And I felt sad for that lost nirvana. After my family home had exploded apart, I'd valued those companionable evenings together, that relaxed way of chilling with people you feel at home with. And now it was lost.

I sat in my room and couldn't wait for tomorrow. I pushed Margaret to the back of my mind and used the mistress's mantra. If *he* doesn't care about his wife, why should I? She's his wife. He's the one who's cheating. Wherever she was, I promised myself her shadow would not spoil my date for tomorrow. So much for personal lectures.

I remembered the reverence with which he'd unloaded those boxes, the fact that he was storing them, preserving them.

Whatever my resolve that night, my dreams were of her. We were sitting in a country pub, eating, when a shadow fell across the table and a wild woman stood there, her eyes burning with accusation, her finger pointing. She was thin, wearing black, her hair loose, straggly, long and grey, and I felt her hatred as sharp as a knife. I tossed and turned in bed, knowing she would like to kill me. In my dream I tried to stand but her glare pinned me down. I tried to speak but my tongue was glued to the roof of my mouth. I knew who she reminded me of, Bertha Mason, aka the first Mrs Rochester. Mad and violent. She would kill me if she could. I awoke in a sweat, my forearms crossed over my chest trying to protect my heart. I knew then I would not sleep. This 'dinner together' was the beginning of something else. I climbed out of my bed to peer out of the window, hoping to reassure myself that the valley was still green. But it was too dark to see.

In the moonlight I imagined I saw a shadow, dark and fluid as an ink blot, cross the valley, turning green to black as Mr Budge would like to have done with his open-cast mining. I believed it heralded something vengeful and malicious. Margaret would wreak her havoc on me somehow. She would punish me. I would not escape her. I sat, staring out of the window, waiting for dawn, longing for the light. We are more afraid of the unknown than of a visible foe, because our imaginations endow the invisible foe with impossible powers. Margaret was an angry, cheated woman with supernatural powers. She would invade my dreams, have her revenge. My mind turned round and round like the cogs on a clock. I was doing the wrong thing and I would pay for it.

At some point I must have gone back to bed and dropped back to sleep because I awoke again in the early hours still in a cold sweat, terrified of something that had no shape or form. I felt the radiator. It was stone cold. I climbed out of bed to open the window and strained my eyes. But could see nothing. The moon was hidden and now the ground was a uniform black.

There was nothing there and yet the feeling of dread persisted.

It was too early. So no green fields, no coal dust. No nightmare woman roaming the valley crying like a banshee, wearing a white nightdress and flapping cloak. The first rays of sunshine crept towards the horizon and, with it, when I threw open the windows, there was the scent of a new morning. The morning of my date. I smiled and heard the radiators creak into warmth, watching the sun creep down the slope of the moors. I could see more clearly now. No broomstick. Out there, there was nothing. But just as I reassured myself, I felt something light brush my right shoulder. I spun around and saw a stray moth fluttering towards the window. I opened it wider and let it escape.

I left my dreams underneath the pillow, along with my conscience, drew in a deep breath and headed for the bathroom.

It is usual to say that a day crawls by when you have a 'date' in the evening. That wasn't so. The day flew by. People coming and going, and at three p.m. Serena the hairdresser came and I told her I was having dinner with Steven Taverner that night. Her eyes opened wide as pebbles. 'What about . . .?'

I shrugged and blew out my lips. 'Phh.'

'No, really,' she insisted, a frown struggling to crease her Botoxed forehead.

I tossed my head. 'I can find everything out tonight when we have dinner.' Oh, how I loved the sophistication of those words, *having dinner*. Not supper. Not a drink. Not a quick fuck in the back of the car. Not even afternoon tea.

Dinner.

'If he's married,' I added airily, 'I can soon finish it.'

'Be careful.'

I reflected on her warning all the way home. Why had she felt it necessary to warn me like that? Why did I need to be careful? I didn't. I felt I understood him now. There was nothing to be nervous about. Back home I hogged the bathroom for an almost unprecedented twenty minutes. I washed my hair and shaved my armpits. And in my bedroom, wrapped up in a towel that might once have been thick and white, but was now thin and grey – like a young woman faded and aged, I dried myself and lathered on some smelly body lotion I'd bought in the Pound Shop. It didn't take me long to rummage through my wardrobe. There wasn't a lot of choice. There was the grey dress I'd worn the other day to work, a tiny black dress that left little to the imagination. Too tarty. I put that one back in the wardrobe. The blue dress was too posh for a local pub. Swanning in in a floor-length gown to a country pub would look pretty stupid. But that only left a black dress with big red flowers splashed all over it. I didn't much like the material: polyester, shiny and cheap, showing every tiny lump and bulge. I guessed someone had bought it, worn it once, seen the damage it did to their appearance and disliked it after that, giving it to the charity shop where I'd bought it. But I'd really gone on the flowers, whatever they were. Something tropical, at a guess. That was it then. I managed to find a pair of tights with no ladders and pinned my hair back on one side, letting it fall over my face on the other. I thought that made it look sophisticated; besides, it was handy if I needed to hide behind anything. My high-heeled black *leather* shoes and I were ready by ten to eight. I knew he would be bang on time. The next ten minutes dragged and I felt stupid. What the heck was I doing, dressing up, going out for 'dinner' with a married guy probably twice my age? I didn't even have a chance to answer myself because I saw his car glide along the road, probably looking for my address.

Oh well, I thought. Here goes!

He actually got out of the car as I opened the front door to let myself out. I did not want him seeing Jodi or Jason or them seeing him. He gave me a tight smile. 'Hello, Jennifer.' No Spinning Jenny. No Jenny Wren. No Jenny Lind. Just Jennifer.

Behind me I sensed a swish of air as Jodi curtain-twitched. I anticipated her voice in the morning, sharp, mocking and critical. 'Your dad, was he?' When she knew I'd had nothing to do with him for years. If I got a birthday or Christmas card it was a red-letter year. She noticed everything.

It was then that I noticed he was wearing a suit and felt my mouth drop open. A smart, navy blue suit. Embarrassing. In my book, men wore suits to two occasions. Strictly weddings and funerals. Definitely not *out for a drink* or *going for dinner*.

So this, I thought, was what a real, grown-up dinner date was like. He was taking it seriously. He held open the passenger door and I climbed in, feeling even more vulnerable and out of my depth. I didn't know what to say, how to act, what to do. I'd hardly known what to wear. I clipped my seat belt and gave an uncertain smile, staring ahead.

'I thought we might eat at The Traveller's Rest instead of The Plough?' His voice was gentle and soft.

My mind pinned to what I considered a significant fact. I'd seen his hands wrap around the steering wheel. He was not wearing his wedding ring. I could still see the dent in his finger and a pale line where it had sat. Now, I guessed, it was in his pocket.

He was cheating on Margaret.

But something else registered. He lived in Stanley. The Traveller's Rest was his local pub. If you're going to cheat on your wife you hardly take your date to your local.

I licked my lips and wondered.

'That would be lovely. I don't think I've been there before.' I borrowed a phrase I'd heard on a film. 'Is the food good there?'

He turned his head sharply, as though he suspected this wasn't *me* speaking, and gave the ghost of a smile. 'I believe so.' He still looked tight-lipped and I worried that he was regretting this. Then his mouth relaxed. 'I'm sorry, Jennifer,' he said in a soft, apologetic voice. 'I'm unused to this' – pause – 'dating thing.'

I settled back in my seat. So that was what this was? A dating thing. I wasn't sure about that but I was sure about one thing. It beat my parade of wankers any day.

NINETEEN

There was much about Steven Taverner that still mystified me. I couldn't quite get a handle on him. I watched his driving to find a clue. He was a cautious man, his driving careful and precise, pulling in tight to the side when anything approached on this narrow country lane and giving a soft beep of the horn as we mounted the humpback bridge over the canal.

We arrived at The Traveller's Rest; the car park was almost full. He advised me to get out before parking close to the wall and folding in his mirrors. The Traveller's Rest proved to be a traditional sort of pub, draught beer and home-cooked food. Low ceilings and big black beams framing the collection of local beers: Rudyard Ruby, Danebridge, Double Sunset, a tribute to a phenomenon which can be observed from a point just above Rudyard Lake. The scent of cooking wafted in through the kitchen door. The customers looked up sharply as we entered and the woman behind the bar (wrinkly, sun-damaged skin, dark mahogany tan, big white wolfish teeth and long dangling earrings) greeted him. 'Hello there, Steven,' she said in a stiff Potteries accent, 'haven't seen you here for a while.' She gave me the once-over, heavy with curiosity, eyes wide open, mouth slack. I resisted the juvenile temptation to stick my tongue out at her. Tonight I was grown up. On a 'date', and I felt happy.

Steven Taverner gave her a curt, embarrassed nod, devoid of friendliness. Did I imagine it, or was there also something furtive about it? He led me to a table in the bay window. 'Now,' he said formally, 'what would you like to drink, Jennifer?'

I knew I was sitting awkwardly, bolt upright, shoulders tensed, hands primly on lap, knees together, staring ahead as though I was at an interview. 'A glass of wine, please.'

He laughed. 'Give me a clue.'

And when I looked confused, he enlarged, 'Red, pink or white.'

'Oh, white, please.'

'Any particular preference?'

I shook my head. I was already out of my depth. I didn't know the names of any wines, white, red or pink or even fucking blue. And even if I had I wouldn't be able to pronounce them. Half of them would be French or Italian or Spanish. At the wine bar I asked for the cheapest and got house white. He came back with a large glass of straw-coloured wine in one hand and a pint of beer in the other. He handed me the wine which was ice cold and flipped two menus on to the table, encouraging me with, 'Hungry?'

'Yeah.' It was my first lie of the evening. Truth was, there were so many butterflies flitting around in my stomach that there was no room for food. But . . . I scanned the menu and recognized something. 'Fish and chips, please.'

He smiled, returned to the bar and, presumably, ordered food. Whatever the barmaid had said to him – and I could guess – he didn't like it. She shot me a malicious look and I saw his shoulders stiffen, heard a firm denial, almost a shout, and as he walked back to the table there was a scowl on his face that hadn't been there before. He was muttering something to himself but I couldn't decipher the words.

I was starting to feel uncomfortable. What was I doing here, playing the sophisticate with a man I didn't know, whose circumstances were also unknown?

He sat down heavily, still frowning and abstracted. Instinctively I sensed he was feeling the same as I, full of doubts. There was a distance between us that seemed strange, a disconnect which I wanted to bridge.

I felt the need to fill the silence, say something, even something as fatuous as, 'What are *you* having to eat?'

He didn't answer me straight away. He was still internalizing, his eyes flickering. I felt embarrassed and very awkward. I repeated my question and he came to with a shake. 'Same as you,' he said, back to smiling now.

I was still curious as to Margaret's role in all this. How did she fit in? Where did she fit in?

He leaned forward and began what felt like an interrogation. 'Tell me about yourself, Jennifer.'

I was startled. The blokes I went out with didn't say, *Tell me about yourself.* They told me about *themselves* – all bloody evening. So I was unprepared with a story. Which is probably why I gave him a sanitized truth.

'There isn't much to tell,' I said. 'Mum and Dad split up years ago. Don't see much of either of them. They've both got new partners.' I thought for a minute, reluctant to mention Thailand. 'Mum's guy, George, he's got a nasty temper.'

I'd felt the back of his hand a few times while my mother had watched, impassive.

'And your father's new girlfriend? Partner,' he quickly corrected.

I made a face. Decided not to mention Dad's sad exploits in Thailand. 'Doing his own thing.'

He giggled at that. Another of my borrowed phrases, I thought.

The latest bulletin from Thailand had mentioned a hot little hooker named Malee. I hoped I would never have to meet her.

But borrowed phrases make you bold. They give you another identity. Someone else's cloak to wear. 'So what about you?'

His face changed. He dropped his eyes, frowning. His expression was steely. 'Jennifer,' he said, voice broken. 'Oh, Jennifer. I lost her.' He reached across the table and touched my hand. His felt cold.

Luckily for us the fish and chips arrived then.

At first we ate in silence. I kept stealing little glances at him but he was focusing on his meal, chewing thoughtfully and staring into the distance. Then he looked up and I sensed he was considering telling me something. Something that stuck in his throat. And it wasn't a fishbone. Finally he did speak, but I had the feeling it was not what had been on his mind. 'Is your food all right?'

'Oh yes, thank you. It's delicious, actually.' I'd pinned the word, *actually*, on because I thought it sounded posh. But it didn't. It sounded fake. The person I was becoming or rather trying to become. People talk about 'not being yourself'. That was how I felt, a fake who trotted out other people's phrases.

'I'm glad you came out tonight,' he said next.

I stopped chewing.

'Do you have a current boyfriend?'

'Steven,' I said, putting my knife and fork down, ready for honesty, 'I wouldn't be out with you tonight if I had a current boyfriend.' As soon as the words were out I knew I'd nailed my colours to the mast. Challenged him.

And he knew it too. He raised his eyebrows as though I had told him off.

I tried to retrieve my bluntness. 'I've had a few . . .' I slipped past the word, wankers, choosing instead, '*unsuitable* boyfriends.' I managed to laugh it off. 'I never seem to find a decent one.'

He fixed me with a bit of a stare. 'What do you call unsuitable?' he said so quietly it was barely above a whisper.

I shrugged. 'Cheats, lazies, liars, guys who take drugs, weirdos, guys into S&M, guys with nasty tempers. I've had the lot.' I eyed him. 'And then there's the married ones.'

He was silent as he digested my words. Then . . . 'Weirdos?'

'Into bondage and stuff. Strange practices.' I didn't want to remember Scary II.

He was frowning with his next question. 'How old are you, Jennifer?'

'Twenty-three.'

'I'm forty,' he said. 'Would you consider a man nearly twice your age unsuitable?' He tried to turn it into a joke though it wasn't one. It was deadly serious. 'Would you consider a forty-year-old man unsuitable, or one of your . . . weirdos? Tell me now. Don't let me find it out later.'

'I would if he was married.' There – I'd thrown down the gauntlet. And now I waited.

He opened his mouth to speak, thought better of it. Then . . . 'The boxes, the clothes, the stuff I've put into store. They were my wife's. She died almost three years ago now. Cancer.' He wasn't looking at me as he blurted this out. So – was it a lie?

'I'm sorry,' I said. But I wasn't. I was exultant. He wasn't cheating or going through a troublesome divorce. She was dead. Hang on a minute . . .

'Have you got any children?'

He shook his head and spoke quickly, as though to hurry the phrase through. 'She didn't want children and, as it turned out, we didn't have time.'

'I'm not sure I want them either.' I recalled my brother's early years. 'Nasty, smelly, crying things.' But it was a lie. I did want children. My own.

He gave an abstracted smile aimed somewhere beyond my shoulder. 'I think that's what she would have said.' At the time the wording puzzled me. Later it made perfect sense. Then I felt vaguely creepy, haunted, as though he had asked her, was still communing with her. Goodness knows why. He was a quiet, pleasant, unattached man. Nothing messy here, I told myself. No drugs, no kinky ways, just a sad man who'd lost his wife. I wasn't under threat.

'I like children.' He spoke defiantly, again looking past me before focusing back with a look that was so intense it drilled into me. Now I wanted to own the truth, but it was a little late.

'You remind me of her,' he said, leaning across and touching my hair. 'You're very like her. You could almost . . . be her.'

I shifted in my seat. I felt uncomfortable.

When he looked up his face was quite different. It was determined, intense, decisive. 'And now I have found you.'

I wanted to hold my hand up, *Whoa. Stop right there. You're going too fast for me.* But then I had a quick think. *Why shouldn't I? Why shouldn't I have the luck for once? Have a nice, decent boyfriend, someone solvent who drove a car, opened the door for me, took me out on 'dates' and 'for dinner' dressed in a suit? Someone who invited me to tell him about myself instead of listening to boring stories about football or motorbikes or what weights he was lifting in the gym or how many pints he'd downed a few nights before. Or lied. I could go out with Steven for a bit and if it didn't work out . . . Hey-ho. I would lose nothing, I reasoned. I could have nice evenings out. Anything was better than being stuck in my room with Jason and Jodi downstairs alternating between lovey-dovey and bitter arguments. Dinner at the pub was nicer than my micro-wave meals. The ambience felt safe and normal. And if he was old enough to be my dad, well my dad had followed in the footsteps of my mum and buggered off, hadn't he? And the girl he was currently with was probably younger than me. So what was the problem? That was where I stopped, aware I was walking into the unknown.*

I was brought down to earth. 'Are you sure your fish and chips were all right?'

'Yes. Lovely. Thank you.' Was this how these evenings would go? With stilted conversation and an unaccountable awkwardness? Or would he gradually learn to relax with me, become light-hearted and easy to be with? Would marriage change him once he had the security we both craved?

'Do you want dessert?'

Dessert? Was that what I would call pudding? I shook my head. 'I'm full. Thank you.'

He crossed over to the bar then to pay the bill. Another big tick in the box, I thought. He hadn't even asked me to go Dutch, unlike Mr Mean aka Lee Williams, who started patting his pockets the minute the bill was due to be paid. Oh, and surprise, surprise. He'd forgotten his wallet . . . again. So it was a choice. I either paid the bill or we did the washing up or did a runner. And I can tell you, in six-inch stilettos my running is not great. So I'd pay up rather than face the police or mountains of greasy water. Mr Mean and I rarely went to the same place twice. So I felt reassured that there was never a tip for the waitresses who watched us leave with a sour expression on their faces.

Another of my fears displaced. Until I watched Steven speak to the barmaid, before both turned and looked at me. I couldn't read their expressions.

Steven drove me home and I was quiet, worrying what was the right thing to do next? I couldn't ask him in. Jodi and Jason had made it perfectly clear that I was *not* to invite boyfriends in. With the result that they were lucky. They'd missed out on Scaries I & II. What was he expecting now? A quick snog in the car? Full-blown sex? If I didn't know the rules of this encounter, did he? I felt completely out of my depth as I studied his profile. Very calm now, steady hands on the wheel.

In the end I needn't have worried. He pulled up in front of the house, climbed out, opened my door for me and kissed me – on the cheek with cold lips. It was a strange and worryingly passionless expression which left me even more confused.

'Good night,' he said.

I let myself in.

TWENTY

Through my window I watched his tail-lights wink and blink as he drove away, slowly, cautiously, while I digested the fact. Margaret was dead. He was a widower with no children. As I pulled my dress off I wondered if this evening would be repeated.

Or had he seen through me, seen me for the damaged, sad little loser I was? I went to the bathroom, cleaned my teeth and lay on my bed for a while, thinking. I had met some very odd men. I thought I had understood all the types. But there was something about Steven that was different. Something strange. Not on the surface but buried as deep as a grave. Something was down there. I sensed it but could not put a handle on it. Should I be wary? Of happiness?

We had a suicide once at The Green Banana. It was in B7 which I've never liked entering ever since. It still holds the dank, damp-earth, depressing smell of the dead. Is that instinct or a product of my imagination? His name was Ted and he was probably in his early sixties. He'd lived with his mum all his life. When she died he brought over an assortment of her old furniture: a longcase clock, a sofa that looked like leather but wasn't, a 1950s' Dansette record player to play vinyl on and a rack of old ladies' dresses. It was a sad little collection but unfortunately not unusual at the storage facility. On the screens I'd watched him unload the stuff, one of the lorry men giving him a hand with the sofa. I watched Ted thank him and try and give him a note, presumably a fiver. Ted wasn't wealthy. He wore cheap, chain-store clothes, well-worn, and drove a Skoda, also well-worn. As was he. He looked bent and battered by life. The lorry driver was a kind guy who worked for a local haulage company. I'd met him a couple of times. A fat, good-natured man called Lennie with a kind, ruddy face. Lennie shook Ted's hand, clapped his hand on his shoulder and tried to tuck the note back into Ted's top pocket. There was a brief toing and froing between the two men, Lennie finally accepting the note. But I knew later he'd put it in the Médecins Sans Frontières charity box that stood on the desk. Ted stood and watched as Lennie climbed back into the lorry. Even on the subduing black-and-white CCTV screens, I'd picked up that he'd seemed sad but surprised at the lorry driver's generosity, both in his help and his reluctance to accept the money. Ted had paid up front for six months but one afternoon, not long after he'd moved in, I'd passed by B7 and seen him sitting on the sofa looking forlorn, so I wasn't that surprised when a few weeks later he strung himself up by one of the steel beams that crisscrossed the store. I was the one who found him. It was November, my least favourite time of the year. Short days, getting shorter, dark by four, so when I checked my books I realized Ted hadn't checked out.

His ten-year-old Skoda was still sitting in the parking lot, waiting. I had a nasty feeling even before I went to check what was going on. Luckily, just before I'd set off on my rounds, Andrew had turned up to take some cash to the bank and he'd waited while I voiced my concern, so he was just behind me when I raised the shutter and saw Ted, dangling like a puppet, white and still hanging from the beams, his face expressing an apology.

I felt weak and dizzy and fell back against Andrew, who'd already pulled out his mobile phone to dial 999.

He half turned to me. 'What time did he log in?'

I hoped this wasn't going to turn into a Blame Jenny episode. 'Three thirty,' I said, hearing a prickly note in my voice. 'He nearly always stays for over an hour.'

'In the dark?'

I shrugged. 'I guess he brings a torch or plugs a light into one of the sockets.' None of the units had electric points. The plugs were in the corridor and accessed with an extension lead.

'Mmm.'

We waited.

I saw blue lights flicker. The police were here.

Within half an hour the place was swarming with all sorts of people, a police doctor and goodness knows how many uniformed policemen, and then finally, after a few hours, two guys came with a sort of stretcher thing and loaded Ted's body into a black estate car with a curtain to hide the contents in the back. He hadn't even left a note. But then who would the note have been addressed to? Me? Our customers don't fill in next of kin so it would take a while for the police to track someone down.

Our problem was we couldn't rent out B7 until it had been cleared, and the police – God only knows why – wouldn't let us empty it for nearly six weeks. And then, having had an inquest and Ted being buried alongside his ma, we were finally allowed to contact the next of kin (who didn't want any of the contents of B7), hire a skip and empty out. A mate of his came and picked up the Skoda. There were still three months to go on his contract but we re-let it without giving away its past and never refunded the difference.

Heaven protect us from another suicide. And it was strange but the person who rented B7 left after his initial six months saying there was something tainted in the air and he felt uncomfortable there.

'Really?' I'd said, faking ignorance and surprise when really I knew it was poor old dead Ted's soul.

The person who followed on after that, however, had no such problems. The ghost had gone.

Something about Steven reminded me of Ted. Except I couldn't work out what.

The day after our date I hung around the phone, wondering whether he would ring. Would this be the beginning of a romance? Or would that be it? One date? I'd so enjoyed the warmth of a date, of having a man open a car door for me, of politeness and attentiveness.

I watched the entrance obsessively, but there was no sign of the Ford Focus.

The day after was the same and the day after that was a Sunday and I was aware he didn't have my mobile number, only the landline to The Green Banana. I was preparing for this 'romance' to go the way of all others – in the bin.

But on the Monday he turned up again. It was four o'clock and I was looking forward to going home when the white Ford Focus slid into the yard and he parked up. I watched him walk towards the door and wondered how I should respond. I had just decided on 'neutral' when the door was pushed open and he was inside.

He gave me a broad grin, transforming his face from bland with small features, eyes, mouth, nose, into something approaching attractive, though not quite. 'Jennifer,' he said. 'Sorry I haven't been in touch. Work, you know.'

I felt reassured. Wherever this was heading, the future looked brighter than anything in my past. What possible harm could there be?

He regarded me for a minute or two, his head on one side, before saying, 'Shall we go out again? I mean – would you like to?'

'Yes.'

'Wait there.' I watched him cross the yard and disappear into the store. He was gone for about ten minutes. When he returned, he was holding out another dress, draped across his arms, just like when I'd watched him from the corridor. Patterned this time, navy background with a splash of flowers, pink, white, pale blue. 'Here,' he said and held it out. I tried not to look at the label but saw it all the same. Parakeet.

'Are you sure?'

He nodded, smiling, and held it out further towards me.

Questions were building up inside me now. I knew where the dresses had come from. But why did *he* have them in the first place? The obvious answer was that he had bought them for Margaret but she had been ill so had never worn them. But why had he kept them? That I couldn't work out. She must have been the same size as me. A coincidence?

I looked at him for an explanation but his smile seemed to have stuck.

Our second 'date' was a blueprint of the first. We went to another pub, this time in Leek, a town on the edge of the moorlands just a few miles away. He asked me questions to which I gave evasive answers. And when I asked him questions he was equally evasive. I felt neither of us was being open or truthful.

'The house where you live, is it yours, Jennifer?'

I began with an evasive, 'Sort of.' Thankfully he didn't pursue the subject. Not then. That came later.

Over the next few months, Steven and I fell into a routine. We'd go out a couple of times a week. Usually to a pub, once or twice to an Italian restaurant, where I learned to twiddle spaghetti round my fork using my spoon, say yes to parmesan cheese and black pepper which arrived in an embarrassing grinder. A time or two we went to a curry house in Leek where I learned to order the mild ones. I recognized names of different wines: Rioja, Cabernet Sauvignon, White Zinfandel, Merlot. I knew which ones I liked and which ones turned my stomach to acid. I was becoming sophisticated. And well dressed. I now had five new dresses hanging in my wardrobe, a choice for every date, which he'd removed from the boxes in D5. I shoved aside the breathy whisper: *You are dressing as Margaret.* Wearing a dead woman's clothes, clothes meant for her.

I shoved the thought aside.

He always picked me up and drove me home and, apart from a quick peck on the cheek, Steven Taverner didn't make a move on me, which also puzzled me.

And so it came to July. We were sitting outside a pub, a little farther away, The Mill near Worston, which had a river nearby providing a periodic backdrop of ducks and swans, and beyond that a railway line from which came the occasional whoosh of a train. The evening was balmy. I decided it was about time I started telling the truth. Or at least selected bits of it.

'Actually, Steven,' I said, 'I have something to tell you.'

He waited. I had learned that Steven was economical both with words and gestures. He was quite happy in his own silence, seeming to live inside himself. 'When I said I lived in that house in Brown Edge, what I should have said was that I rent a room there. The house belongs to a couple called Jason and Jodi. They needed some extra cash and so decided to rent out a room.'

He thought for a bit before responding. 'Don't you find that a bit strange, a bit demeaning?' He looked at me hard.

I shrugged. 'I don't have a lot of choice. I'm only twenty-three and couldn't afford to buy somewhere of my own and this was a cheaper option.' I felt ashamed. He would see me differently now. A scrounger. There was a silence while I pretended to be absorbed in the ducks swimming around. When I looked up he was looking pleased. Pleased? He was trying to hide it but there was a definite gleam in his eye. 'Do you find you lack privacy?'

'Of course.' I tried to shrug it off but something snagged. I found it an odd comment.

By the middle of September, I was troubled by the fact that our physical relationship had gone no further than a brief peck on the cheek at the end of the evening. Let's face it, in most relationships you're fighting them off not willing them on. But then I was learning new rules. Steven remained an enigma. I was even beginning to wonder if, in spite of his marriage, he was a closet gay, or else I'd lost my attractiveness to the opposite sex. Was he still mourning Margaret? He never mentioned her now. She remained locked in D5. And I had replaced her. He had given me a few more gifts, a peach-coloured nightdress that felt and looked like satin, the sort Hollywood movie stars swanned around in, fag held in a cigarette holder inches long. There was an odd dress, the least glamorous of them all, calf-length, brown with a geometric pattern, two blouses, a pair of cream-coloured trousers, loose.

All the right size. Every time he visited the store I had another gift. They had obviously been stored up.

Something else bothered me.

I hadn't told Scarlet that I was dating one of our clients. I didn't think she'd have minded – it was something else. I hadn't quite worked out what footing our relationship was on. Were we simply platonic friends of the opposite sex or boyfriend and girlfriend? Sex would have sealed it. I would know then. But instinct told me something was out of kilter. Maybe his long silences, which seemed more like absences. So how could I describe our relationship to Scarlet when I couldn't describe the attraction even to myself? Not truthfully.

Jodi and Jason were still fairly frosty towards me but I didn't mind so much now. I had a boy – or rather man – friend who picked me up in a car and took me out for dinner. I was out a couple of nights a week these days and the rest of the time I was quite happy to stay in my room and read or watch TV. It was all fine.

The big surprise (disappointment) was Stella, in whom I had confided. She was my best friend. When I'd been sleeping rough, I'd sometimes go round to her place to take a shower when her parents were out. (They didn't like me, surprise, surprise; no one did in those days.) I'd have thought she would have been glad for me. I'd had such a catalogue of disasters that I imagined she would have been pleased that I had some sort of steady, decent relationship. But when I said I was dating an older man, one of our customers (without mentioning the dead wife or the container or the contents of D5 and certainly not sharing with her that we didn't even have sex), she started the Spanish Inquisition.

'Older?' she snapped. 'How much older?'

I told her, wishing she would not make a seventeen-year age gap quite such an issue. I began my spiel about film stars and celebrities . . .

And she jumped in with both feet and an expression of pity. 'They're film stars, Jenny, they don't even live in the real world.'

I'd always thought they did. They were always quoted in *Closer* magazine as saying life was quite ordinary most of the time. That they didn't *live* on the red carpet but in the same mundane world as you or me.

'Married? Divorced?'

When I said, 'widower', she gave me a horrified look.

'Someone sad.'

'He isn't sad,' I said. 'He's just quiet.' That was an understatement, but she didn't need to know about Steven's long abstractions or the way he tilted his head and listened – to what?

Her next comment was even more insulting. 'What does he see in *you*?'

Truth was I didn't know.

And how could I explain that I was happy as I was and I had the feeling that if I tried too hard to analyse our relationship it would dissolve like sugar in hot tea?

'Has he taken you to his home?'

I shook my head. 'But we drink in his local sometimes.'

I hung my head and defended him. 'He's quite nice looking.' Honesty prevailed. 'Well – OK, anyway.'

She just continued to look at me pityingly so I listed a few more of his assets.

'He's solvent. He has a good job. And a car. And he speaks nicely.'

'Ri–i–ght.' She annoyed me with her doubt and I was cross at having to defend him. My first properly decent boyfriend.

She moved in for the kill with a dirty little grin. 'Does he press all the right buttons?'

Another sore point. He was attractive to look at but he wasn't pressing any buttons. I wasn't 'in love' with him. I wasn't even infatuated. I just wanted someone. Someone of my own. Someone to take care of me, lift me out of my mundane life. I wanted some-*where* of my own too. A home. I hadn't had one since I was fifteen and I really did want this. I wanted to stop worrying about Jodi and Jason having a baby and throwing me out. I wanted to stop worrying about being homeless again and poor and hungry, having no job, standing at the bus stop in pouring rain, getting soaked and splashed by other people's nice cars. I wanted a life. And it looked like Steven Taverner might just provide me with one.

That would have to be enough. Stability, comfort, someone who loved *me*. There was something more. I felt I was being manoeuvred down a corridor. It was meant to happen, bound to happen.

I knew he didn't come with bells and whistles. I wasn't 'in lerve'. I didn't hear lovely music playing in my head when he kissed me. I felt a big empty nothing. But I did feel safe and secure and comfortable in his company. When we weren't together I didn't worry he was dating my best friend. I didn't worry he'd steal money from me or do drugs or come in pissed and violent, being sick all over me. When I was in the car with him I felt safe, not worried he was about to erupt like a volcano and leave some poor sod lying bloodied on the side of the road because he'd cut him up. I didn't feel frightened of him tying me up or being into kinky sex. Sex?

That was where my thoughts stopped abruptly, colliding into one another like a motorway pile-up. I looked at Stella – my best friend – and couldn't confess this one detail. Sex? What did that matter anyway? Did it *need* to happen? I couldn't ask any of my mates and my mum had recently gone to live in France. I'd had a postcard from Chamonix without, I noticed, George's name on the bottom. Just Mum, no address and one lonely, solitary X, so she wasn't exactly on tap for parental guidance. And my dad was still currently surfing the Net for more Thai girls. The last I'd heard of him was a jaunty text – 'Back in Asia' – with lots of heart emojis and a couple more that bordered on the obscene. So he was hardly going to advise me on the sexual side of relationships. (I'm not sure I'd have either wanted or accepted any advice he might have given me on that score anyway.) I definitely wasn't going to confide in Stella or Scarlet. I could hardly discuss our lack of a sex life with Steven. I didn't want to embarrass him – or myself – or risk spoiling whatever relationship it was that we had. So it was up to me. I was on my own.

TWENTY-ONE

T he nearest I got to it was one warm day, in late September, when we were sitting in the beer garden, again coincidentally, outside The Mill at Worston. We'd gone there early, to avoid the crowds and feed the ducks. Later on the place would be heaving on such a warm night, the hint of a dying summer in the bright gold that dappled through the trees. It was a pretty gastro-pub, film-set pretty. For some reason – maybe the tranquillity or the warm sunshine, the approach of winter with its long evenings and threat of snow or floods, or maybe it was simply the rural ambience of the place – I felt particularly relaxed and close to him early in the evening. I never felt threatened by Steven's presence. His build was slight and he was only an inch or two taller than me. It was more what brewed inside him that could, at times, make me uneasy. His silences and abstraction could stretch into many minutes. I could not follow him down this rabbit hole so I had no idea where his thoughts were leading him.

We were sitting outside underneath a huge orange umbrella which, angled against the sun, threw a long shadow across the grass, when he put his arm around me. I leaned in to him and thought how very nice and clean he smelt. He was stroking my hair, winding it around his fingers, his eyes half closed. And he too looked relaxed, almost asleep, his breathing steady. He gave a tiny snore. Perhaps, I thought, I might tease him about it later. I drew in a deep breath. If anyone was going to broach this most sensitive of subjects it was going to have to be me because Steven was too shy. It had to be here and it had to be now. The time was right.

Or so I thought. 'What a lovely evening,' I began, looking at him. He was dressed less formally this evening, as the weather was unseasonably hot, the Indian Summer we all enjoy so much and value over a fine summer's day. The Indian Summer is a bonus tacked on to the tail end of summer, tucked in just before the onset of autumn.

He was wearing a short-sleeved, pale blue open-necked shirt, khaki trousers (he never wore jeans or shorts) and brown Vans instead of the brown leather shoes. Yes, I thought. He looked OK. And I felt a stirring of pride and desire. I wouldn't mind him making love to me . . . and we could have children. Perhaps soon he would invite me back to his house and there, on his bed, we would finally make love. Everything would be all right. Maybe what was holding him back was the fact that it would be in Margaret's house, Margaret's bedroom, Margaret's bed. Perhaps, like the suicide ghost of poor old Ted in B7, *her* ghost was still there and that was inhibiting him from taking me there. More than ever, I wanted to exorcize this dead woman. Meet her and dismiss her. So I touched his mouth, put my finger inside and waited for him to suck it. A well-known preamble to the act. Not for him. He removed it gently, as a mother might remove a child's hand from a biscuit tin, reprovingly. He half opened his eyes, giving a lazy smile. 'What are you up to, Jennifer?' Maybe his tone should have warned me. Cold and rapidly distancing.

I took the bull by the horns and whispered into his ear very softly and, I hoped, *extremely* seductively. 'Do you want to sleep with me?'

He opened his eyes wide. Shocked? Then took my chin in his hand and gripped it hard enough to hurt. 'Do I *want* to sleep with you?'

I nodded.

He laughed and the tension was over, or so I thought. 'Of course I do,' he said. 'But first I want to be sure.'

Sure of what?

Sure I didn't get pregnant?

Sure it was what I wanted too?

It was neither of those.

'I want to be sure,' he murmured into my ear, 'that you are the right one.'

'The right one?' How many interpretations can you put on this apparently simple phrase? I waited for clarification.

He took his arm from around my shoulders and moved away, frowning into his beer glass as though the foam created shapes. 'When I married Margaret,' he began. And stopped.

'When I married Margaret,' he repeated carefully, 'I made a vow. Till death us do part.'

Which is what had happened.

'Do you want to talk about her?'

'No,' he said decisively, 'I do not.' Then, in a softer tone, 'I don't need to any more.'

Part of me rejoiced. But now I had picked the scab off. 'Is that because you've stopped grieving?'

He gave me a sharp look. 'I'll never stop grieving.'

I shrugged. I didn't have a response.

'Jennifer,' he said gently, closing his eyes against the glare of the sun. 'Margaret is no more. She's the past. You are the present. And, I hope, perhaps the future too.'

I didn't know what to say.

But his face was set. He shook my shoulders. 'Listen to me, Jennifer. I don't want to talk about Margaret. Not ever. Please don't bring up the subject again. I do not want *you* to talk about her or wonder about her. The subject is closed.'

'So why keep hold of her stuff?'

He had no answer.

He shook his head from side to side. 'I don't know,' he said. 'I don't really know.'

His mouth was moving but no words came.

'I'm sorry,' I said, touching his hand. 'I didn't mean to upset you.'

'You haven't. You just don't understand.'

'How can I if you don't tell me anything?'

'Why?' There was anguish in his face. 'Why do you want to know?'

'Perhaps because . . .' I took a chance. 'Because I like you.'

The change in his face was as marked and abrupt as though someone had flipped a switch. Off to On. Normal Steven was back.

'That is sweet of you. Sweet. Thank you.'

I was silent but the questions were stacking up all the same.

How long were you married for?

When were you married? Where were you married? Was it a big fancy white wedding?

What cancer did she die of? Were you heartbroken? Grief-struck?

And the one that affected me most: *Why have you stored boxes and a suitcase containing her new clothes?*

I asked none of them but they wouldn't go away. They would never go away.

And now he was smiling but sharing the inner amusement to himself. 'Perhaps I should take you to my home, Jennifer. Perhaps you would understand then.'

He was reminiscing now, not really sharing this with me. 'I sometimes smell her around the house, you know?'

Light Blue.

'I used to wake in the night and feel her beside me. Expect her to move. But she doesn't. She lies there. Quite still. And very cold.' He wrapped his arms around himself and gave a little shiver.

I could say nothing because I realized he was lost inside himself.

'I hear her footsteps.' He tapped the table. One . . . Two . . . Three.

I touched his arm, trying to bring him back to the present. I didn't want some ghost story. I wanted him back. Without her. The thought flitted through my mind. Was my Mr Perfect boyfriend in actual fact just as weird as all the others? A more heavily disguised Scary I or Scary II. Was he, in fact, Scary III? I watched him and he didn't realize. He was too absorbed in his memories. I felt my heart drop. He was just like all the others after all. I'd attracted another loser. I'd sussed him. He was, I was now convinced, Steven Strange. I'd had Scary I and II, Mr Mean, Mr Married Man and The Wanker. And now I had Mr Strange, Mr Spooky, Mr Downright Fucking Bonkers all rolled into one to add to my collection.

He was still talking to himself, his eyes half closed. 'In the mirror, watching me, waiting.' He touched his right shoulder with his left hand and rested it there. 'The house,' he said, 'is very dark and quiet. It waits,' he said. 'It waits.'

I didn't want to hear any more. And I certainly wasn't going to ask what the house was waiting for.

Then he seemed again to be aware of me. He scrutinized me and then leaned forward and grasped my hand. 'Do you think it's fanciful to believe that a house waits for its mistress to come home?'

I didn't know where this was heading. He gave me a hard stare. 'Well, do you?'

'No,' I said. 'Houses are made of bricks and mortar. Not minds and feelings. Of course they don't wait.'

On my observation there are two sorts of married people: Type A – those who crow about their *perfect* spouse, *perfect* marriage, *perfect* children, *lovely* home. And then there's Type B – the ones who do nothing but moan about their 'other half'.

Not many married people are honest enough to be truthful, say their marriage is a mixture of A&B. Good and bad. Happy and downright miserable.

Steven was Type A. Margaret was practically canonized. She had been the perfect spouse. One I could never live up to.

'I was heartbroken,' he said next. 'Damaged.' Then his face changed. 'But now I've met you.'

'I can never live up to—'

He looked puzzled, tilted his head. 'But you don't have to live up to her.'

He was Type A and didn't even know it.

'You remind me of her.' He touched my hair, but instead of it feeling affectionate or sexy, it felt threatening. He was still smiling and at the same time gripping a lock. I tried to pull away but his grip tightened. A moment later he released it. 'I'm sorry,' he said, bright again now. 'I'm sorry. I didn't mean to hurt you.'

I didn't respond. My mind was jumping around like a Mexican Bean. I should get out of here – and away from him. This was no dream. This was a nightmare.

Maybe if I'd had any sort of alternative, I would have done exactly that. But I didn't. The void that had been my life so far was as unappealing as continuing into the unknown.

Was my dream slipping downstream? Floating away in the

current? Should I swim after it or let it drift? I breathed in and out avoiding reaching a decision there and then.

He must have sensed we'd reached an impasse because he stood up. 'It's time I took you home.' I stood up too, oblivious now to everything except the urge to return to the safety of my room.

As we reached the car he put his arm around me and turned me to face him. 'Next Saturday?'

I nodded. If I'd tried to speak I wasn't quite sure how the words would come out.

'By the way,' he said. 'I've bought you a gift.' He produced a small package tied with a bow of golden ribbon. 'Perfume,' he said encouragingly.

I already knew what it would be.

TWENTY-TWO

I felt so uneasy that on the following night I called in to see Stella after work. I wanted to pour my heart out to my best friend, but she was distracted and not in a listening mood. She appeared to be having a bad evening, even though I'd taken round a bottle of Prosecco which usually cheered her up. Not tonight. Geraint was in bed and quiet but there was no sign of Sonny. Maybe that was why she was having a bad evening?

When I told her about Steven's first wife she took a gulp of Prosecco and pursed her lips. 'So what happened to her?'

'Cancer.'

'Hmm.' She was thoughtful. 'When?'

'Three years ago.'

'So what's your problem?'

And I knew I couldn't put it into words. 'I don't know.'

'You don't know?'

I shook my head. 'Oh, Jenny,' she said. 'Please, don't get into another pickle.'

'Not if I can help it.'

I'd tried to make my voice sound positive but it sounded weak, defeated. Truth was I didn't want to let this one chance of having a better life slip away from me. I liked Steven. He was sweet and kind and not at all aggressive. He was – I chose the word – unusual. But good chances don't swing around twice. Call it greed if you like. I call it self-preservation. I was determined to cling on to this one chance. Stella looked at me pityingly. 'Oh, Jenny,' she said. 'Can you never see what's staring you in the face? If you feel there's something weird about him there probably is.'

I threw up my weak defences. 'You haven't even met him. You don't know him. You're just jealous.'

'Of what?'

'Because I have a decent guy for once.'

She countered with, 'You think so?'

I didn't respond.

She took a huge swig of Prosecco. 'Look at it this way,' she said. 'He's giving you clothes obviously meant for her. He's buying you *her* perfume. He tells you that you look like her. I mean, think,' she appealed. 'What is he up to? It seems plain to me he's trying to turn you into her.'

'Men usually go for the same type.' I didn't like the way I was sounding, weak and pathetic.

'You think he's still grieving for her?'

I shrugged.

She persisted. 'So how long can you put up with a grief-stricken boyfriend?'

'You're being ridiculous. He isn't like that at all. He's good fun.'

'Fun? Really?'

'Yes, really.'

Her response was to take a disbelievingly large swig of Prosecco, eyeing me over the top of the glass.

I sensed something was wrong with her. I could hear Geraint grizzling upstairs and, although it was nearly ten, Sonny was nowhere to be seen. And there was something different about Stella. She'd lost her sparkle (in spite of the Prosecco). She'd lost her confidence too and her mouth looked smaller, tighter. Meaner. Unhappier.

Married woman A was merging, in front of my eyes, into married woman B.

She put her glass down on the coffee table. So hard the top shivered.

'Stell,' I said, feeling a flood of affection for my friend. 'Are you OK?'

She shut the subject down. 'Course. Why wouldn't I be?'

I persisted. 'Only . . .'

'Some things,' she said soberly, 'aren't all they're cracked up to be, Jenny.'

In a sudden burst of confidence and maybe desperation she added with a touch of urgency,

'Jenny, be careful. Marriage isn't a bed of roses, you know.'

I tried a joke. 'More a bed of nails?'

Though she tried to laugh her face crumpled and she stole an unhappy look at me. 'Sometimes.'

I left five minutes later – the first time I'd ever left without us polishing off the entire bottle. I put her misgivings about Steven down to envy and ignored them.

I didn't hear from Steven for a couple of days. I wondered if, realizing how young I was, he'd thought the better of our liaison, seen how unlikely it was. And then he rang me on the Saturday afternoon about three o'clock. 'How about,' he said slowly, 'instead of us going out, you come back to my place?'

It was what I'd wanted but I felt apprehensive as well as excited. Perhaps I would unlock the secret once I stepped over the threshold. I would understand him and our relationship.

'That'd be great,' I said, lighting up suddenly inside. 'I can't wait.'

'Good.' He sounded happy, confident, as though he'd just solved a problem. I put the phone down. Scarlet was watching me out of the corner of her eyes, weighed down with the biggest false eyelashes I'd ever seen. They were two great big black hairy caterpillars on her eyelids. She looked at me disapprovingly. And my happiness shrivelled. Grape to prune. 'Anything you want to tell me, Jenny?' Her voice was tight, a note I'd never heard before.

I felt shifty, ashamed and vulnerable and couldn't find the right words. 'I've been seeing Steven Taverner.'

'On the sly?'

'He isn't married. His wife died. He's a widower.' I realized how much I hated the word.

She was watching me very carefully.

'You don't like me dating one of our customers?'

'I'm not sure,' she said, her face screwed up. 'I don't think it's that. What else do you know about him?'

'Not a lot. His wife died of cancer a few years ago. We've been out a few times. He's invited me back to his home.'

She still looked troubled and I felt a snag of terror. Was I going to lose my job over this?

She was reflective.

While I considered . . . I got paid well here, I liked the conditions. If this job fell apart, where would I be? I wasn't qualified to do anything else. And the thought of returning to The Stephanie Wright Care Home for the Bewildered filled me with terror. I just couldn't do it. Not again. I as good as had no family. My lodgings were unsatisfactory; I might be kicked out at any time. If Steven and I were heading nowhere, I could be scuppered over this. I watched Scarlet and felt vulnerable.

Then she smiled and put her arm around me. 'Oh well,' she said. 'Takes all sorts. Just be careful, Spinning Jenny.'

She didn't say careful of what. I breathed again.

After fussing around the desk for a few minutes and pretending to give great attention to the silent monitors which were observing absolutely nothing, I went into the kitchen and made some coffee, bringing a mug out for her to seal our peace. As for her words? I just tossed them aside. Buried them deep. I could ignore them for now.

We sat for the rest of the afternoon in uncomfortable silence, neither wishing to widen the rift that threatened to slice our friendship in two. I watched the hands on the big clock turn with painful slowness and was glad when they reached 5.28 and I could shut up shop. I put some lipstick on and sprayed myself with perfume.

Steven had arranged to pick me up after work and take me straight back to Yr Arch, which I'd translated, erroneously as it turned out, as The Arch. One day I would ask him where the name had come from, and who chose it, him or Margaret. Why *Yr* instead of *The*? But at the moment I was feeling too vulnerable to ask questions.

At five thirty his car rolled in, just as I was locking up. Scarlet was already sitting in her car having an animated conversation with Andrew. I could see her arms waving around and they both glanced across at me as I climbed into Steven's Ford and, for their benefit, pecked him on the cheek with deliberate warmth.

But as soon as I shut the car door I was aware that something was different about the relationship between Steven and me. I didn't want to focus on it but something had shifted. The nearest I can get to it is the smoker who ignores a cough or the woman who ignores a lump in her breast. Ignore it if you like but you know it's there. That is how I felt, a sense of unease, of a deep malignancy that I was trying to ignore. Steven did not respond to my kiss when I got in but sat very still for a while, as though my kiss had paralysed him. At first, he stared ahead, through the windscreen, out of the car. Then he turned and met my eyes, not quite smiling, but appraising me, maybe wondering what lay behind this forwardness, while the car stayed in neutral, engine running, his feet not touching the pedals, both hands on the steering wheel. I couldn't work out what this scrutiny meant. What did he feel for me? Love, pity, condescension, exasperation? Lust? I didn't have a clue because my 'boyfriend' was as inscrutable as Buddha. At the same time, thoughts drifted through *my* mind, but like a rainbow glancing across the water they were elusive, ripples of brilliant colour shimmering across a murky pond, nothing substantial enough to hold in my hand or to interpret.

As I strapped myself into the passenger seat I tested the water. 'You don't seem so bothered about your stuff now,' I said. 'Are you sure you still want to pay to keep it here?'

He looked amused. 'Are you trying to eject me? Isn't that bad for business?'

I wasn't sure how to take this.

'At least I know it's safe there,' he said, quite calm now. 'It's enough to know that. I don't need to keep seeing it, reminding myself it's there.' He tapped the side of his head. 'It's in here as well,' he said. 'I'm always aware of it, Jennifer. I know every single item in there.' He turned to face me. 'I need to keep it there. I need to preserve it.'

'To remind you of Margaret?'

The words were out before I'd had time to think.

He didn't answer. And the look he gave me was as strange as snow is in summer or a heatwave in December. There was something inappropriate about it. I felt cold. I waited for him to speak.

'I don't need proof of her existence,' he said finally, staring straight ahead, his face taut. Then he turned to face me, his skin waxy pale. He looked unhealthy. 'I won't forget her. Not ever.'

It wasn't exactly what I'd hoped or expected to hear.

I could have put an Elastoplast on it, assured him she had been his wife and of course he wouldn't forget her, but the words choked up my throat. He was staring through the windscreen now, his expression blank while I tried to figure things out. I'd never seen him look grief-stricken about his wife's death. Yet, surely, preserving all her stuff must mean that he still loved her?

He turned around. 'You smell nice,' he said, then he slipped the car into gear and edged out on to the road. I breathed easier now we had left The Green Banana behind and Scarlet and Andy's watchful gaze. Their car was behind us but soon turned off. Steven drove carefully, taking no risks, always within the speed limit. I felt safe.

Which the traitorous little voice that lies within all our skulls countered with: *Until . . .*

We headed out of Tunstall, turning into the Leek Road and travelling through Stockton Brook and Endon until we reached farmland. He kept silent all the way but seemed to be arguing something within himself. Then he turned right, over the canal bridge, beneath which, years ago, a man had hanged himself. I never knew his name or his circumstances. We headed towards Stanley village, driving past scattered cottages, barn conversions, and the two sixties' houses beyond the pub, turning left into a curving tarmacked drive which ended at the front door of a very neat, characterless bungalow, its name engraved on a slate plaque set into the brick wall. This, then, was Yr Arch.

TWENTY-THREE

I felt a wisp of disappointment as I took in the lawn to the side of the drive, one solitary tree in its centre. I'd built up Steven's house to be so much more than this plain, unobtrusive, uncared-for house, which begged to be ignored like a plain girl in a plain dress at a noisy party. But then I should have expected this. Of course Steven would live in a quiet, simple house. It fitted. As he parked the car, I studied its unexciting exterior and started to wonder about Steven's relationship with his dead wife. Had she been like my analogy of the plain girl? Perhaps seeing me studying it, Steven glanced across at me, raising his eyebrows. 'Is this what you expected?'

Unable to stop myself I shook my head. 'Nothing like it,' I said.

He gave a chuckle and one of his almost-smiles. 'So what *did* you expect?'

I turned to face him then. 'I thought it would be an old cottage,' I said, 'with white walls and black beams.'

He looked at his house and smiled again, tight-lipped. 'Sorry to disappoint,' he said, sounding hurt.

I touched his hand. 'It doesn't.'

'This was built in the 1960s,' he said. 'They didn't go in for mock Tudor then.' We were still sitting in the car, the uninspiring bungalow in front. I realized he was waiting for me to say something complimentary. I have never been good at smothering my negative feelings with false bonhomie. I couldn't think of a thing to say so I simply looked around me and tried to find something nice to focus my eyes on.

There was only one thing. 'What a lovely tree.'

'Apple tree,' he said shortly.

I had to find something to break the taut atmosphere.

'Is the tree the same age as the house?'

'No.'

I turned back to study the house.

It was brick built, with plain, UPVC windows and three wide steps leading up to a white-painted front door. Obviously compared to living on the streets, my single bedroom at Jodi and Jason's, or the earthquake zone that my quarrelling parents' house had become, it was a palace. But my cursed imagination had filled in the blank with something else. A pretty garden. An archway of flowers. Something quaint. Maybe, I thought, it would look prettier in spring when the garden came to life. But what garden was there, except lawns and that one solitary, lonely tree?

But if I lived here I could make a garden. My imagination coloured the picture. Bulbs in the spring, flower beds through the summer, roses climbing those plain walls.

'So,' I said, squaring my shoulders, 'this is it.'

It did the trick. Filled the void of silence and lack of appreciation. 'Yeah,' he said, sounding pleased now, putting his arm around me and drawing me to him. 'This – is – it.'

We climbed out simultaneously in a smooth, almost choreographed move.

I followed him to the steps and the front door. He inserted his key, threw the door open and stood back, letting me enter first.

Maybe that was a mistake.

The first thing that you notice when you enter a house is its smell. Some places have pleasant scents: meals cooking, wood smoke, potpourri, plug-ins, bathroom deodorant, shampoo, air freshener, scented candles. Other homes have less pleasant odours to offer – tobacco, recent toilet activity, stale cooking. Or just stale air.

That was the scent of Yr Arch – musty, fusty, like the home of an ancient aunt: old fashioned, old clothes, moth-eaten curtains, upholstery that has sat for too long, cloying and a bit sour. Underlying that was the vaguest hint of Light Blue. Basically, the house smelt of *her*. Dead her. Even two steps in I was being reminded that this had been *her* house and she had left her scent. Houses usually have sounds too. They are rarely completely silent. Washing machines whirr, central heating crackles, radiators expand and contract, electronic machines finish their cycle and bleep, as a message left on an answering machine alerts you to its presence. I had never been in such a quiet house before. Even the air seemed muffled and dead, and so I stood in the hallway and soaked in the oppressive silence. They say as silent as the grave. Is the grave, I wonder, silent? No one has been able to tell us.

The complete lack of sound felt hostile, resentful of my presence. I would have liked to turn around and run away from this. I felt as though I couldn't breathe in the atmosphere, which was as heavy as the air before a thunderstorm. I imagined her drifting towards me, studying me and rejecting me before drifting back down that long hall. One brief look was all she'd needed before she had turned her back on me and retreated, sucking the air behind her.

Steven was behind me, waiting for a comment. I needed to stop this and get back to normality. He had told me she was dead and that, I told myself, is that. *I am in a long narrow hall*, I told myself. *It has no windows so of course it's dark. The windows and doors all need throwing open and this (imagined) smell will soon dissipate. Steven is standing behind me, waiting for me to speak. He wants appreciation. I can feel his hand on my shoulder. No one else is here. The doors off the hallway are all closed. No one is behind them. The rooms are all empty. And I can soon throw them all open. Windows too and let the spirits out.*

I leaned back into Steven while I absorbed more of the scene before me. I was not reassured. The carpet was beige with a few faint stains here and there, maybe muddy feet or spilt drinks.

Someone had tried to scrub the stains away with little success. Each stain was encircled by a paler patch. The walls were white with a hint of something – almond, cream, green, blue. Not quite pure, ice-white, yet just as cold. And it felt like that. It was like standing in a freezer. I actually shivered. A few sepia prints did their best to relieve the spartan feel but even those felt impersonal. Steven was still behind me, his hand gripping my shoulder. He was close enough for me to feel the warmth of his breath but, perhaps still waiting for my verdict, he said nothing. I turned around to search his face and had a sudden panic. I did not recognize him. I turned to face him. He looked different here. Maybe it was the light, but it was as though I was looking at a stranger. I play-acted and took a step into his arms, laughing, trying to shatter the atmosphere with jolly words and a lie. 'It's lovely.'

I knew instantly he was relieved. He exhaled; his arms relaxed and I followed my sentence with another of those fake laughs, 'I don't know which door to open first.' To me my voice sounded hollow, echoing down the corridor and bouncing back towards me. I could hear the ring of insincerity. But, apparently, Steven did not.

He pressed his lips down on mine, and for the first time I sensed some passion behind the gesture. 'You're here now,' he said, stroking my hair and drawing me in close. 'And I'm *glad* you're here. I worried about bringing you. I worried what you might think. A woman looks at a house differently.'

'But Margaret liked it.' I opened my eyes to look straight into his, which were troubled now and evasive.

But he agreed with my statement. 'Yes.'

He put his hands either side of my face now. 'I worried,' he said. 'I thought it might hold too many ghosts.' His words were light, almost jocular, but his face was deadly serious.

'Ghosts?'

We laughed together and he stepped forward while I followed.

But the truth was I did feel uncomfortable here, watched and criticized, just like at home. Something did not feel right, but I could not work out what it was. I consoled myself with saying; this is just my first time. The feeling will melt away with each succes-sive visit. As I followed Steven along the hallway, I sensed her beside me, tut-tutting. And knew already she disapproved.

I shouldn't have asked. 'Have you ever brought anyone else here?'

He couldn't seem to give me an answer.

And even more stupidly, I asked again. 'Have you had other girlfriends here – since Margaret?'

I waited but he shook his head. 'No.'

I did not ask him to enlarge.

He opened the door at the end of the hall and I followed him into a kitchen.

It was old fashioned, fitted with dark oak cupboards at floor level, while the eye-level cupboards were glazed displaying china plates, cups and saucers. They looked like bone china and had pink, gaudy flowers over a white background and fine rims of gold.

The floor consisted of terracotta tiles and the worktops were pale oak. The effect was dull brown and uninspiring. I could picture 'Margaret' here but not me. I half closed my eyes to see her standing at the sink in M&S 'slacks' and a polyester blouse. (No need to iron, she would say.) I saw her as beige-coloured, someone polite and unobtrusive, with a soft, pliant voice. Very like her husband. But towards me I felt waves of unmistakable hostility. My picture acquired detail. Her skin was pale, like Steven's. She wore no foundation. Her hair was similar to mine, light brown, the colour soft and shining in the light, falling not quite straight to her shoulders. Knowing it was her best feature, she would touch it often, drawing attention to it with her hands. Her eyes, without make-up, would look small and shrewd, and her lips with clumsily applied lipstick too pink – the wrong colour for her complexion – were in danger of appearing tight, mean and ungenerous.

Picking none of this up, of course, Steven crossed the floor to pick up the kettle. 'Coffee?'

I'd have preferred a glass of wine – whatever colour he had in the house – but I nodded. 'Thank you.' I felt stilted and awkward and my voice was muffled, as though I had spoken from outer space, sending the words floating down to the three people in this room. I scanned the kitchen, searching for a clue as to the source of this resentful vibe. But I found nothing. It must be all inside my mind. A by-product of a fertile imagination. Now it was I who tut-tutted – at myself.

The kitchen was neat and tidy, the smell in here one of bleach and surface cleaners. Apart from the white plastic kettle, the oak surfaces were clear, the cupboard doors closed, the tea set tidily placed on a tray. I moved towards the windows over the sink.

Through the gloom I just made out a small square of back garden bordered by a low hedge, and beyond that fields which stretched into foggy invisibility. Steven handed me a mug of coffee. Though he was smiling, his face was anxious now, perhaps picking up on both my scrutiny and my uncertainty. Or maybe he was sensing her presence too – and her disapproval. Maybe I didn't fit the mould after all. He was still waiting for me to say something. But I fumbled for words. He prompted me.

'Like it?' There was a touch of pride in his voice.

It's a terrible feeling when you are expected to say something nice and you can't find a single appropriate word out of the thousands of adjectives swimming around in our language. Even a simple *nice* would have been something, but the words collided in my brain. I had told enough lies for the day.

I couldn't say I loved it; neither could I say it was homely, so I said nothing as I nodded. But I did manage a smile. Which reassured him. He gave me a light kiss on the cheek and his hand slid down my arm as the kettle boiled. He handed me a coffee, took one himself.

'Come into the sitting room.'

TWENTY-FOUR

I didn't see it straight away.

Clutching my coffee mug, I'd followed him into another square beige room with UPVC patio doors taking up almost an entire back wall. Outside the light had almost gone but I could just make out a rotary washing line over a paved area and pictured her, pegs in mouth, hanging out his and her clothes. As I stood at the window and stared out, the last of the light faded; the picture was gone, replaced by a black void.

In spite of my experiences with Mum and Dad, I had thought a home could, possibly, be a haven, somewhere you could kick your shoes off and feel relaxed. You left your troubles outside. This house had a different feel to it. It felt uncomfortable, uneasy with itself. This place felt more like the ugly open-cast destruction Mr Budge had planned for my pretty green valley. Disturbed, I turned back into the room, eyes sliding over the three-piece suite (beige Draylon) and television. Turned my gaze upwards and froze.

Have you ever been on a continental holiday where you are stopped in your tracks and a street artist offers to sketch you? My mother has. In the far-distant days when she and Dad were happily married, it happened to her. And the vain, silly creature had had it framed and put over the fireplace. We looked at it day after day.

The same must have happened to Margaret. Obviously the picture must be of her. It could not have been me. The eyes mocked me. *Work this one out.* I stepped forward and looked up into a pair of eyes that were a mirror image of my own.

I couldn't say anything at first and then I found some words. 'Is that . . .?'

'My wife,' he said proudly. He walked up to the fireplace and touched the picture with reverence, spreading his hand over the glass.

'That's Margaret?'

It was a rough sketch, the sitter square-on to the artist. A few strokes indicated shoulder-length brown hair, full lips, blue eyes. It could have been me or it could have been almost any woman with the same colouring. I didn't like looking at it, putting a voice, mannerisms to it, bringing her back to life. Was she my doppelgänger, was that why Steven had picked me out?

I watched Steven's face. He was rapt as he focused on the picture, transported to happier times.

Sometimes we absorb a fact at the time but only realize its significance months later. He still wasn't wearing his wedding ring. I noticed when he'd put his hand up to touch the sketch. The slight indentation and white line was still there, too.

But at the time my mind was grappling with my interpretation, substituting logic for wild fantasy. Men and women often 'go' for the same type. Partners divorce only to find another spouse with the same physical appearance – and the same faults. This is why having divorced an abusive husband, a woman frequently selects her next partner with the same characteristics. Teresa Simpson (A9) would likely fall for another philanderer. And me? As I have said, I attract bad men as flies are attracted to rotting meat. All types except Steven.

He was the exception.

I looked again at the picture and seemed to read uncertainty in that mouth, drawn in a too-bright red, a deeply held doubt in those pale eyes. In that too I recognized myself and touched my own mouth.

This was a picture of a person who doubted herself too deeply ever to be convinced she was worthy. And no shade of lipstick would mask that.

So, I thought, this is Margaret and this is me.

Margaret and I were the same. Steven had done the predictable, been attracted to a similar type. She wasn't the M&S beige trousers I'd imagined. She was me.

I stared. Sometimes when you stare at a portrait you swear you see the person move. I could have sworn she blinked or winked.

I turned around. 'How old was Margaret when she died?'

It was, surely, a simple question, but it seemed to throw him. He didn't know the answer.

I waited.

Then, with a smile, he finally responded, 'Thirty-six.'

I had the feeling this wasn't true but covered up my doubt with a bland statement.

'Not very old then.'

He shook his head.

'Was it cancer of the breast?'

He shrugged. 'I can't really remember, Jennifer. In the end she had it everywhere. I don't want to dwell on it.'

I was quiet while I thought this through and made my decision.

Steven, with his quiet ways, was better than my usual dish of life's gifts. He was *not* another bad man to add to my collection. He was just different.

My man of mystery stood behind me while I tried to untangle knotted mysteries and supress doubt. He draped his arm around my neck and we both gazed at the portrait. 'I told you you looked like her.' He sounded pleased with himself. And me.

I wondered then. What had her life been like with Steven? Happy? Until she got sick.

'How long were you married?'

Again, the simple question seemed to throw him.

Then. 'Six years,' he said curtly.

'What was she like?'

'What was she like? That's a strange question.'

'Not really.'

I looked into the painting and thought I recognized something else. Had she too had a difficult life before she'd met Steven? Had men been unkind to her too? Had she always picked the wrong guy – until she met Mr Right-Guy Taverner? Had the wrong men been attracted to her as they were to me, sticking like flies to flypaper?

I wondered.

'Like you.' He nuzzled the back of my neck and I felt his groin harden against me. At last, I thought, with a touch of triumph. It had taken six months to get to this point. I didn't turn to see where his gaze was focused. I felt simply triumph while his wife watched. I felt relieved. He was normal after all and I *did* have the power to turn him on. I ignored my own response, simmering. Did I want him? Yes? No? I made my decision, turned around and returned his kiss, licking his lips and pushing my tongue inside his mouth. Which was when his desire seemed to cool, his erection shrink. He held me at arm's length and looked hard into my eyes.

'No,' he said gently. 'Jennifer, no. Not like that. That isn't the way.' He held me close then. 'Do nothing.'

I felt oddly ashamed. I didn't know what I'd done wrong. I'd only encouraged him with a saucy kiss, but he held my chin in the angle of his hand between thumb and forefinger. 'Are you ready for this?' he whispered.

I wasn't sure what the question meant. I'd never been asked it before. Guys just assumed I was up for it. I felt myself redden, shrink back, unsure. Men have a physical sign their desire is waning. Women's wilting desire is more subtle. Hidden deeper. Harder to interpret. I nodded anyway. It was going to happen sometime. If we were going to have a normal relationship, sex had to play its part, so if not now then later. He took my hand and led me back along the hallway, turning right and pushing the door open.

The bedroom walls were painted white with a couple of flowery prints and a plain blue carpet. It had that fusty scent with the under-lying Light Blue that I was already beginning to recognize. The bed was covered with a thin duvet with a blue and white spotted cover and a valance hiding the base, pillowcases with frilled edges.

Men don't keep house as well as most women. And once you enter a bachelor's, widower's or divorcé's lair, you see a man in his most human and vulnerable form.

He was aroused. I could tell by the film that covered his eyes, by the slow, heavy, deliberate breathing, by the way he was pressing himself into me. And the obvious. But instead of dissolving in a sea of lust, my mind was filled with facts, delving into D5. I saw the boxes standing on the concrete floor, the suitcases, the name written in the thick black marker pen.

My spine was frozen so he had to back me towards the bed hard enough for me to fall.

'Take your clothes off.' I have heard more romantic overtures, but most of my past boyfriends had simply ripped off any articles of clothing without so much as a by-your-leave. I complied, slipping my dress over my head and stood, a bit embarrassed and exposed, in my bra and pants, thankfully matching purple from New Look.

But he shook his head as though I was disappointing him. 'Everything.'

I was frankly mortified. Call me a prude, but naked as the day you were born doesn't quite match up to a purple push-up bra and lacy matching thong. I looked at him with a silent plea. He could have held me then, touched me, kissed me, loved me, reassured me, aroused me. But he didn't. He just stood back, cold as a block of ice, as I slipped out of my two minuscule remaining garments. He was appraising me as though I was a cow in the farmers' market. If I had felt any warmth towards him, any sexual desire, it would have melted away as I shivered. I felt awkward, exposed, embarrassed and, for some unknown reason, ashamed.

I was conscious of something else. The bedroom was on the ground floor, the window overlooking the drive. It was dark but a lamp was on and the curtains weren't drawn.

What if someone called?

'Now lie back and close your eyes.'

This was foreplay?

I did as he asked, aware that none of this was going according to plan. I felt an odd sense of confusion. Where was the romance?

'Jennifer,' he said, speaking so low and close into my ear that I felt the drum vibrate. 'Don't move. Lie perfectly . . . still.'

I looked up at him. Puzzled. 'Close your eyes.' And then he was on top of me. I felt his erection against my belly.

Later, he drove me home.

TWENTY-FIVE

Two nights later.

'Weirder and weirder,' Stella said when I gave her a potted version of the event. Sanitized, of course. I was too embarrassed to describe my situation in graphic detail. Then she started giggling. 'You have to admit it, though, Jen.' She opened her eyes wide. 'He just wants you to lie back and think of England.'

I was uncomfortable as I nodded. That wasn't it. It wasn't England I had been thinking of. And as for Steven – what had he been thinking of?

'Bloody hell.' And she took a long draught of wine. Then she frowned. 'Jen,' she said seriously, her hand on my arm. 'I know you think Steven's a great catch and the answer to all your problems . . .'

Sensing a *but* hovering in the air I felt bound to stick up for him and protested. 'Well, at least he's not a wanker like the rest of them.'

'Jen,' she said again, frowning now. 'There's all sorts of men out there. There's wankers, accepted. But there's weirdos too.'

'I know that.' I felt bound to put in, 'You're just jealous.'

'No, I'm not.' I knew that was the truth as she continued. 'I know he seems nice. But there's obviously something strange about him. Something . . . not right?'

I defended him hotly. 'You've hardly met him. Once at the store and another time when you called in on your way to your holiday and we were just heading out. You *are* jealous.' I counted his attributes on my fingers. 'He has a good job. A nice car. He's not a married cheat. He's available. He doesn't get road rage. He isn't mean. And he has a lovely . . .' But I stopped at that, knowing I was heading towards what it was that made me uncomfortable. The dead wife who hovered around the house. The portrait which could almost have been me, the contents of D5. And worst of all the lovemaking, which felt nothing like it should. Not one of my boyfriends had made me feel as though I was descending into . . . What? I could hardly put it into words – not even to myself. And then I did. Had his fantasy been that he was making love to his dead wife?

Stella gripped my hand then. 'Don't even think . . .'

'Think what?'

'You wouldn't . . . move in with him?'

I shook my head. 'I don't think it's his scene. He's more the . . .'

She clutched my arm. 'You wouldn't *marry* him? No. Jenny, no.'

I tried to turn it into a joke. 'He hasn't asked me yet.'

She looked aghast.

And I turned on her. 'Look. It's OK for you, Stell. You have a life. You've got a lovely husband, a child. A house. A family. A mum and dad who help you out when they can, in-laws. I've got none of those and I'm not likely to get them either. For some reason I'm always left with the rotten apple in the bottom of the barrel. I don't know why. Maybe it's some vibe that I give off. But that's the way it is. This is my chance. Probably the only one I'm going to get.'

'Don't.' She still looked a bit frightened. She pulled my arm. 'Please. You're my friend.'

I carried on, steamrollering over all her reservations. 'I don't have any qualifications that are likely to see me into a super-job. I have no money behind me. I barely scratch out a living. I rent one small room in a small house. And Jason and Jodi can't wait for me to leave. And then what, Stell? *My* mum and dad don't want me and I don't earn enough to have a nice clean place all of my own. I'll be homeless again. On the streets. I've been there, Stell. It's shitty. It's also dangerous and very cold. You get dirty and everyone thinks they can just hit on you because you're a druggy or desperate. And that's the trouble. You *are* desperate. *I'm* desperate.'

'Rent another room.'

'They're not much better.'

She drew in a sharp, frustrated breath and I carried on trying to convince her. 'Don't you see it? Steven is a way out of all this. He has a lovely place in a pretty village. He's quiet and he's my lifeline.'

'And he loves you?'

I answered as honestly as I could. 'In his own way.' I thought I'd spoken with dignity and finality. But Stella countered with, 'Which is?'

And that, even I with my verbal gymnastics, couldn't answer. Or rather didn't want to. Put it into words and it would have seemed too real.

Stella's eyes were wide as she waited.

And my response sounded pathetic. 'Stell, I want some*thing*, some*one* of my own.'

And now she looked alarmed. 'Jenny,' she said, 'you're sounding dangerously desperate.'

And the truth was I was. Life was slipping by. I know I was only twenty-three but I felt much older. I wanted that home, a family of my own. OK, Steven didn't set me on fire, but he seemed safe. I hoped he *was* safe. I believed I could be with him. And if what he wanted was a compliant, naked wife who lay still as a dead person, if that was what aroused him, I could hack that. There were worse ways of having sex. I'd experienced most of them. Sordid, violent, as near to rape as stayed this side of the law. I could play-act for now because that would mean security. It would be worth it. People who have never lacked security don't know what a precious thing it is, to be able to sleep at night, in a bed, secure, safe, comfortable. Warm, well fed. Try being homeless when a kick or worse will wake you from a freezing cold nightmare into some new terror. Try wandering the streets because you daren't sleep. Try having a couple of drunks stumble over you and have a go at raping you but they're too pissed. Try being so cold you've forgotten what warmth even feels like. Try being so hungry you practically vomit at the thought of food. Just try it. And then pass judgement on me. Steven was decent and he seemed to love me – in his way – which was, admittedly, unusual. There was always the chance that he would change. Forget about Margaret and replace her with me. And then he would be the ideal husband. It would just take time. That was the version with which I convinced myself.

When Mum and Dad split up, just before my GCSEs, they had sold the house for less than they'd paid for it; the property market at that time had plummeted because of the economic downturn and their semi had nose-dived even more because prospective buyers sensed the misery and desperation. This dumped them into the nightmare land of negative equity. Lives that are going wrong result in their own economic downturn. Everyone wants a *happy* house. My parents had, disgruntled, gone their different ways, searching for the elusive land of happiness with new partners, but with the albatross of debt hanging around their necks. That was the time that I had nowhere to live. ('*Oh come on, Jen, you're a big girl now. You should be able to look after yourself,*' and, '*You wouldn't rob your old dad of this chance to be happy, to be really happy, with a gorgeous stepmother, would you?'*)

Parents can be so selfish.

So yes. I joined the homeless. Became one of the great unwashed. An inhabitant of cardboard city. The sky was my ceiling, the pavement my floor. Anywhere my bathroom and toilet.

I'd used up my friends' sofas and goodwill and my grandmother didn't want me. So I slept rough and it was hell.

TWENTY-SIX

absolutely loved Scarlet. She was funny, interesting, clever, kind and honest. I liked her style and her happiness. That was her abiding characteristic – a joyous, golden optimism. I trusted her too. The question was, should I trust her judgement?

She was sitting, swinging her legs from the stool as we chatted.

She was looking proper hot today – in skinny faux-snakeskin silver jeggings and a cropped top she could have passed for a girl of seventeen, except for her face which was ravaged, sun damage plus cigarettes plus a sort of streetwise, wary look. Scarlet was beautiful but she looked as though she'd had a hard life. I didn't want to have a hard life. I wanted an easy one.

But at least she *knew* about life – and men. Not like Stella, whose experience outside Sonny was limited. They'd been together since school. And she was not above a little cattiness and envy. I was learning not to trust my best friend.

I knew that whatever Scarlet said I'd listen. Besides, she knew Steven. Not well, admittedly, but better than Stella. And her life experiences must have included quite a few 'unusual' men and probably a few 'bad sorts' among them.

So I risked it. 'What do you think of Steven Taverner?'

She drilled right into me with those black gimlet eyes. She looked a bit startled and a bit wary. 'Why do you ask?'

'Just wondering.'

'He seems a decent sort. But, Spinning Jenny, I can't say I really know him. Not like you do.'

She hesitated before adding, 'He's quite a bit older than you.'

And followed that up with, 'And he has been married – and widowed.' And then she twigged. 'Is something wrong between you?'

I tried to sound both nonchalant and sophisticated. 'No. We're getting along just fine.'

'So why are you asking?'

'Sorry?'

'If everything's so fine,' she said perceptively, 'why are you kind of checking up with me?'

'I'm not.'

'Come on, Spinning Jenny,' she coaxed. 'You can confide in me.'

'It's our—'

She guessed. 'Sex life?'

'Mmm.'

She burst into great guffaws of laughter. 'Darling,' she said, 'show me a couple whose sex life is satisfactory.' Then, 'Maybe he needs a few lessons.'

'But he's been married. He must have—' I stopped short but I *was* listening to her.

That was my first mistake.

She touched my hand with hers (long scarlet nails with big silver rings on every finger). 'How well do you know him?'

'We've been going out for more than six months now.' I knew my response was prickly, defensive and ultimately uninformative.

She repeated her question. 'I mean, how well do you know him? What do you know about him, Spinning Jenny?'

'As well as . . .'

'For instance,' she continued, 'do you know what job he does? Have you met any of his friends, his family?'

I knew the answer to all this. No.

She put her arm around me. 'Wait until you know him better before you make any sort of commitment. Don't be in a hurry. Don't rush into anything.' She tapped my nose with a long, painted nail. 'And if, at any time, you just have to find out a little more about him, there's always . . .' She dangled the key to the top drawer. 'This.' She leaned in. 'A sneaky little preview?'

I was tempted.

'Be careful,' she said. Then added, 'How serious is this relationship?'

And that was the trouble. I couldn't answer because I didn't know. After that one visit to his house we seemed to have returned to our previous footing. A 'date' a couple of times a week. We were returning to our old haunts now. Bar staff and baristas were recognizing us as regulars. I wondered if in that one encounter I had disappointed him. After our evenings together he'd drop me off with a chaste goodnight kiss. There was no more sex. Not even weird sex. Which had set me thinking. Men like sex, surely? Hadn't he enjoyed it? Did he have someone else? Was he still grieving for Margaret? Was he a closet gay? I couldn't work him out and wondered incessantly. It ate me from the inside like a canker.

And then, quite suddenly, seven months, one week and two days after our first date, he asked me to marry him. And I nearly died of shock.

It was November. We were at the Mermaid Inn, a beautiful, remote pub high over the moorland with views that stretched for miles in all directions.

A Mermaid Inn? So elevated and far from the sea? The inn is named after the nearby pool. There are two legends which explain how the mermaid came to be there. The first is effectively a rather charming love story between water nymph and seafarer and claims that she was taken there hundreds of years ago by the sailor who was from the nearby town of Thorncliffe. But when he died the mermaid became angry and – unable to return to the sea – started to haunt the place.

The other legend is more sinister and tells of a beautiful young woman who rejected the advances of a local man named Joshua Linnet. Unable to accept the rejection, Joshua accused her of being a witch and managed to convince the local townsfolk to drown her in what was then called Black Mere Pond. Mere being a local term for a pond. With her final breath the young woman muttered a curse against Joshua and three days later *his* body was found by the pool, his face covered with claw marks. It is said that her spirit still haunts the pool in the form of a demon mermaid. Which is the true version? Take your pick. In my opinion neither. But up here, so remote, so far from civilization, it is only too easy to believe in these legends of demon mermaids and water nymphs, convince yourself that somewhere, in the murky past, there was a true haunted, tragic history. And you might fear to be up here, on a dull lonely night. The name must have originated somewhere.

The legend grows legs as it is said that livestock refuse to drink water from the Mermaid Pool, and birds will never fly across it. The water, oily, peaty and black, has given rise to the legend that it is bottomless, a gateway to the underworld. In the 1850s a group of determined locals attempted to drain the lake to see how deep it really was. But soon after the men began digging at the southern end of the pool (where a drainage ditch can still be seen), the mermaid herself appeared from the lake and threatened to flood the nearby towns of Leek and Leekfrith unless they stopped digging.

Needless to say, they packed up their shovels and went home.

Even driving up to the pub that cold Sunday afternoon, something of the eerie atmosphere penetrated the car, and the walk to the front door was a struggle, the wind so strong it practically cut you in half, as though the mermaid herself was buffeting you. When we entered the pub we both laughed out loud. It was such a relief. On such a wild late afternoon only a few tables were occupied.

We sat in the corner while Steven fetched drinks and suddenly happiness burst out of me. 'I feel so happy,' I said, 'I could die. Right here and now. Nothing in my life will ever measure up to this beautiful, wild afternoon. Thank you.'

He turned to face me, surprised. 'Really? You mean that?'

Which bit, I wondered, but repeated, 'I never thought life could be so kind.'

He looked even more startled. Then he brushed my cheek with his hand. 'So easy to please?' He followed this up with, 'Marry me?'

Now it was I who was amazed. 'What did you say?'

He gave a little chuckle. 'You heard.' And now he wasn't looking at me but out through the window, at the vista. As I have said, it was a wild afternoon, but a shaft of light had found its way through a few clouds. When I was a little girl I believed that those beams of sunshine stretching down to earth were a stairway to heaven, thrown down by God to give us mortals a chance of ascending. These days I am not so sure. If there is a stairway to heaven then, surely, there is also one in the other direction? A child believes life will be good to her. An adult knows that life can be the opposite.

But outside I could see where he was looking, at that shaft of light, pathway to heaven.

His proposal had shocked me into silence. The afternoon felt very strange, out of kilter.

Steven tilted his head, that strange movement which looked as though he was listening to something or someone, seeking their approval. He gave a nervous laugh. 'Take your time, Jennifer.'

I turned to look at him. Not in the usual way but searching his face for clues. I liked his brown hair, slightly thinning. I liked his straight nose. I liked his eyes and the small, quiet mouth, out of which I had never heard a swear word or a curse. As I studied him he studied me back with a half-smile. 'Well? Do I pass the test?'

I knew what was missing. He hadn't said he loved me. Like many little girls – before everything had gone so wrong – I had had my dreams. White lace, a gold wedding ring, a home, a husband, children. This was my stairway to heaven. He was my stairway to heaven.

But . . .

'I know so little about you.'

'You only need to know one thing,' he said. 'I want to marry you.' He still hadn't said it.

This was my chance. My *only* chance. Carpe diem. I threw all caution to the wind; what came out was a shocked and breathless, 'Yes.'

He smiled, kissed my cheek and it *was* tender. 'You will, Jennifer?' He sounded very certain of this. I nodded again, firmer this time, but still feeling as though I was jumping off the edge of a tall building into thin air. Unknown territory. The stairway descending.

'Yes.'

He murmured something but it wasn't addressed to me.

TWENTY-SEVEN

Weddings have to be arranged, don't they?

And for some reason – God only knows why – I tried to get in touch with my mother.

My mother's name is Sylvia. She is tall and angular with sharp, unpleasant features. I don't look like her at all, thank goodness. She is a selfish woman who, without a backwards glance, walked out on my brother and me when I was a teenager, to be with 'the love of her life', George Harris, who turned out to have an evil temper and subsequently walked out on *her* a few years later. When I think of life in the years before my parents split up, I can only remember everyone being cross. Cross because we didn't have enough money. Cross because my bedroom was untidy. Cross because my mother didn't want to make the tea or do the ironing. Cross with Dad, cross with me, cross with Josh. I never ever remember her being affectionate towards Dad. (Later on, he got an overdose of that from Gloria – and later still from Malee the Thai child bride, his latest squeeze.) When he was with Mum he always seemed downtrodden and a bit unhappy so my image of marriage wasn't exactly bliss. When I tried to imagine them joyous, happy, in love, getting married, I couldn't. How the hell did those two ever get married in the first place? It was only when I was a bit older and knew a bit more and could work a few things out for myself that I realized. They'd had a quickie. Mum had got pregnant with me. The two families had threatened them and they'd caved in and got married. So it was all my fault. No wonder she wasn't exactly fond of her daughter.

Marry in haste, they say. Big mistake. Better not to marry at all.

I came along months later, squawking like a screech owl, Mum said, and the scene was set for a tragedy. Misery, unhappiness, lies, quarrels, disaster. A resentful bride, a cornered groom. Two incompatible people. Wasted lives. To be honest, apart from being left homeless (living in a bedsit, Dad only had room for Josh who must have been, at best, an accident), I was glad when she vanished from our lives. And my dad seemed happier too. My dad's name is Gregory (don't ask!) and he never speaks unless you talk to him first. He is one of the world's quiet folk. But he's gentle and kind. And he never gets angry. I guess some people would call him passive. I call him lovely. I love my dad. But he moved on. Three years after Mum left, Gloria abandoned him too. Not sure what really happened. One day she was sprawled all over him like an octopus and the next she'd just vanished and been replaced by various Thai girls, culminating in Malee with her singsong high-pitched voice. Men are such fools.

So that's my family.

And Steven's? I knew absolutely nothing about them.

Brothers, sisters, mother, father? Nothing.

When I told my mum, having tracked her down through *her* mum (my grandma whom I never saw – I didn't even get a Christmas card from her), she snapped, 'So I suppose you want some money from me.'

That was my sweetest moment. 'Oh no, Mum,' I said. 'We don't need your money. We have enough. Steven is financially secure. He has a good job.'

'What?' I could hear the vitriol in her voice. 'So what is his job then?' She couldn't resist an extra jibe. 'Not a brain surgeon is he, sweetie?' I particularly hated it when she called me sweetie. Besides which, I didn't actually know what he did. So I made it up.

'He works for the government.'

'Really,' she scoffed. 'MP, is he?'

I didn't bother to answer.

'I just thought,' I continued, 'that as I'm your daughter you might like to know. You might even like to buy a bloody hat.'

And I slammed the phone down, only too aware that all I'd had was a mobile number. I didn't know where she lived now. I didn't even know whether she was still in France or not. All I knew was that my gran, whom I'd tracked down to Eccleshall, sixteen miles away, hadn't suggested we meet up as a threesome. That didn't surprise me. When I'd lived rough, I'd asked her once, just the once, if I could stay with her. She lived in a council flat at the top of the High Street and there was probably a rule about having guests to stay. But hell, I'd just told her I was camping out in Hanley Park, along with druggies, alcoholics and rapists. You'd have thought she'd have broken just that one little rule. But I found more kindness, more generosity, in the other homeless creatures – like Minnie Ha-Ha, who didn't have two pence to rub together – than in my own flesh and blood.

'Absolutely not,' she'd said. I could picture her sour expression even now. So now I knew where my mother's nasty streak originated from. Like mother like daughter. It was in her genes. Thank goodness not in mine. *I* was nothing like my mother. One of the rare occasions she'd agreed with me once, she said, 'Just like your father.' Well, I'd rather take after my dad and be a gullible fool than that miserable, nasty, mind-polluted piece of crap.

Of course, it was different with my little brother, Josh, three years younger. He was like mum, with a nasty, suspicious turn of mind and a mean streak. When we were kids, he'd say or do anything to get me into trouble. Telling tales whether they were true or not. From the second he was born I knew what the word hate meant. I hated him. I would look at his nasty, tiny blackcurrant eyes, see them slide into malice as he plotted the best way to hurl me into trouble, and when Mum walloped me he'd stand right by her, savouring every smack. And then I'd go wailing to Dad looking for a bit of sympathy – if he was home. If he wasn't, I'd sit on the front step and wait for him. Even when it was dark, rainy, cold, snowing, I'd sit on that bloody step and the minute he turned the corner I'd run to him. Dad always stuck up for me.

So no Mum to the wedding. Grandma probably wouldn't bother even if I sent her an invitation, so I wouldn't waste one. And there was no chance I'd waste a stamp on inviting my horrible little brother. I wouldn't want him there. And I wasn't sure exactly how to get hold of Dad with his plastic Thai lady. Last I'd heard he was on a long vacation somewhere. I wanted to warn him, tell him about Ruby Ngoma. Careful. When the money goes so will she. I tried the last mobile number I'd had for him but it didn't even ring.

When I told Stella we were getting married she was noticeably appalled. 'What on earth are you getting into, Jenny? You don't know the guy. He could be a serial killer. You don't know about his previous marriage. He's creepy at best. At worst . . . Oh, for goodness' sake, Jen, you don't even know what's in that bloody store.' And then she homed in on the weak spot. 'You don't even know for sure that his first wife is dead. Have you seen her death certificate?'

'No.'

'You must have lost your marbles.'

'No,' I said with dignity. 'I have not lost them, Stell. I've found them.'

The person I really wanted to get hold of was Minnie Ha-Ha. But how do you find a homeless person? No fixed abode means exactly that. I thought I might trawl the streets of Hanley on the off chance that I'd happen upon her.

I finally tracked Dad down through an old friend who had a more up-to-date number for him than I did. Apparently he was back in good old Blighty and, surprise surprise, had brought Malee with him. Even more of a surprise, he was living in Stafford. I visited them in an ex-council house and broke the news.

When he opened the door to me my first thought was, *Goodness, he's grown fat.*

Malee was hanging off his arm. Tiny, bad teeth, big smile. Lots of black hair.

They invited me in and over a cup of tea I broke the news. 'Darling,' he said, beaming. 'My beautiful little girl. Getting married.' He paused, then glanced at Malee, a little embarrassed. I could see what he was thinking. She and I were roughly the same age, which was probably one of the reasons he'd clearly been avoiding me.

He moved on pretty fast. 'So,' he continued far too heartily, 'when do we get to meet him?'

'Soon. I'll arrange something. We can have a night out at the pub all together. Eh?'

Malee giggled.

My dad put his arm round her. 'What's he like, love?'

'A bit older than me,' I said. 'Married before. But his wife died.'

Malee butted in. 'Children?'

'No.'

Dad chipped in then. 'Just give us the date, love. Tell us where and when. And we'll be there.'

No offer of financial help, I noticed. And I didn't have much spare for my wedding dress. Do bridegrooms often have to buy their bride's dress?

Dad tried to sound cheery, but I could hear unhappiness in his voice tinged with insecurity. Like he knew Malee would walk out on him sooner or later. And he would be left all alone again and a lot poorer.

'So, what's he like, this Prince Charming who's captured the heart of my beautiful daughter?'

I didn't respond with, *Yeah, the beautiful daughter you abandoned so she lived on the streets, the beautiful daughter you didn't even bother to tell that you were back in the country. The beautiful daughter who didn't even have a mobile phone number for you. Yeah,* that *beautiful daughter.*

I told him the little I knew about Steven, that we'd met because he'd stored some stuff of his wife's at the place where I was now working. I said he had a nice bungalow in Stanley where I would be living and that he was welcome to come and visit. Everyone knew Stanley as being a smart, pretty village near Endon, gateway to the Staffordshire Moorlands, and my dad looked suitably impressed. Malee just looked thoughtful. I could read her mind. How could she benefit?

'So, when is it to be?'

But his question focused my mind. When and where *was* the wedding to be?

I didn't know. When you accept a marriage proposal your mind fills with a vision of white tulle, lace, flowers, veils. Or at least mine did. The actual detail, the ceremony, the nitty-gritty, the time and place to fill in on the invitations, et cetera et cetera, that all comes later.

Only it didn't.

TWENTY-EIGHT

Two weeks after that happy evening outside The Mermaid Inn, Steven had not followed his proposal up with anything concrete. No ring, no discussion about when and where. I was beginning to get worried. Maybe he'd meant that bloody phrase – 'get married sometime'. Maybe I'd imagined it or read too much into his words. Maybe I'd dreamt it, like the stairway to heaven. Maybe the mermaid had bewitched me.

I was reluctant to bring up the subject – it would look too desperate. And I was nervous that he would back off. When we met he seemed his usual self, friendly and relaxed, a bit distracted sometimes, but I was beginning to be doubtful that this wedding would ever take place. I hadn't told Jason and Jodi that I was engaged because . . . What's the first thing people ask when you announce an engagement? Where's the ring? And the second? When's the wedding? I could answer neither question.

Until we had discussed the detail it didn't feel real.

Detail. I picked the word out like debris from between my teeth. I wanted the details. Not just about the wedding. I needed to know more about the man I'd agreed to marry.

In early December he took me back again to Yr Arch. It was a Sunday, late afternoon. We were having a takeaway and a bottle of wine. And I began my interrogation. We were sitting on the sofa, a small lamp lit in the corner. Once we'd finished our takeaway, Steven took the dishes into the kitchen. I heard the tap running as he rinsed the plates then the sound of plates being stacked. While he was gone, I eyed the picture over the fireplace and wondered about his life with Margaret. I couldn't imagine it. I couldn't quite picture her here, and then he was back.

I inched in. 'I know so little about you, Steven.'

He gave me one of his 'looks'. A sort of quizzical expression but with a nervousness behind it. 'You're not going to call it off, are you, Jennifer? You're not regretting saying yes? You aren't going to abandon me, are you?'

I was surprised at the level of anxiety in his voice.

'No. No.' I kissed him and patted his arm. But I could tell he was worried where this conversation was leading. He'd tucked his mouth in so it felt tight, unyielding, ready for a let-down and I felt his body tense.

'I don't even know what job you do.'

His smile now was indulgent. *Is that all?* 'Nothing very glamorous, I'm afraid.'

I waited.

'I work for the council.' Maybe sensing that wasn't enough, he added, 'For the Highways Department. Coordinating roadworks.' He spoke the words slowly, enunciating with deliberation.

'So you're the guy who shuts the roads?'

His face was serious. 'Only when it's necessary.'

I sighed. On the Sense of Humour Scale, Steven Taverner did not score highly.

'Did you have to go to university to get that job?'

'I did.' He was still relaxed, leaning against the back of the sofa. 'Birmingham. Engineering and then a Road Management MSc course.'

'Gosh.'

He was watching me, his face softening into an indulgent expression as he let his guard down. 'Your family,' I continued. 'I don't know anything about them.'

'We're not close,' he said quickly.

'Do they know about me?'

'I haven't told them . . . yet.'

'And Margaret? Did they get to meet her?'

'Of course.' If Steven had a degree in Road Management, he also had first-class honours in shutting down a conversation. I persisted.

'And Margaret,' I said. 'I don't know anything about her.'

'You don't need to know anything about her.'

'But if she was your wife and you were happily married . . .'

'Of course we were happily married.' He was getting angry now. 'What does that matter to you?'

The truth? I wasn't sure, except I believed that the state of his previous marriage would reflect on our own.

I felt defeated but made one more lame attempt. 'Did she have a job?'

'Yes.'

I waited but he was giving nothing more away.

'Have you finished your interrogation?' A simple phrase which could have been spoken in a few different ways: teasing, funny. Serious. Even hostile.

'I have . . .'

He stood up abruptly, straight as a soldier, crossed the room towards a small oak bureau and dropped the flap, taking out a small square box. He opened it and handed it to me. The name of a well-known jeweller's in Hanley was inside, together with a ring, sapphire surrounded by tiny diamonds. These days they would call it pre-loved or pre-owned. Basically second-hand. In this case literally. 'Put it on.'

I obeyed the order.

It was a bit big. 'Like it?'

I nodded and he looked pleased, but I was aware that this had been a distraction and stuck with my line of questioning.

'What about *her* family?'

He looked genuinely puzzled. 'Whose family?'

Was one of us mad? 'Margaret's.'

'I don't see them.' His tone was unmistakably dismissive, the irritation compounding.

There was an awkward silence before he stood up. 'Time to take you home, Jennifer.'

At some point I would be living here, eating, sleeping with Steven. And yet he was still an enigma. A man who buried his emotions so deep they were irretrievable. If they existed at all. I'd never heard him mourn his dead wife or express regret even though, fairly obviously, so young, her death must have been tragic. He didn't talk about her as a real person and that disturbed me. Maybe, I consoled myself, he was simply considering my feelings. Perhaps I had replaced her so completely that he no longer mourned. One day it would be *my* picture that would hang over the fireplace. Slightly more disconcerting was the thought that followed so closely it bumped into me, who would be looking at it? One day, would a case and boxes with *my* name arrive at some store? Jennifer 1,

Jennifer 2. All the clothes I would never wear, labels still dangling from them? Would he shell out money to store *my* possessions?

They would fit in one small trunk.

I had a lot to learn about the man I was about to marry. Too much.

Once in the car I pursued my original line. 'Had you thought when you would like the wedding to be?' I didn't dare broach the subject of who was going to pay for it.

'January?'

'Lovely.'

I pictured a winter wedding, fur-hooded cloak, sparkling frost.

'A quiet wedding,' he said. 'I don't suppose your family will be coming, so just a couple of friends. Registry office.'

I lowered my expectations.

The evening ended with the usual peck on the cheek. But not without affection.

I let myself in as he drove off.

Jodi was watching a soap on catch-up TV. She didn't turn around. 'You're *always* going out these days.'

I wasn't the only one. There was no sign of Jason.

Soon it'll be for good, I thought. *You'll have to find someone else to share your fucking mortgage.* I went upstairs.

Two nights later we were going out. 'To discuss our wedding plans,' he'd said grandly, so I was actually excited. It was time for some passion.

'I am so excited.'

'I've booked the date,' he said. 'And somewhere for our honeymoon.' He turned to look at me, an indulgent smile. 'And don't ask where.'

'OK.'

'We have a busy night ahead of us,' he said and put the car into gear.

I didn't ask where we were going.

I felt nervous entering The Quiet Woman. I found the inn sign of the woman with her mouth stopped by a scold's bridle ominous. I stuck my tongue out at her and followed Steven inside. He went straight to the bar without asking me what I'd like to eat and returned with a glass of wine for me and a beer for himself.

He pulled out a notebook and flattened it on the table, then looked at me expectantly.

'Right,' he said. 'First of all, the date. How does two o'clock on Saturday the twelfth of January sound?'

I drank some of my wine and nodded. 'Good,' I said. 'Sounds good. I would . . . I feel I should invite my parents. Though my mother won't come,' I added hastily.

'OK,' he said.

'I suppose Jodi and Jason. But they won't come either.'

'Anyone else?'

'Scarlet and Andy, Bethany and her new guy, Stella and Sonny. I'd like to ask Ruby Ngoma. She's one of our customers,' I said.

'You aren't thinking of inviting *all* your customers?'

'No. Maybe Serena. She's always done my hair for me.'

He reached out and stroked it. 'And she does a nice job. Anyone else?'

There was someone else, but I had no idea how to get hold of her. Homeless people have no address.

'How about you?'

'I think I'll just stick to my best man and his wife.'

I was shocked. 'Not your parents?'

He shook his head. 'Remember, Jennifer, it's my second marriage. I want it quiet.'

'But . . .'

He put his finger to my lips and pressed so I could feel my teeth sharp against the inside of my mouth.

'I've booked a hotel for a reception.'

I changed the subject. 'So . . . our honeymoon?'

'A secret.'

'OK. Just tell me hot or cold.'

'Cold,' he said, 'and wet.'

'Wow. You have been busy.'

'I have. There is something else.'

Money, I thought with a sinking heart.

'Obviously I'll pay for the wedding.' He gave me that kind smile again. 'I can't see your parents coughing up.' I'd given him a sanitized version of my relationship with my parents, and explained that we weren't exactly close.

'No.' I felt slightly ashamed. 'But I have enough for a wedding dress.'

'Good.' We clinked glasses.

I made a small decision. 'Where do your parents live?'

He must have been off his guard. 'Macclesfield,' he said, without thinking.

Taverner is not a common name. I could track them down, I thought.

'Brothers and sisters?'

But he'd twigged. His face was wary as he shook his head. I waited but that was it. He should have got a job with the Secret Service. They needn't have bothered to get him to sign the Official Secrets Act.

The food arrived. Lasagne. I hate lasagne. Did he even know that? Had I ever told him? He picked up his knife and fork and started eating.

My mind was busy. I was not going to have Stella outdo me in terms of a wedding dress. Hers had been a-ma-zing. I dreamed on. But halfway through the evening at The Quiet Woman, something changed and I never quite worked out what it was. Steven stopped eating and regarded me. 'You won't regret this, Jennifer, I promise you. I *will* make you happy. And you will never leave me.' It was romantic but little voices started pinging in my brain like incessant text messages.

And the sudden closeness tempted me into taking a bold step. 'You're still a bit of a mystery man to me.' I softened the words with a smile but held my breath.

He was on his guard. 'How so?'

'I'm not sure I really know you.' I'd softened the words with a smile, but nothing was going to dent his good humour.

He laughed quite openly. His face was different. 'You soon will,' he said. 'We're getting married. Remember? Of course you know me.' He chucked me under the chin like a favourite uncle. 'I'm Steven,' he said, eyes wide open. 'Your . . . Oh, God,' he said, 'soon-to-be husband.'

I could hear my granny's voice taunting me. 'Sell yourself cheap, my girl. Because that's all you're worth.'

Sometimes taunts are so cruel you can never really shed them. They stick to your skin like lizard scales; when you shed the top layer they are on the layer beneath. That is the valuation which sticks. So you never quite lift yourself off the floor.

TWENTY-NINE

Right through Christmas we planned our wedding, and I was getting excited. Our guest list was small, mine consisting of my dad and Malee or her replacement (whatever he'd said, I doubted they'd come) and my mum (she wouldn't come either). I wouldn't waste a bloody stamp on my brother Josh and you could forget my grandmother, old sourpuss. But I could invite Stella and Sonny, Bethan and her new bloke, Scarlet and Andy and Serena and Ruby, and I felt I ought to ask Jodi and Jason too. When I handed Jodi their invitation, she looked at it as though it was poisoned. 'So you'll be leaving.' Her voice was so acid I could hardly believe it was the same person who had welcomed me a few years before with open arms. But this is what happens, I suppose, when you live in close quarters with the wrong person. I found it hard to respond to my imminent departure without a certain amount of glee. The next day she made some excuse. I'd always known they wouldn't want to come. They didn't, and after I'd moved out I never saw them again. All I meant to them was the loss of £300 a month.

I couldn't ask Minnie Ha-Ha because I had no way of getting in touch. I would have liked to have invited Miss McCormick just to show I hadn't made a complete mess of my life, but I didn't have an address for her either – except, maybe, via the school, if she was still teaching there. I bottled out of that. I hadn't fulfilled her dream for me – to study English at Oxford. She would look at me with disappointment.

On Steven's side he had one friend called Colin Ripley, married to Kara. I assumed he was a workmate. Colin was to be his best man. Had he been his best man at his first wedding? I wondered. 'No one else?'

When I asked him the question he said nothing. A little like the boxes locked away in the store, my husband-to-be was unfathomable.

I reassured myself with his qualities. He was generous, kind, honest, even-tempered, considerate, polite. I ticked them off on my fingers. It was enough.

Almost.

In the weeks leading up to the wedding I became obsessively curious about his previous marriage. So many unanswered questions. Like where was she buried? But it was no use talking to Steven. He closed like a clam and refused to say anything. So my frustration was compounded. Why was he so reluctant to tell me anything about her? He came occasionally to the store and usually emerged with another garment. And so one day, when he had given me a sweater, lovely, soft, pale blue, eye-watering price label still attached, I asked him outright.

'Did you buy it for Margaret?'

He gaped; his mouth worked but he couldn't seem to find the words. And he seemed distressed.

In the end he nodded adding, unnecessarily, 'She never wore it.'

'I know that, silly.' And I held up the price label. Something in his face changed. He looked shifty, as though he'd just deceived me. However, it was a beautiful sweater, and when I slipped it on the colour was flattering. It was a perfect fit, my colour.

One man's loss . . . or in this case woman's.

We went back to Yr Arch twice, both times to start moving my meagre belongings over. The bungalow was larger than I'd first thought. All plainly decorated but obsessively clean now. The whole place smelt of bleach. The fusty smell had dissipated as I had been opening windows, vacuuming and cleaning ready to move in. And that was another odd thing. Apart from the picture which hung over the mantelpiece, nothing of Margaret remained. I had been through every single cupboard and drawer. There wasn't a stitch of her clothes, not a photograph, no female clutter in the bathroom. Absolutely nothing of her except that rough sketch.

I mentioned this to Steven one evening when I was hanging some summer clothes in the built-in wardrobe. 'You've done a good job,' I said.

His smile was indulgent but curious. 'Doing what?'

'Clearing out her possessions.'

The look he gave me now was undeniably shifty. His smile looked false and his eyes wouldn't meet mine. In fact, he looked troubled. At such an innocent comment?

What had I said?

Yr Arch had been built in the sixties; it was dated, but not without its charm. A long corridor led from the front door straight through to the kitchen. A corridor to the right led to its three bedrooms (all double) and a generous-sized bathroom. To the left was a long sitting room which had French windows overlooking the washing line and a sunken garden reached by four semi-circular steps. There was a dining area at the back of the room. The kitchen overlooked the garden too and had a side door reached through a utility room.

The garden at the back was also plain, a wide lawn bordered by a hedge, but the views were far-reaching along fields and, below, Endon, a small village, with Leek to its northeast and Stoke-on-Trent to its southwest. Snaking along the bottom of the valley was the Caldon Canal. As the green valley had provided my room with a view, so did Yr Arch.

The drive to the front was equally uninspiring, lawns bordering a tarmacked drive, at the end a small asbestos garage.

But to me it was paradise. A home of my own. My first. Correction. A home of *our* own. I still didn't stay the night and our relationship remained curiously sterile.

Stella was very downbeat about our approaching wedding and she didn't hide it.

'I think you're making a big mistake.' It was the first week of January and we were at a pub. She had a night off. For once, *he* was babysitting. Hoor – fuckin' – ray! I felt like saying. *So Daddy's taking his turn, is he? About time too.* Stella had hair that changed colour almost every week, amateurishly. She always missed a bit. Her bathroom was testimony to every single different colour she'd ever used. This week she was bottle-blonde with dark brown bits at the back. And it didn't suit her. The hair colour plus the fact that she had a scar on her chin and one of her front teeth was chipped made her look rough, a bit worn out. She'd fallen off a swing when she was eight and that was what had chipped her tooth, but it could have been a fight and she'd made up the story. Stella was like that. She was someone who always wanted to put her good face to the fore. She was very conscious of the chipped tooth, running her tongue over it constantly – a habit, I guessed, that she was completely unconscious of, but it drew attention to the tiny irregularity. She was the same with her scars. Half the time when she spoke her hand would steal up to her face, and she would run her finger down the scar, frowning, subconsciously spiralling back into the fall off the swing – or whatever else had caused the imperfections. She was doing it now, her frown deepening, and then she dropped her hand back into her lap and gave me a hard look. 'Don't,' she said. 'Call it off. You don't know him,' she said with some force. 'You don't know the first thing about him.'

I trotted out the usual – good job, widower et cetera, et cetera – which only stopped her for a moment.

'You don't *really* know him, Jen.'

The trouble was I knew there was more than a grain of truth in her words. I knew Steven was secretive. I sensed that he was hiding something. I just hoped it wasn't something that would have a major impact on our married life.

'Jen,' she appealed, 'what are you letting yourself in for?'

A house, security. A home, a living wage. A car. A family. A husband.

Two nights later I repeated a potted version of her words. That night, when he gave me my final kiss, his hand wandered towards my breast and he squeezed it. Not hard enough to make me cry out but the gesture was a warning.

As I climbed the steps to my front door, I still felt the pressure on my breast. Inside the house was silent. Tonight there was no telly, no lovemaking, no snoring or bed creaking. But I had seen Jason's car outside so I knew they were in. Just lying low.

With nothing to distract me I tried to sleep, still wondering what was behind that squeeze. When I undressed, I could still see the imprint of his fingers.

But when I pulled the ring from my finger it was a visible sign. I now belonged to him. I looked at it and wondered how Margaret had felt when he had given it to her. I imagined her easing it from her finger too, night after night. Until she had died. Had she been wearing it when she had breathed her last? Had this been pulled from her dead finger? I shook that thought away quickly. But my next instinct was equally uncomfortable. It felt like a borrowed object. Like Steven. Temporary.

The next moment I was scolding myself. Steven wasn't a borrowed person. He was mine. All mine. My love. My fiancé. Soon to be my husband.

Yours? I could hear scorn in her response.

Do objects retain something of their previous owners? I picked it up and searched it for some indication. Sapphires are not as hard as diamonds and I could see a tiny mark on the surface. I wondered how it had got there.

Like Stella, Scarlet was odd about my approaching nuptials. 'Why get married?' she said. It was exactly the response I'd anticipated from someone I'd marked as being Bohemian.

'Me and Andy – we never tied the knot and we're happy as larks. Getting married,' she said, hand caressing my shoulder, 'Jen – it's so final. There's only one way out of marriage and that's divorce. Or death.' She gave me a funny smile. 'Like it says in the marriage service Till death . . . and so on.'

'Steven isn't like that,' I said. 'He's conventional. He wants to get married.'

She gave me a funny look.

Her hand gripped my shoulder. 'Spinning Jenny,' she said, 'you don't know what you're getting into.'

'We love each other. That's what I'm getting into. What's wrong with that? Why can't you be more pleased for me?'

'I'm sorry.'

But I hadn't finished. 'Other women get married, have a home, a family. Up until now I've had no one, Scarlet. Not even a mum and dad who really care about me. I rent a room in a couple's house and if they weren't so hard up they'd have chucked me out a year ago. I'm not rich and I never will be. I don't even care about that, but why shouldn't I have something of my own? Understand?'

I could see nothing but doubt in her eyes. 'But, Spinning Jenny, he's so much older than you, and what do you really know about his past? His family?'

'Enough,' I said defiantly. 'Enough. I'm marrying Steven. Not his family.'

Her eyes narrowed. 'You haven't even met them, have you?'

'Not yet. But I will, I'm sure. In time.

I felt *all* my friends were against my good luck. I could only think of one mate who would definitely be glad for me. Who would see that I had lifted myself out of debt and poverty, walked away from living rough on the street, healed the scars of my parents' horrible divorce and 'made good'. I looked everywhere for Minnie Ha-Ha, on the streets of Hanley, around the bus station. I searched doorways, asked other homeless people if they'd seen her. I walked the park and even explored the cave where I'd hidden with her, but I couldn't find her.

Trouble was I didn't know her real name. I assumed it was something like Minnie, the Ha-Ha added by me because she was always laughing. And what did she have to laugh about? I went to Stoke, which still had a bit of a town centre, not one of these nasty 'malls' and I found a person. Just one person who said she knew her. A young girl with a ring through her nose and sad, sad eyes. 'I think she got a place in one of the hostels. Ask at the soup kitchen. They do breakfasts at seven from the shelter. Someone there will know her.'

I thanked her, gave her two quid and a packet of fags. (Steven hated the smell.)

THIRTY

I didn't have time that day as we were meeting Stella and Sonny later on that evening after work. We'd arranged to hook up at the Indian opposite the bus station. We arrived early and were lucky to find a parking place in front and stuck four quid in the meter. Daylight robbery but cheaper than a parking fine – or having the car towed away. We sat in the window at a table for four and looked out on a roundabout with cars circling at dizzying speed, a few lumbering buses and pedestrians, heads down, hurrying somewhere or other, like figures from a Lowry painting but missing the dog. I saw a blue Fiesta pull in and dart off again when the driver realized all the spaces were filled. We must have taken the last one and Stella and Sonny had had to hoof it from the multistorey, which wouldn't improve their mood. They were both lazy. A minute or two later I spotted them approaching. Right from the start I could tell the evening was not going to be a success. Steven's eyes followed the direction of mine. Stella and Sonny looked tense and they were rowing as they walked, heads jerking towards one another, fingers jabbing, their faces taut and angry, their speed too fast. Couples rowing instead of walking hand in hand, smiling at the thought of a very good Indian meal, is a dampener on any evening. Trouble in the land of love?

I could see the tension in Stella's face as they walked in. And the anger in Sonny's. He didn't want to be here.

Steven's greeting to them was stilted, almost designed to make them ill at ease. He was at his formal, polite best, actually shaking hands with Sonny and simply nodding and smiling at Stella. We all sat down. And Stella did nothing but grill him. I could have killed her. Eyes wide open, as though trying to pretend it was all just normal, innocent conversation, when I knew she was doing a thorough check-up. So what was that going to achieve? She was going to stop the wedding if she didn't approve? Sure.

'So how long were you married for?'

'Where was your wife from?'

'What was her name?'

Even, 'You must have felt terrible when she was diagnosed.'

And, 'I bet you were grief-struck when she died.'

Steven responded to the grilling in a steady voice, his face fixed in a neutral smile while I sulked and fiddled with my engagement ring. But even that didn't make me feel better. Stella gave one look at it before saying to Steven with another innocent look. 'Was it your wife's?'

I am about to become his wife, I thought, resentful.

'Yes,' Steven said without embarrassment or apology, as his hand reached out for mine. I treated him to a light kiss on the cheek and an eye-to-eye smile. I felt like winking at him. It's true that a common foe is very bonding.

Stella gave me a supercilious look right down her nose while Sonny focused on crunching his poppadom, which was about to snap into a thousand pieces and spray us all with mango chutney.

Then Stella changed tack. She turned a full smile on Steven. 'You're nothing like Jenny's previous boyfriends.'

Who were all wankers.

And Steven knew that. I'd confessed to him the stories of my previous boyfriends. In fact, we'd laughed over them. He bypassed the bait neatly and stopped her dead with, 'I understand Jenny's previous boyfriends weren't exactly George Clooney.' He gave her one of his glittery glances which I could interpret. He didn't like her. And then, cleverly, he pre-empted any further onslaughts. 'And of course I am a bit older. So I've settled down, sown my wild oats. I know when I have found someone of value.' I could tell from his bland expression that he just knew he was going to win this one.

His composure flustered Stella. 'Well, yes, but—'

'Lots of successful marriages have an age disparity.' He put his arm around me. 'We're right for each other. We both know that.'

I gave him a soppy look back.

She didn't like that. Stella had to fight – and win. As she stared at him I could see her brain working out how to achieve superiority. And she did it by returning to . . . 'Was there an age difference between you and your first wife?' Such an innocent question. Not.

'No,' he said bluntly. 'Margaret and I were almost exactly the same age.'

Something else I'd learned about the lady with the *Mona Lisa* eyes.

I changed the subject. 'So when are you—'

She patted her fattening stomach. *More fat than baby*, I thought, spitefully.

'Late March.'

Sonny looked down at his plate. *He hadn't wanted another one*, I realized.

We finished the meal, paid the bill and left.

Halfway home, he said, 'You did say she was your friend.'

'Yeah.'

'It's just that . . . she seemed to want to trip me up. Why?'

'I don't know. Maybe a sort of jealousy? I mean, she and Sonny don't seem exactly ecstatic together, do they?'

'I hope, Jennifer. I hope . . .'

'We won't end up like that.'

'Well, only a few more days.'

He kissed me, dropped me off and didn't wait to see me into the house.

I hold that night in my mind, boxed into the treasured-memories box, because that night Steven was at his most normal.

Jodi and Jason were arguing like crazy downstairs. I could hear venom in both their voices as I passed the sitting-room door. I crept up the stairs and lay on my bed, too many thoughts running through my brain to even think about going to sleep. Besides, when I closed my eyes I was confronted with a horrible vision. My second-hand wedding dress hung on the wardrobe door. My second-hand ring I placed on the table next to the bed. And I could hear my second-hand husband drive off into the night.

I woke – well, I hadn't really gone to sleep – early and left the house at six o'clock to catch the bus to the soup kitchen. I felt desperate to speak to someone who would laugh away my fears, someone optimistic who could banish these thoughts and restore my conviction that all would be well when we were married and I'd moved into Yr Arch, taken down the portrait and replaced it with a pretty picture. Maybe I would get pregnant. Steven had said he wanted children but time and/or circumstances hadn't allowed it. I wanted my own family, though. I vowed I wouldn't get as fat as Stella and we wouldn't be such terrible parents as my own had been. And Steven's family? It did seem odd that I had not met them; neither were they coming to the ceremony. But like any unwelcome thoughts, I pushed it away. I couldn't afford them.

The soup kitchen was held in a church hall at the top of Hanley, overlooking the rest of the city. Hanley, the city centre of Stoke-on-Trent, sits on the side of a hill, so whatever shops you want to visit you will have to climb. At its centre is The Potteries Shopping Centre, with its empty shops and the rest sparsely populated with shoppers. I left the bus and entered through the side door. The soup kitchen was contained in a spartan room that owed more to the 1950s than the 2000s. The tables were Formica, the chairs stackable plastic, the floor worn wooden parquet marked with the prints of the shuffling shoes of the hungry homeless. And the people? I looked at the queue waiting to be given their breakfast, bedraggled, heads down, moving like sad Lowry figures, in unison. Trudge, trudge. I breathed in the familiar scent of the poor: tobacco, stale clothes, unwashed bodies, dirty teeth. Once, I thought, I was one of them. Now I was about to soar. And then I saw her at the end of the queue. A little taller than the others, head up, proud of accepting the food. And in the same moment she spotted me.

I'd crossed the room in less than a second and, stink or no stink, ignoring breath that smelt of tooth decay and old food, plus alcohol and stale cigarettes, I hugged her hard. Then she held me at arm's length. 'Jen,' she said, 'is it really you?'

I nodded, recognizing how much I loved her, how much I owed this girl – this survivor, this woman who had taught me to survive, this splendid, generous being who invariably found something to laugh at. And look what life had done to her. Don't ever tell me life is fair because it isn't.

'Come on,' I said. 'Let's get out of here. Let's go somewhere else. I'll treat you to a proper cooked breakfast.'

She looked a little dazed at that but I took her hand and together we left for the small café down the street where I noticed even the waitress looked down on her, recognizing her as one of the great unwashed. Well, she wouldn't be if she had access to a bathroom, I thought, feeling like standing up for her.

Minnie (No Ha-Ha today) slurped her coffee. 'Fill me in, Jen,' she said. 'Tell me all that's happened.' She touched my hand and I noticed how ingrained the dirt was under her broken fingernails. 'You look wonderful.'

I told her about the nursing home and the old lady who . . . She burst out laughing. 'Tell me again. So are you still working there?'

I shook my head.

I told her about living at Jodi's, the awkwardness of house-sharing with a young couple. I told her about working at The Green Banana. And finally, as a climax, I told her about Steven and pulled out a photo I'd taken of him on my phone.

She stared at it for a very long time, puzzling over something. Which I took to be his age. I felt inexplicably anxious.

'He's forty-something,' I put in.

She shook her head. 'Not that.'

'He works for the council.'

She shook herself. 'Doing what?' Her voice was sharp.

I shrugged. 'Road Management.'

She blinked, swallowed, took a huge bite out of her bacon butty. A little brown sauce trickled down towards her chin. She didn't wipe it away, although the rivulet had left a trail where a tiny part of this great unwashed face had been stained even further.

'He's got a lovely house,' I added, showing her the picture of—

'Is it in Stanley?' she asked quietly.

I nodded. 'How did you know that?'

She looked up, eyes bright as buttons, and shook her head. She looked worried. I didn't pursue it but ploughed ahead with my plan. 'I wanted to ask if you'd be my bridesmaid,' I said. At which point Minnie Ha-Ha lived up to her name.

'Look,' I said, feeling that something was very wrong here. 'I have to go to work now. Can we meet again?'

She didn't answer.

'Please,' I said.

She gave me a hard look. 'And you are marrying him?'

'Next Saturday,' I said.

She began to rock then, backwards and forwards in her seat. It was a habit she had when she was troubled.

'What is it?'

She shook her head, looked away. Drained her coffee cup. 'Jen,' she said. 'Are you sure?'

I didn't know how to answer. The truth was I wasn't. But is anyone sure about a lifelong commitment? Had my parents been? Had Jason and Jodi? Stella and Sonny? Maybe on the day they just convince themselves. Had Steven and Margaret?

'Will you at least come?' I asked.

THIRTY-ONE

And so the day dawned – not quite how I'd imagined it. But when can reality ever compare to our fantasies? No bridesmaids, my meringue getting mud-splattered as we stood on the pavement and cars raced by. Cold in spite of the velvet bolero. I stood alone in the rain watching my beautiful, dream wedding dress get stained. Remembered my mother's carp: *White shows up everything.* Yeah, right, Mum. And why was I thinking about her, today of all days?

Happy is the bride the sun shines on? Well, in that case I was doomed. The persistent drizzle felt a really bad omen. And I picked up that Steven, in a smart grey suit, looked nervous, almost afraid. He could hardly smile at me. Or did he think I was overdressed for a January wedding in the Hanley registry office?

At least my dad and Malee were there, she embarrassingly in a gold micro-skirt, looking about fourteen and clinging on to my dad who seemed to have aged even in the short time since I'd last seen him. As expected, there was no sign of the bride's mother. Selfish bitch couldn't even be bothered to send me a card, let alone cross the Channel to attend. And having no address for her other than 'France', which if I remember my Geography lessons, is a bloody huge country with lots of people in it, any invitation I'd sent her would have been unlikely to have found her. I hated my mum; even so, her absence made me feel even more alone.

Stella and Sonny had met up with Scarlet and Andy and travelled in together. Stella was heavily pregnant now and had the girth to prove it. Andy and Sonny were talking football. Both Stoke City fans. I think they hardly noticed they were even at a wedding. But Ruby seemed really happy for me, chucking confetti all over the place and ignoring the notices outside. 'Be happy, darling,' she said, and landed a smacking, smoky kiss on Steven's cheek which he barely tolerated. I hoped she hadn't seen him wince. Serena had done my hair, helped me into the dress and driven me there. I was touched that she'd decorated her car with white ribbon. The Barbie-doll-pink Fiesta, festooned with white ribbon and silver helium balloons, made a gaudy sight. It looked like a little girl's birthday cake. But at least I would be recognized as a bride.

There was no sign of Minnie Ha-Ha, which was no surprise but disappointing all the same. She hadn't said she'd come but neither had she said she wouldn't.

I'd packed up most of my stuff from Jodi and Jason's the week before and moved it over to Yr Arch, leaving only a few things to collect after our honeymoon. It looked bare without my stuff and I spent a moment reflecting on my change in fortune.

The wedding ceremony was over in the blink of an eye. And I was now Mrs Taverner, my sapphire ring joined by a gold wedding band.

We had our wedding reception at The Grand in Hanley, which sounds posher than it is. In fact, we had a small room on the first floor, with a glorious view of The Potteries Shopping Centre. With the window slightly open, we could hear the furious honks of car horns and some wailing police sirens, but the food was good, a lovely Staffordshire beef roast with all the trimmings and apple pie and custard to follow. Throughout it Steven started to relax, sharing jokes and chat with Colin Ripley, his best man, who had brought Kara, his wife, also, coincidentally, pregnant, so she and Stella had plenty to chat about. Colin was somewhere in his forties, a pale, bald man with bowed shoulders and a shiny suit, like a clerk from a Dickens novel. As we greeted our guests, Steven grinned at me and clutched my hand, giving me a tender look which I returned, adding in a full-blown goofy grin. Colin made about the shortest best man's speech I've ever heard, simply saying that Steven had had 'his fair share of tragedy' and they 'enjoyed working together'. He managed to compliment me on my appearance which drew a sniff from his wife, Kara, who seemed a jealous, possessive sort.

Then he sat down abruptly. Thank goodness my dad didn't even try to make a speech. He'd apologized the day before in a text message. 'Sorry, Darl. Don't expect me to make a speech. Not really my style.'

There was no mention of money. His sole contribution to the festivities consisted of fumbling with a giggling Malee throughout the entire ceremony and reception.

Steven's speech was equally brief, simply saying he couldn't believe his luck. To my relief there was no mention of Margaret. She was out of the picture for the day.

At my insistence Steven said he *had* sent his parents an invite, but that they had rung him saying they hoped we'd be very happy but were unable to attend.

I tried to find a reason that didn't include dislike of me or resentment at their son's remarriage. 'Is it because they were so fond of Margaret?'

He hadn't seemed to know how to answer this, finally settling for, 'They *were* fond of my wife.'

Afterwards I realized his answers were all evasive, but at the time I was too upset at him calling her his wife. *I* was now his wife. *She* was his dead ex.

I should have remembered the score for ex-wives in fiction isn't great. Mad, cruel, damaging, a rival, unattainably beautiful. And that's leaving out the supernatural hauntings. And the First Wives still living, bitter and angry, determined to have their revenge.

But I was realizing that mention of Margaret was taboo. Too touchy for casual mention. She was a subject we both skipped around, but never too close. I'd never asked him to tell me more about her death. It all seemed deliberately vague. Maybe it was all still too painful. Even for him. Even now.

But the details were still missing.

There was still so much that puzzled me, and as we ate our wedding breakfast I tossed them around in my mind.

New clothes? Why hadn't he given them to her? Why hadn't she worn them? Where was she buried? Had they had a funeral? A memorial service? Had she died in hospital or at Yr Arch? If so, in which room, so I could avoid it? How had he cleared any sign of her from the house so completely? Not even a hair from her head remained. I knew because I'd scoured the entire place, searched every cupboard and drawer. Twice. He had obliterated every single sign of her, as completely as though she had never existed. Never lived there. But he had owned the house for years. She *must* have lived there.

Halfway through the reception I saw a slight figure inch in, sticking to the wall, pressing herself against it as though she wanted to remain invisible. But I saw her and jumped up, my dress rustling as I hurried over to her. 'Minnie.' I was touched to see that from somewhere she'd begged, borrowed or stolen a pink blouse to wear over her ripped and stained jeans and I caught a waft of perfume. She'd made an effort, probably gone to Boots and sprayed herself from one of the perfume testers.

When I reached her, her eyes were fixed on Steven with a look of horror. 'No. Jenny,' she whispered, her voice hoarse. 'No. Please tell me he isn't . . .?' I glanced across. Steven hadn't noticed our surreptitious guest and was chatting easily to Ruby. I looked back at Minnie. 'What is it?'

'Tell me that isn't your husband.'

'Yes,' I said. 'That's Steven.'

She grabbed me and dragged me outside and I felt sure Steven had noticed now.

Outside the door she spoke softly. Underneath the 'borrowed' perfume she still smelt unwashed, stale. 'Jenny,' she said, steadying her voice now. 'You know sometimes – if the girls are really short. You know hungry. No money. You know sometimes . . .?'

I nodded. I knew what girls who were desperate did for money.

'They called him . . .'

I put my hands over my ears. Not today, not on my wedding day. I didn't want to hear anything that might shatter my dream. 'No,' I said firmly.

'You have to know.' Her voice was gentle now but she looked determined. 'They called him Coffin Man.'

I shook my head from side to side, as though I was a terrier shaking the life out of this mad tale. 'No,' I said equally forcefully. 'No.'

But she wouldn't stop. 'He likes you to lie still? Very still.'

I knew then. No one could have made this up, thought it on a dark night, dreamed it in a nightmare. It was Edgar Allan Poe.

My mouth was dry now. I couldn't find a word. Minnie, my adored friend, my mentor, my mate, had shattered my dream with these few words. I shook my head, but regretfully now. 'Please,' I said, 'go away.'

She took one last look through the frosted glass in the door. There were sounds of laughter. It was a wedding breakfast. My wedding to Steven with whom I had felt safe – until now.

'Go away, Minnie,' I repeated.

She looked at me for a brief moment, knew I believed her story, turned and left, slinking away like a shamed wolf, loping steps, shoulders bowed, head down.

She had ruined my day.

I took a deep breath, turned around and re-entered the room.

Andy and Sonny were still deep in conversation, both with beers in their hands. Ruby and Serena were cackling over something Ruby had said. Dad was still fumbling with Malee and Colin and Kara appeared to be having a bleak sort of row. The cold-shouldered, silent sort. She looking away, he staring ahead, lips pressed together. Looking at their faces I imagined this was one of many. Steven and I would *never* be like this, I swore.

He rose and came towards me, kissing my cheek. 'Was that one of your friends?' He looked beyond me. I read curiosity but no guilt.

'Yeah,' I said, 'but she couldn't stay.' And I hoped and prayed that he hadn't recognized her.

He smiled at me, took my hand. 'I'm so glad,' he said, 'that we're together. That you can't leave me now.'

Can't?

I managed to prise Colin Ripley away from his wife. He was Steven's best man. He must know him really well. 'Did you ever meet Margaret?'

'Sorry.' He obviously didn't have a clue what I was talking about.

'Steven's first wife.'

He shook his head. 'No. I came to work with him after she'd . . . Look,' he said, putting his hand on my arm. 'Today isn't the day to talk about this. It's your wedding day. Enjoy it, Jenny. Just enjoy it.'

Like Steven, Colin Ripley was basically a nice man. Minnie must have mistaken Steven for someone else.

Everyone started drifting away soon after and we went home to Yr Arch. Our wedding night. Tomorrow we were going on our honeymoon. I comforted myself with a fable.

And they all lived happily ever after.

THIRTY-TWO

I woke early. And for a moment I couldn't work out where I was. And then it all came flooding back. I lay on my back and stared up at the ceiling, remembering. I wished Minnie Ha-Ha hadn't said it. Hadn't used that particular phrase that resonated like a knell. Coffin Man. Why had she said it?

Steven pushed the bedroom door open and handed me a cup of tea, sitting on the bed. He was already dressed in his brown leather loafers, beige chinos and a maroon sweater. 'We need to get going,' he said. 'It's a long drive. A long way from here.'

'How long?' I was trying to guess our destination.

'Most of the day.'

'Where is it?'

'Wait and see.' Then he relented. 'It's a lovely little place. By the sea.'

'In January?'

'It has its own microclimate. It'll be lovely walking weather.' He pulled back the bed clothes. I was lying naked, exposed. I put my hands over my breasts and tugged at the duvet.

'So where is it?'

'A lovely, beautiful little village in Pembrokeshire. By the sea.'

'Lovely.'

'There are lots of cliff walks and other places to visit.'

I was getting excited now. 'Are we staying in a hotel?'

'In a pub,' he said, grinning. 'Even better. Food and drinks on tap. It's the right place.'

What a curious phrase, I thought.

'Time for you to get dressed now, Jennifer.'

It sounded like an order but I protested and drank my tea. He stood in the doorway, waiting, watching me all the time, occasionally turning his head to peer along the hallway. I felt hurried and uncomfortable. And this was my first morning as a married woman?

I showered in the bathroom. (Pink with a plastic shower curtain around the bath, but it worked well enough.) I locked the door and felt safe. Alone under the gush of warm water I could reflect. Last night had been . . .

They call it lovemaking. It was nothing like. There was no love, no affection, simply a mechanical act. I'd had boyfriends before, most of them inept at making love. Except David Ganger who, obviously, was a practised expert. But Steven's advances were nothing like any of them. He wasn't rough or thoughtless. Simply strange.

Don't move.

Stay perfectly still.

Don't make a sound.

Play dead?

He stripped me naked, pulling off my clothes. Minnie's words resonated. *Coffin Man.* It was what it felt like. I had to play dead.

Minnie wouldn't have used that phrase out of spite. She was not like that. But how else did she know?

He'd laid my clothes out for me on the bed, labels dangling. Black trousers. Black sweater. I protested. 'Black? Not very honey-moon-y.' I'd planned to wear jeans with a new pink sweater that I'd bought.

He was standing behind me, running his hands up and down my arms. He whispered into my ear. 'Wear them for me.'

I got dressed. I wasn't going to start my married life with an argument.

He'd already packed up the car so less than an hour later we were edging down the drive of Yr Arch and heading out towards Endon and the A53 which we'd take to Shrewsbury before heading down to Newtown and then southwest towards Pembrokeshire.

It was a long journey, taking most of the day. Every couple of hours or so we'd stop for a coffee, stretch our legs and then get back in the car.

'I hope this is worth it.' I was teasing but his response was deadly serious.

'It is. Believe me – it is.'

I would far rather have been heading towards an airport and somewhere hot where I could stretch out on a sun lounger, soak up the sun and acquire a winter tan. Things that had seemed out of reach only months before.

It was getting dark and I was dozing when he nudged me. We were rounding a corner. It was almost dark. Below us were the twinkling lights of a village and the moonlit ripples of the sea. I sat up. 'We're here?'

'Yeah.'

I sat up as the car juddered to a halt outside a beautiful half-timbered pub across the road from the sea. It was beyond a dream. I climbed out of the car and flung my arms around Steven, who was stretching his legs and looking rather pleased with himself. 'Well? This is Dale.'

'Wow,' I said and did a little skip. 'Wow.'

He looked at me indulgently, like he really loved me. 'You like it?'

I nodded.

I kissed him good and proper then. 'I love you,' I said. 'Thank you.' He stroked my hair away from my face, kissed my mouth. 'And I you.'

A cool wind blew in from the sea, bringing with it the scent of salty seaweed and fish. The sounds were of the pennants on the masts of the boats, covered for the winter, tinkling in the breeze. I could see fishing nets stretched out to dry. I pushed open the heavy front door, oak studded with huge bolts, and feasted my eyes on the interior. Ancient beams with the scent of wood smoke mingled with frying food.

Only a few people sat at tables. All turned to stare at us.

Steven went up to the bar and spoke to the lady who'd watched us enter. She seemed to know him. 'Mr Taverner,' she said. She had a pronounced Welsh accent, speaking with a long 'a', emphasis on the first syllable.

'Gwen.'

'Nice to see you again.' She was a large lady with brassy hair but a kind expression. She looked past him to me and raised her eyebrows.

'So this is her, is it?'

Steven's response was stern. 'This is Jennifer, my wife. We were married yesterday.'

'Oh.' She seemed confused. 'I'm so sorry, my dear. I was mistaking you.'

I didn't know what to say. In the end I simply smiled and linked arms with my new husband.

'I've put you in the best room,' she said. 'Right at the front with a gorgeous view of the sea. Now why don't you decide what you want from the menu and I can be preparing it while you unpack.'

'Good idea.'

The menu was chalked up on the board and consisted (unsurprisingly) of various fish dishes and a steak and kidney pie that claimed to be home-made. I chose the pie while Steven decided to have halibut.

By the time we'd carried our suitcases upstairs and hung our clothes in the wardrobe, Gwen was calling up the stairs. 'You'd better come and eat before it gets cold.'

The room was similar in style to the bar. With blackened beams and a drunken floor. Through a planked door with a thumb latch, there was a small shower room. I peered through the window, hearing waves splash against the wall, visualized long walks along the seafront, full English (Welsh) breakfasts and perhaps days out at some of the nearby towns: Haverfordwest, Milford Haven, Pembroke. Even, if the weather permitted, boat trips out to Skomer or Skokholm. I'd seen the pamphlets fanned out on a table. Maybe this would turn out well.

The food was waiting for us on a table in the window, bowed with small, bottle-glass panes.

Steven sat back in his seat – an ancient, curved pew with a tall wooden back.

His eyes were closed. I put my hand over his. 'Tired? It's been a long drive.'

'I was dreaming,' he said, eyes still shut.

'Pity I can't share the driving. Maybe that's the first thing on my to-do list, learn to drive.'

'Maybe,' he said and fell silent. His eyes were still closed, his lips moving. He was having some urgent conversation – with himself.

Which I ignored because I felt a bounce of youthful energy. 'You'll feel better when you've had something to eat and a beer.' Gwen bustled across. 'Going to have your usual Bluestone?'

I looked at her, querying. 'Local beer,' she said. 'Steven loves it, don't you?' She turned her glance to me. 'Food all right, love?'

'Yes. Fine.'

'How about a glass of a local wine for you, *cariad*?'

I didn't know what *cariad* meant but it sounded friendly. 'Thank you.'

'They do a lovely red, see.'

Steven's eyes opened as she returned with a beer for him and a generous glass of wine for me. We clinked glasses and started to eat. But I sensed he was distracted. My bounce of youthful optimism took a nosedive. 'Is anything the matter?'

He shook my question away and I felt a snatch of concern.

'You are happy, aren't you?'

He nodded. 'Mmm.'

He ate his food mechanically, without enjoyment. Turning away from this worry, I told myself over and over that I, at least, was happy. Very happy. So why did I feel the need to pick at the scab? 'What were you dreaming about? You seemed to be having some sort of . . .' My voice tailed away.

He seemed to be focusing on a point the other side of the bar, where three people were sitting, drinking, laughing. Two men and a woman.

I realized he was caught up in his own world, abstracted, somewhere else. Hard to reach.

He turned to me with a strange look bordering on hostile. 'You want to penetrate my mind?'

'Would that be such a bad thing to do?'

He batted the question away with his hand. I felt a distance between us.

The door opened and closed, bringing in a waft of cold, briny air. A dog trotted in.

'How do you know this place?'

He was in a world of his own, far, far away. Lips moving. I would learn that he often retreated to this 'other' place. But I was a new wife then who didn't know her husband very well. I asked again.

'Steven. How do you know this place?'

He didn't answer and I persisted. 'You've been here before.'

He turned to look at me then but it wasn't a warm look. He could have been looking at a stranger.

I fell quiet then. Asked no more questions.

I believed that he had brought Margaret here. On their honeymoon? Which struck me as creepy.

He remained distant while I tried to make small talk but I couldn't seem to tear him away from past recollections.

I ate my food without enjoyment.

I looked across the table and smiled at him, at the same time realizing that I still hardly knew him, this pale-faced, polite, quiet man, who sometimes retreated into his own dark corner. I wondered what secrets he held inside that head of his. I reached out for his hand, trying to establish a reconnection, and he looked back uncertainly. 'Jennifer?'

'Are you happy, Steven?' It's the question no new bride should have to ask her husband.

Instead of giving an ecstatic, instant reply, he looked uncertain, a slight frown crumpling his forehead, and he seemed almost to delve right inside the back of his head. 'Am . . . I . . . happy?' He teased out the words, considering each one individually. His hand in mine felt like a dead thing, his eyes far away, his face set.

I dreaded what he was about to say. I almost put my hands over my ears.

'Eat your food,' he said, in a perfectly normal voice, 'or it'll go cold.'

Then I comforted myself with the thought that he was tired. We would feel different in the morning.

THIRTY-THREE

And to some extent we did.

The day began with what Gwen called a Full Welsh Breakfast.

Bacon, eggs, tomatoes, mushrooms, and something I'd never eaten before – lava bread. A seaweed, found on the coast, washed until it was free of salt and prepared. She'd cooked it with oatmeal until crisp and it was delicious. We had lashings of coffee to drink and freshly squeezed orange juice.

I caught Gwen watching me with a puzzled expression, but she was polite and friendly. Later, I thought, I would ask her some of the questions that had seemed to slide past Steven.

After breakfast we put our coats and walking shoes on and I had a better look at The Lobster Pot from the outside. It was small, stone, modest, only yards from the sea. It looked as though it might have been a smugglers' tavern. Did they have smugglers in Pembrokeshire? I guessed so. It had plenty of character, built out of what looked like large, irregular boulders. Judging by the seaweed and the tide mark, the sea almost reached its door at high tide. Fishing tackle and lobster pots lay on the ground. Laughter spilled out through the open door, rippling across the bay. It felt a friendly fairy-tale place.

I smelt the tang of the sea, salty seaweed, fish. I breathed it in like a tonic, listening to the sound of the waves.

Exploring the village was a brief affair. It was tiny – no more than thirty houses. Gwen had provided us with a packed lunch and the winter sunshine poured down, encouraging us to walk.

Dale was one of the prettiest villages I had ever seen. It was its own picture postcard, the perfect place for a honeymoon – even in January. A few houses were scattered along the road around the bay before the road turned inwards, ending in The Brig, four or five houses grouped by a chapel. The tide was out so the scent of the sea was strong, boats pulled up on the beach. The rocks were covered in seaweed, slimy and shining, smothering the rocks, which looked lethally slippery. The main road turned to the right, but we climbed the hill behind The Brig, the sea dropping below us.

Steven still seemed disstracted and, while he was quiet, I planned the questions I would ask Gwen. I was coming to terms with the fact that this honeymoon was a rerun. Steven was always reluctant to talk about his previous wife, which had the result of making me feel jealous and insecure. One can never live up to the sanitized memories of the dead. As usual, I supplied my own narrative. He had adored his dead wife. He was still stuck in the past, a little. It was up to me to drag him into the present and lead him towards our future. And a family. I felt smug and optimistic. I could sort this. If it took every ounce of will, I would make this work.

I grabbed one of Stella's well-worn phrases, one we had giggled over many times.

A little wine, a little time. We would get there, reach Nirvana.

We climbed the hill. It was quite a pull and I was puffing and panting, but finally we'd reach the top; the path narrowed and we looked down on the sea, still sparkling in winter sunshine.

The view seemed to release something in him. He laughed and pulled me towards him. He tilted his head out towards the sea as though greeting an old friend. I heard the waves gushing over the rocks, the *phut-phut* of an outboard motor and the distant tinkle of bell buoys marking the locations of lobster pots. Far out towards the horizon a huge oil tanker, probably heading for the refinery at Milford Haven, moved like a great leviathan.

'I love it,' I said and buried my face in his jacket.

'That is good.' He responded mechanically and I realized he was still in that *other* place.

We carried on walking. The wind whipped up and all of a sudden it felt like January. I thought with longing of the flagged floors, log fire and welcome warmth of The Lobster Pot.

And I was anxious to find out what I could from Gwen.

I shivered. 'Can we turn back?'

He seemed to see me then. 'You're cold?'

'Yeah, I am a bit.'

'Let's just round the headland. I want to show you St Anne's Head. And the fort. Then we can drop down to West Dale and head back, if you like.'

'I do like. Fort?'

'It's a funny old place,' he said. 'But it'll keep till another day.'

So we battled on, the wind stronger than ever and the path narrow and slippery. I hardly dared look down on the waves bashing against the rocks with fury. Towering above us were grey walls, presumably the fort, but we skirted past it, our heads down against the wind. The noise of the wind and the sea made conversation impossible.

At last the path descended, and with it the weather and the din subsided. Way below us was a wide empty sandy beach where the waves rolled in more tamely.

An hour or so later we were back at The Lobster Pot.

Gwen fussed over us and made us a pot of tea.

As I watched her, I was lining up questions in my mind. She would be someone who found it easy to talk. She would be a provider of information and would have observed Steven with his first wife without prejudice.

But I was in for a disappointment.

Steven said he needed a hot shower. His clothes were soaked and mud-stained where he'd slipped on the path. 'You go first,' I said. 'I'm desperate for a cup of tea.'

As soon as he was gone, I asked her, 'What was she like?'

'Sorry?' She seemed very confused by the question.

'Margaret,' I said. 'Steven's first wife.'

'I didn't actually meet her.'

I stared at her.

'They didn't stay here,' she said. 'They had a house – along The Brig.'

'You didn't see her?'

She laughed. 'No. I think she must have been the indoor sort. And the weather wasn't kind.'

I couldn't work this out. 'How long were they here for?'

'Four or five days.'

'And you *never* saw her?'

'No. As I say – the weather wasn't great. He'd pick up some food a time or two, a couple of our home-made pies, take them back.'

'Where did they stay?' I wondered then whether she had been already ill. 'When was this?'

'Oh, a year or two ago.'

I was even more confused. 'But she died three years ago.'

'Oh, I don't think it was that long ago, love. I'll ask my Noah.'

Sometimes you regret asking a question. I had wanted to know so much more: what she'd looked like. Like me? How she had spoken? Why had they come here? But the questions were sliding away. I had the feeling that each answer would take me further from the version I had constructed from Steven's story and the bits I had pieced together.

I twisted my wedding ring around on my finger. Welsh, Clogau, rose gold. It had, at some time, been enlarged, with a let-in of a slightly different coloured gold – more yellow and without the pink tinge of the extra copper. My fingers were fatter than hers? But the sapphire engagement ring had been too big. Another anomaly.

Who was she, this woman who had never worn the clothes he had bought her, had never been seen on an entire holiday, who had been on that invisible holiday after the date she had died? Whose fingers were either bigger or smaller than mine?

Was she still alive?

Had he committed bigamy? Was she dead? Had she died? I had no evidence, no death certificate, no headstone. No one I knew so far had been able to corroborate the story. I thought back to the wedding and Steven's sole friend, our best man, Colin Ripley and Kara, his wife. They had never met Margaret either. I knew instinctively that there was no point asking Steven for the true version. He would deflect the query as deftly as a Wimbledon tennis champion returns a shot. I reflected how little I actually knew him. And even less about her. Minnie's warning floated in front of my mind again like a grey chiffon scarf which I wafted away. She was mistaken. It wasn't him.

He emerged from the end of the bar then, his hair still damp. 'Hi,' he said.

I responded coolly. 'Hello.' Couldn't prevent myself adding, 'Feel better now?'

'Yes.' But he must have sensed something different. He looked from me to Gwen and back again and apparently digested some of our doubts. He made an effort to be hearty. 'Are you going to have a shower?'

'In a minute.'

It was a long wait, the three of us awkward in each other's company. Steven pinned Gwen down with a stare. 'I'm sure you're glad,' he said, 'that I've found love again.'

Gwen said, 'Umm,' while she fished around for a suitable response, but she was looking at Steven in a very odd way. Almost a panic. She looked from me to him and back to me again, as though she wanted to tell me something and for some reason she was refusing to agree with his sentence. Her brow crinkled in confusion. I got the feeling she wanted to ask, *Does she know?*

There was an awkward silence which even Steven couldn't fill. Luckily a bearded Captain Pugwash entered the bar, dressed in a navy fisherman's jersey, denims, and still wearing waders.

'This is my husband,' Gwen said, without even looking at him because her eyes were still wide open and fixed on me. Captain Pugwash stretched out a meaty paw. He smelt of fish, beer and tobacco and his hand was as coarse as sandpaper. 'Pleased to meet you, Marg—' His wife shot him a warning look. 'This is *Jennifer*,' she said. 'Steven's wife.' The deliberation in her voice warned him. 'They're here on their *honeymoon*.' He looked taken aback but soon recovered. 'I'm Noah Rees.'

I smothered a smile. Noah? What a reassuring name for a fisherman. I couldn't have named him better myself, unless I had given him my instinctive name, Pugwash.

'If you fancy a trip out to the islands, I'm your man. Particularly if you're keen on seabirds.'

I liked him instantly. 'I am,' I said, 'especially—'

I got no further. He wagged a finger at me, blue eyes sparkling. 'No. Let me guess,' he said. 'Puffins.'

'How . . .?'

'The funny little sea parrot.'

I nodded.

'Well, now's the wrong time of year for those . . .' He still looked uneasy. 'But you might be lucky and see some porpoises and seals. There's plenty of those out there, and other birds as well. Perhaps even basking sharks or whales.' He winked at me and I liked him even more. 'You never know what you'll see out on a boat.'

I was in heaven. Stoke-on-Trent is about as far from the sea as you can get on this island and I'd hardly ever been to the coast. A couple of day trips to Prestatyn, with my parents warring even then, a coach trip to Blackpool out of season and one to Formby, but they hardly counted. I'd been more aware of my parents' arguments, embarrassingly loud on the coach, while I was more concerned about being thrown off than appreciating the beauty of the seascape.

Steven had moved away from me, distancing himself from the exchange. I had the feeling that while he liked Gwen, he didn't feel the same about her husband. He was watching Noah, an odd look worrying at his face, which I thought at the time I could interpret. A sea trip was not on his agenda. Perhaps he hadn't taken a trip with Margaret. Maybe he or she hadn't been able to swim. I felt a warm wash of satisfaction. Like I'd got one over on her. I felt bound to make some contact with him and touched his arm. 'Hey. Sounds great, doesn't it?' The look he gave me took me aback. It was part panic and part this uncomfortable distancing, as though he didn't know who I was.

We had become virtual strangers again.

'Right,' I said, 'I'm off for my bath.'

I spoke so much more brightly than I felt.

I'd enjoyed my soak and had just dressed when the door opened. He was frowning. He stepped towards me, his eyes very wary. 'I need to talk seriously to you,' he said, and my heart skipped a beat. He pushed me back towards the bed and I plopped down, still wary and apprehensive. He sat beside me. 'You need to make a will,' he said.

Whatever I had expected, it had not been this. I gaped like a goldfish, finally stuttering out, 'But I haven't got anything to leave. Who would I leave it to?'

He wiped my hair out of my eyes, gentle this time. 'You don't understand,' he said. 'Marriage automatically revokes any previous will. And now we are married you are entitled to half of anything I own.'

My mind was busy then exploring this. 'Half of everything?'

He nodded.

And my mind worked it out. Half his house, half his car, half any money he had saved up. I scooped in a very deep breath. This sounded good to me. But he hadn't finished. 'If I die,' he said, 'you get the lot.'

I was silent for a moment, then asked the obvious question. 'You're not ill, are you?'

He smiled then. 'No.'

'Good.' Then another thought felled me. 'And if I die?'

He simply smiled. Smiles come in all shapes and sizes and this one was bland. Nothing tucked behind it. It was Steven's meaningless smile, empty of everything – humour, recognition, friendliness.

We spent the afternoon wandering around the tiny village. 'Tomorrow,' he said, 'we can go to Tenby if you'd like.'

'Oh, yes.'

At six o'clock, he stood up. 'Time to eat.'

I waited until we were sitting down at dinner, full of tasty fresh fish, happy and relaxed, when I made my first mistake of many.

I leaned forward on my elbows and God-only-knows why said, 'Tell me about Margaret. Why do you never talk about her?'

Immediately his face hardened. He looked suspicious. He picked up a chip from his plate and chewed the end off, not looking at me. 'Why do you want to know? *What* do you want to know?'

I was shocked at his hostility. His eyes were hard as granite. I felt unnerved but ploughed on regardless.

'I wonder,' I continued boldly, 'if I am anything like her.'

'You could be,' he said thoughtfully, his face a little softer. 'You could well be.' He touched my hair, stroked it away from my face, tucked a strand behind my ears. 'You could be her.'

I realized then that the months we'd spent 'dating' had been a rehearsal. But what the next act was I couldn't even guess.

THIRTY-FOUR

As a honeymoon I wouldn't say it was a great success. Nothing like the romantic break I'd imagined; not like the stuff I'd seen on the telly and dreamed about for years: dancing cheek to cheek, long sessions in bed. In fact, the sessions were more like

me playing a waxwork while Steven . . . well. Put it like this, it
was over almost before it had started, which was probably a good
job as he preferred me to lie perfectly still and hardly breathe.
Lovemaking? Not exactly. Sometimes I'd reflect. Why didn't he just
buy an inflatable doll?

The weather didn't help. It rained steadily right through the first
couple of days. And however beautiful, however picturesque,
however fabulous the seaside is, when it rains it rains. All you can
see is raindrops bouncing off a dull, hostile stretch of grey water.
The sea looked cold and uninviting. The country is the same from
north to south, east to west. When you go outside you are wet and
cold, whether in the middle of Wolverhampton or down in beautiful
Pembrokeshire. You get wet and you get cold if you venture away
from the fire. I was bored and fed up. It was OK for Steven. He
could sit half the day with a crossword and a pint of beer, ignoring
me once he'd realized I wasn't going to supply him with any of the
answers.

Which irritated him.

I tried to speak to Gwen, but Steven seemed to sense it. And she
deflected any questions. Noah had given up on the idea of taking
us out in the boat. He spent most of the time either doing renova-
tions or else sitting in the corner with his cronies, their conversations
getting louder and louder as the beer went down, accompanied by
loud guffaws.

And then one evening, he was sitting on his own by the fire,
looking pensive. Steven was in the shower, so I judged it safe to
speak to him. 'Can you remember exactly when Steven was here
with his wife?' I'd tried to make it sound innocent, an idle question,
but he looked sharply at me with those faded blue seadog's eyes.

'Why don't you ask him?'

I had my answer ready. 'I don't like to bring up the subject. It
seems . . .' I tried a slick trick, '. . . as though I'm jealous. And
I'm not, Noah.'

'Right.'

He needed prompting. 'So, when was it?'

'A year or so ago.'

'Could it have been three?'

I got another of those sharp looks but he shook his head.

'Do you remember her?'

'Never got to see her.'

I was frowning. This didn't sound right. 'Not once?'

'No.' And then he picked up on my thoughts. 'Strange, I agree.'

Steven arrived then and looked tensely across when he saw me speaking to Noah.

'What were you talking about?'

I was getting to know this oil slick of a question. 'I was talking to him about your previous visit. Where was it you stayed?'

'Seagull Cottage,' he said. 'The pink one on The Brig.'

I tried to make my next question merely an extension of the first. 'When was it?'

He tightened his lips. 'You already know Margaret died three years ago. So it must have been before then, mustn't it?'

I persisted. 'Was she already ill?'

His eyes grew hard then. Had we not been newlyweds, I might have imagined he disliked me.

'I don't want to talk about it. I've told you before. I don't want to talk about Margaret.' His hand, gripping the beer glass, shook slightly.

I dropped the subject but I was dissatisfied.

I knew then that I would have to unearth the rest of the story some other way than to ask Steven for details. And Gwen and Noah had none – except that they believed Margaret, who had remained invisible throughout, had visited Dale less than three years ago. Either both their memories were mistaken, one feeding facts from the other, or else Steven was lying. He couldn't be mistaken – no one forgets the year their spouse died.

Why would he lie? How would he lie? If she had had cancer, that was that. A natural death. But the word 'natural' rolled around in my mind like a marble. The opposite would be unnatural, with all the implications that brought with it.

The next morning, our last in Dale, the weather had finally changed. The sun beamed down and did its best to warm the air. It wasn't quite ice-cream weather but, wrapped up, we could take a picnic all the way to Dale Fort.

The wintry sunshine almost blinded us as we stepped outside. Our shadows were long and swayed in front of us, both of us distorted and huge, only discernible which was which by my hair blowing around my face. We crossed the town and began the climb up to the headland, threading behind the row of houses standing on

The Brig. As we climbed we were, for a while, sheltered from the wind. But the moment we lost the protection of the houses we caught the wind again and quickened our pace. For a while, the coastal path left the road which climbed towards Dale Fort, a field centre for biological studies used by schools and colleges. Steven had described the place to me, but I had not yet seen it apart from its grey concrete walls when we had rounded the headland. 'It's spooky,' he said, smiling, 'with lots of strange places behind bars. Locked areas. It was a coastal artillery and has secret passages, so they say, which go down to the smugglers' bays.'

'Really?'

He nodded, still laughing. 'Really,' he said. 'It's the *oubliette* of the Bastille.'

'And they allow biology students to stay there?'

'They keep the dangerous bits locked.'

'I think you're trying to scare me. Can we go in there?'

'Best we stick to the coastal path, Jennifer.'

Best we stick to the coastal path.

To tell you the truth, I was glad when the honeymoon was over and I could go back to work. I had, mistakenly, thought being married would seal our relationship. But I knew for sure now, deep down, that there was something strange about Steven. Instead of feeling more comfortable in his presence, I was beginning to dread it. And the disquiet was compounding, a drum roll banging in my head leading up to something.

THIRTY-FIVE

'So how was the honeymoon?'

I eyed Scarlet dubiously. I would love to have been able to confide in her, ask her what she thought – really – but I said nothing, and she prompted me.

'Truth?'

I opened my mouth, but no words came out. I couldn't find them. She supplied them for me, a friendly arm around my shoulders. 'A disappointment?'

I nodded, avoiding her eyes, which held sympathy for my

punctured dreams. Sympathy when she should have felt envy? After all, Steven was a catch, wasn't he? I was in an enviable position, wasn't I?

I slumped in my seat, suddenly depressed and looking for solace. And underneath that I was worried. Something wasn't right but I didn't know what. And I didn't know how to heal it. I looked to her for something positive. 'Do you think most honeymoons are a bit of a disaster?'

She picked up on it at once. 'So that's what it was like?'

I immediately backtracked. 'No. No of course not. It was . . .' I summoned up every single ounce of enthusiasm. 'Brilliant.' Spreading my arms wide to encompass all that was good in this world. Except it didn't fool her. She was far too streetwise and experienced. Inside me I felt something sour, something hollow, which was leaching through my skin, giving out messages. I already knew something was missing from my marriage. But I wasn't sure what it was. And then I realized. It wasn't that something was missing. It was that something was present that was poisoning it. Margaret and the attachment Steven had felt for her and which still existed even though she was dead. Or was she? I hadn't seen her death certificate. I'd taken his word for it. So what if . . .? Minnie had called him Coffin Man. And now I felt as cold as if I was inside a coffin.

Scarlet hadn't been taken in by my little play-act.

'Oh, Spinning Jenny,' she said, her voice laden with even more sympathy, and she put her arms around me and gave me a hug.

A couple of customers came in then. Stan, still storing his mother's stuff – for ever – or at least until he died and joined her in tatty-furniture heaven, Teresa Simpson, today minus her son who was, I guess, probably in school. Without the teenager by her side she looked even smaller and more vulnerable as she struggled with a couple of chairs, trying to fit them one way or another into the back of her Vauxhall Corsa. There was something so sad about the droop of her shoulders that I went outside to give her a hand and was treated to the first smile ever. She must have been pretty – once. Which reminded me – looks don't last for ever.

The solicitors played their usual brief visit, their greeting terse nods as though they were angry with us for charging them for the storage space. They were always resentful even though they were handing over money which they wouldn't miss. It was the act of paying for something that ate them from the inside. Serena was obviously having a day off. Our customers these days were a sad lot. All too busy to stop and chat. To my dismay, Tommy Farraday and the rest of the group had moved out following the police raid. I missed them. It's one of the shames of working in a store. Our customers are transient. They go through a period in their lives when they need us. Then they give notice and vanish. And that's the end of that. They forget about us. Of course, you soon find replacements who do exactly the same. Len, who liked a bit of banter, had moved in recently with the contents of his tool shed which had blown down in the wind, but he too would probably find somewhere else to store his tools. Or build another shed. As I checked the database I realized we were almost always full. And only a few stayed for more than six months. But Steven was turning into one of the long-term customers. He'd given no indication that he had any intention of moving out any time soon. I wondered when he would start moving the boxes out. And where he would put them? Belatedly to the charity shop? Or was his plan to sneak them in to the house behind my back, somehow bringing her home with her Light Blue scent.

I wouldn't be surprised if even Serena, one of our longest-serving customers, opened her own salon at some point. And then she wouldn't need us either. Just as I was thinking this she walked in. 'God,' she said, dumping her enormous black leather Marc Jacobs handbag on the desk as though it weighed a ton (and it probably did), 'you looked gorgeous on your wedding day, Jenny.'

At least *she* had appreciated my beautiful wedding dress, making me twirl and pose, taking pictures with her phone ready to put on Snapchat or Facebook.

'I'm glad you let me do your hair. You looked fab. I bet Steven was bowled over,' she continued.

Not exactly. He'd said little about my wedding outfit but his silence had said it all. I'd sensed that he'd hated the look, realized it was second-hand, pre-owned, cheap-looking.

'Yeah,' I said casually.

Showing a sensitivity rare for her she looked hard at me. 'You all right?'

I shrugged, close to tears. The trouble was I knew I wasn't all right. I was frightened and worried.

She looked at me a minute longer then nodded. 'Post-wedding blues,' she said wisely. 'Common as morning sickness in pregnancy.

You put your *all* into the detail, guests, dress, food. Forget that at the end of it is just simple, humdrum married life. You fold the dress away and put it on eBay.' She grinned. 'After you've had it cleaned, of course.' (So she'd noticed the mud splatters.) 'You share toilets, listen to him snore, go back to work. And bingo, you go down like a sinking ship, romance floating away on the tide. It's like the baby blues. Oh,' she finished, putting her arm around me and bringing her face up close. 'Poor you.'

But then Serena reverted to Serena and changed the subject. 'I think I can manage a smaller rental,' she said. 'Save costs. I don't seem to need such a big place any more.'

Scarlet had come back, and she was frowning. 'I'm not sure we've got any spare of the smaller ones,' she said, putting – rather pointedly, I thought – *two* mugs of coffee down. 'I think Steven took the last one. Being cheaper they don't come up so often.' She slurped her coffee in a slightly rude way. 'You could ask him if he's OK to move it out?'

They both looked at me then, Serena voicing both their thoughts. 'What does he keep in there, Jenny?'

I responded without thinking. 'Margaret's stuff.'

Serena gave me a sly look. 'Well surely he can dump it now he's got you?' They were both looking at me, waiting for my response.

'Yeah,' I said lamely. 'I'll ask him again if you like.'

Serena jumped in then with both feet. 'Would you?'

I nodded and drank my coffee until their attention was caught by yet another row over the grey images of the CCTV between Teresa and Philip, who had just turned up, only this time erupting into violence as she raised her hand, took it back as far as it would go and slapped him right in the chops, while we all stared, open-mouthed, waiting for his reaction. We were in for a disappointment. There was no reaction. He just stood there, apparently too shocked to react. And then, surprise, surprise, he covered his face with his hands and looked as though he would burst into tears. 'Shi–it.' Serena provided the expletive.

For the first time since the warring couple had first appeared months ago, I felt sorry for the errant Philip. He looked sheepish, old, shrunken and silly, while Teresa appeared to have grown in stature in the last ten seconds. So what was going on there?

But while there was enough drama to keep them distracted, I slipped away. My curiosity was reaching bursting point.

THIRTY-SIX

I stood outside the padlocked door. The name Margaret, to me, spelt whispered secrets. If I opened D5 I would learn something about the man I had married and my predecessor. Did I want to hear these whispered secrets? I wasn't sure. But the questions were lining up.

Scarlet was standing behind me, the key around her neck. She fingered it as she looked at me.

'Darling.'

'What do you think?'

She shrugged. 'Yes and no.' She tried to reassure me then. 'Probably nothing there,' she said. 'Just a few of her dresses. Personal stuff like that.'

I realized then even more that The Green Banana was the place where people stored their inner fantasies, lost dreams, failed hopes, damaged memories and dirty secrets.

And in a way, though I hadn't taken out a storage facility, I'd joined their ranks with my vulnerability. I'd been needy, desperate for a job, and Scarlet had taken me in. I'd made a choice and I was only now realizing where this choice had ultimately led me. I'd met Steven, ignoring the fact that our relationship was strange, that a connection was missing. I faced that now. I had tried to sanitize his behaviour, explain away his actions and predilections, normalize them. But I needed to face up to something. His wife had died, so he said. So where were the people who had known them as a couple? Where were her family? Her death certificate? Why was he hiding her from me, at the same time as trying to mould me into her? How was it that both Gwen and Noah claimed she had stayed in the seaside cottage after Steven said she had died? And ringing in the back of my mind was the fact that neither had seen her.

'Let's open up.'

Scarlet gave me a look asking the question. *You're sure?*

I nodded.

One of the most evocative of the five senses is the sense of smell, particularly in the muted light of the store. Inside the scent of Light

Blue was strong, almost overpowering. Scarlet used the torch on her phone to illuminate the interior.

The boxes were still stacked neatly at the back, the suitcase by its side.

Scarlet stood in the doorway, keeping watch.

'It's his secret,' I said. 'He wants to keep it. I feel I'm being disloyal.'

'Don't do it if you don't want to.'

I imagined they contained loving memories, photographs, things she had treasured. I touched the top box.

Scarlet was waiting.

I slit the parcel tape with my thumbnail and opened it. As expected (Steven was a very neat man) the contents were folded. At the top a peach-coloured nightdress, its label dangling. 'She never wore it,' I said. 'Just like the other stuff of hers he's given me.'

There was a layer of white tissue paper next. It rustled as I lifted it. Underneath were several pairs of knickers. I spread them out on the floor. They too were new, still on the plastic hangers. I put it all back, the layer of tissue paper between, and sealed it again with tape. 'This is just new stuff,' I said, turning round. 'She never wore them.'

Scarlet was frowning, like me, trying to work it out.

'Let's go.' I needed time to try and puzzle this out.

She tried to make a joke of it. 'Well at least he hasn't got her head in there or some chopped-up bits.'

It wasn't funny. I turned to look at her and she immediately tried to rectify her statement. 'Sorry, darling. Sorry. I'm so sorry.'

Sorry for what, I wondered as we locked the padlock and returned to the office. I was frightened now as I tried to piece it all together.

She'd been ill. He'd bought her clothes in the hope that she would recover but she hadn't.

And out of sentiment he'd saved them. *Aaagh. Sweet*, one could think.

Coincidentally, that very day, he turned up at five o'clock. I saw his car swing in through the gates and panicked. Had I put the stuff back *exactly* as I'd found them? Folded them in the right way, put the tissue paper back? Had we locked the padlock? Alarmed, I looked at Scarlet and she read my panic, put a hand on me and whispered, 'It's OK,' just at the moment that he walked in, looking jaunty.

'I thought I'd give you a lift home. Save you the bus.' I was relieved. He wasn't going in there . . . But then he said, 'I just want to pick something up first. Won't be a minute,' and the anxiety bubbled up again.

Minutes ticked by while I waited. How would he respond to my intrusion, because he would know it was me. It had to be me.

I watched him on the CCTV as he approached the doors, disappeared inside. And now I waited.

Until he emerged carrying something. He crossed the yard and the office door opened.

It was a sweater, pale blue, still with the scent on it. 'Ready?'

'I'll lock up,' Scarlet said, watching me for my reaction. 'I'll see you in the morning.' She was trying to reassure me with her smile.

But that evening something changed. The game rules were different. As soon as we were home he handed me the sweater. 'Wear this,' he said. 'Please?'

'I'll maybe shower first.'

I emerged from the shower to find him standing in the bedroom looking agitated. Silently he handed me my bottle of perfume. I looked at him, wanting to tell him, *You can't turn me into her. I am not her. She is dead* . . . but the words dried up in my throat like a wadi in the dry season. Margaret might be dead; he was trying to make me replace her. No, it was worse than that. He was trying to turn me into her.

Initially I felt powerless, and then something bubbled up inside me.

It was fury. Margaret was dead. I was not. I still had my life to lead. I was Jennifer Lomax.

No, you're not. You're Jennifer Taverner now, and that strength which had seemed so powerful shrivelled up. I watched him, concerned. He was rocking ever so slightly forwards and backwards. 'Steven?'

The look he gave me was confused. I put the sweater on but he was still looking at me as though I was a stranger. His mouth was working as he struggled to find words.

'Steven,' I said, putting my hand out to steady him. 'Darling.'

And then he came to, shook himself like a dog. 'Jennifer. You look nice in that sweater. Mmmm.' He breathed in with a noisy sniff. 'You smell nice too.'

There was only one response I could make. 'Thank you. Shall I make tea tonight?'

'That would be nice.' He wasn't looking my way now. Even his response sounded stilted and false.

I managed some pasta with salmon and anchovies, a recipe I'd found on the internet. I don't think either of us enjoyed it very much. I was trying to analyse our situation. Something between us had shifted. Did he know I had spied on the contents of D5? Why should he be so defensive? There was nothing in there that should be hidden.

But something was very different.

That night I climbed into bed warily, but I must have made some movement. He grabbed my hair, pushing my head on to the pillow. 'Don't move.' It was a warning.

I believed what he wanted to say was *don't breathe*.

I was frightened and lay as quiet and still as I could as he climbed on top of me. As he climaxed, he murmured her name. '*Margaret.*'

And I felt fury shoot through me like lightning.

THIRTY-SEVEN

I spent most of that night shallow breathing. Maybe I dozed. Next morning, he was quiet and subdued enough for me to try and reach out to him.

'Steven,' I said, 'what's happening?'

He gave a silly little smile, embarrassed. 'Sorry,' he said. 'I was miles away.'

I took a big leap into the dark then. 'Steven . . .?'

He looked up.

'Are you still grieving for Margaret? Have we perhaps married too soon?'

He put his head on one side and seemed to think about it. I got the impression he was pleased I'd asked. 'You think that?'

I had no answer except to try. 'There are counsellors, you know, people who can help you through grief.'

'I don't need a counsellor,' he said. 'But thank you for asking,

Jennifer. It's nice of you.' There was something different in his tone, something childlike.

The next sentence I hurled at him was unashamedly a cliché but I didn't know what else to say. 'If ever you want to talk . . .'

He shook his head, almost back to normal. 'I'm fine, Jennifer. I don't need counselling or grief advice or anything else. I really am fine.' He reached out for my hand. 'But thank you for being considerate.'

I left it at that. But there were still great gaps, too much missing. I wanted details now. I wanted answers, finally, to my questions.

'I can't remember if you told me,' I said casually, leaning back in my chair and taking a sip of coffee.

'Told you what?' Unconcerned, he lifted a spoonful of cornflakes to his mouth.

'Which church you were married in.' I struggled to keep my tone casual.

'Mmm.' He turned his attention back to his breakfast while I waited. And got no answer.

I followed that up with, 'Was Margaret Welsh?'

Now that question *had* surprised him. 'No. Why?'

'Oh, I just wondered . . .' I put on an act of being flustered. 'The name of the house. It's Welsh, isn't it?'

He was on his guard now. His whole body stiffened. 'Jennifer,' he said slowly and deliberately, 'you know I don't like you asking questions about Margaret. We have each other and she is in the past. Forgotten.' He stood up. 'And now I must be off. I don't want to be late for work.' He gave me a bright smile, his hand resting on my shoulder. 'You catching the bus in?'

I nodded and he was gone.

I cleared up the breakfast things and went to get ready for work, spraying myself with Light Blue which released a whole raft of emotion.

On the bus I sat, musing.

The sense of smell registers largely in the subconscious. Novelists convey it with a wonderful variety of words: stink, aroma, perfume, scent, whiff, pong, sniff, reek and so on.

Forensic scientists use it. What draws people to the dumping ground of a body? Putrefaction. Vultures smell it from over a mile away. Sharks smell blood from a kilometre away in oceans of water. Scent can evoke love, beauty, loyalty, arousal as well as revulsion, hatred, fear, loathing. It can incite violence or lovemaking, fear as the smell of burning. There are plenty of words to describe this powerful tool and these words invariably have two meanings. Yes, the smell, but also the emotions tucked behind that word. We talk about the *stink* of tobacco but the *aroma* of fresh ground coffee or newly baked bread. Having worked in an old people's home, I could recognize the *stench* of a soiled bed or the *reek* of stale urine from forty paces.

Conversely I have always loved Estée Lauder's Youth Dew, not because I particularly loved the smell but because one of the sisters I worked with at The Stephanie Wright Care Home was so kind to me. She would let me splash some on my wrists and neck from her handbag spray if I'd had a particularly hard shift. The very waft of it made me feel comfortable and happy, though it wasn't my favourite. I'd sneaked into Boots and sprayed on the most expensive perfumes from their testers. Once I'd even slipped one into my carrier bag. But I was so terrified of being arrested and marched out of the shop by the police that I'd chickened out and put it back on the shelf. If I was rich and beautiful, I used to dream, I would wear nothing but five drops of Chanel No. 5 to bed (like Marilyn Monroe).

Wimp, Stella had hissed at me in her pre-married-bliss baby days. *Bloody wimp.* 'So you're going to buy some are you, at eighty quid a bottle?'

I gave back a hoity-toity retort. 'I can't help it if I've got expensive tastes.'

And arm in arm, we'd chuckled and sauntered down the parade, out of The Potteries Shopping Centre.

Light Blue resurrected Margaret. By spraying her perfume on me she was invoked. When Steven breathed in the perfume he could believe I was her.

I arrived at The Green Banana, still disturbed by my musings, to find one of the drivers blocking the entrance with his lorry and impatient for me to open the gates. I keypadded him in, minutes later locking the office and walking to the corridor outside D5, just at the moment that Serena came tripping along in her six-inch heels. 'Did you get a chance to ask Steven about moving out of here?'

I shook my head. 'I'm sorry,' I said. 'I clean forgot.' I felt bad for lying but I hadn't wanted to bring up the subject.

'Oh.' She gave an expression – part disappointment, part irritation. 'I could do with saving some money.' Then, seeing my face, she said, 'It doesn't matter. It isn't important,' before she too sniffed the air.

'Light Blue,' she said. 'Your perfume.'

Moments later I heard her car manoeuvre in the courtyard before heading off. She'd only come in to check on the status of D5. Serena had done me a few favours and now I felt selfish for not considering her request. The truth was, I didn't want these remnants of Margaret in our home.

I returned to the office and my role of gazing at life on flat grey screens. But I was restless that day, my mind constantly asking awkward questions – with no answers. The trouble with curiosity is that, like swallowed acid, it burns you from the inside out. You can feel it erode your stomach, working its way through to the skin. I wanted to bring Yr Arch alive, not treat it as a mausoleum. I wanted her properly dead. I didn't want to ape the woman who watched me from the sketch in our sitting room.

That day I began to feel angry. I had always been a victim, at the mercy of someone else's whims. Now I wanted to break free, take my future in my own hands. I wanted better. Something had shifted. I realized even more now that Steven's world was strange, an alien planet and I was being drawn into it, away from my world and all that was familiar. I couldn't stop. I stood on the crater of a volcano and peered into toxicity. I knew I should draw back but I was powerless, sensing the fumes rising, breathing them in and feeling the damage they did to me. I was trying to ascend on the downwards escalator, watching other people rise on the other side while I continued to head downwards. However hard I tried, I couldn't reverse my direction. I think that was the first time I was really frightened. What had I let myself in for when I had married? Had I left one bear pit only to find myself in another?

I was worrying about this as I journeyed down Smallthorne Bank with its little shops, mostly owned by Asians, many with their plastic wares spread out on the pavement, brightening up the urban scene with eclectic variety, from pink tricycles to red washing-up bowls and gaudy arrangements of plastic flowers. The bus passed Ford Green Hall, an ancient black-and-white house on the left before climbing up towards Norton. I would soon be home.

Home. I still loved the thought of it, the sound of the word, a kitchen, bathroom, bedrooms, garden, all those things I never would have had but for Steven. I felt swamped with gratitude. He was a good man, I was convinced. I wanted it to work. It had to work.

As I was staring out of the bus window, I saw her. Minnie Ha-Ha, rucksack on her back, trudging up the hill as though she was exhausted. I knocked on the window but she didn't see me. So I pinged the bell and jumped off as soon as the bus slowed, then ran towards her, shouting, 'Minnie. Minnie.'

She didn't recognize me at first. Then she did, giving a whoop of delight, greeting me with, 'What the fuck have you done to your hair?' Some things don't change.

I stroked it self-consciously. A week after the wedding, Steven had persuaded me to have it cut to a short and, in my opinion, unflattering bob.

I tossed the remark aside. 'Oh, I got fed up with always washing and straightening. Stuff,' I said carelessly, my fingers tugging at the ends as though to lengthen it. 'This is so much easier.'

'Well, it don't do nothing for you.'

I changed the subject. 'So what are you up to?'

She looked pleased with herself. 'I'm in a hostel,' she said, 'doing some work, helping out there.'

'Paid work?' This would be a first but she shook her head. 'No. Voluntary. I just help with the breakfasts but it gives me an address, a bed to sleep in and food.'

I gave her a tight hug. Whatever she said, I could still smell the scent of the homeless. Maybe it impregnated not only her clothes but her skin, as Light Blue did mine.

'So,' she said, when she had escaped, 'how's married life?'

I answered honestly. 'Strange,' I said. Then, 'Minnie, you knew Steven before, didn't you?'

Her answer was evasive. 'Not really.'

I touched her hand. It felt like a homeless person's hand: cold, the skin dry and coarse, nails grubby. I could almost feel the years of grime underneath my fingers. She said, 'Sorry.'

But I shook my head. 'It was better that I knew.'

She didn't respond straight away, but put her arms around me and I felt a wash of sympathy. Sympathy? For me, the girl who had everything?

I pulled myself away and held her at arm's length so I could read her eyes. What I saw there unnerved me. Evasion, fright, apprehension. She didn't want to upset me She grabbed my arm. 'If he'd just paid for sex I wouldn't have said anything. It's the way he got them to play dead as though they were in a—' She stopped. 'That's why they called him that . . .'

I put my hands over my ears and tried to cover up my revulsion. She gave me a pitying look, as patronizing as an aunt patting a child on the head. 'Play dead. Corpse bride. It's what we call it when the man doesn't want us to move or make a sound. We have to lie there, like a corpse. He was worse than most.' She shuddered. 'He would . . .'

I shook my head. I didn't want to hear any more.

I tried to laugh it off. 'A bit of S&M . . .' I was about to continue that it wasn't exactly unusual, but Minnie Ha-Ha was watching me, a look of pity now replacing the usual tough-girl glare. She put a hand out to touch my arm. 'It's more than that and you know it. You say he was married before.'

'His wife died.'

'Exactly.'

What did that mean?

'Be careful,' she whispered. 'Be very careful. Watch your back.'

Why? I reasoned. All I had to do was to *play* dead. Not *be* dead.

Minnie Ha-Ha kissed me and her breath smelt nicely of toothpaste. 'I'd look into it if I were you.'

'It's nothing serious,' I insisted. But the lie shrivelled on my lips, desiccating my tongue.

I stood regarding her while I picked out the truth in her words, knowing that it was *all* the truth. Minnie was the poorest person I knew. She had nothing. Not a home or a relationship. Just the clothes she stood up in, which weren't so much pre-loved as discarded because they were trash. And yet I trusted her more than anyone else I knew. She didn't lie. She had no reason to.

I put my hand on her arm.

'How do I get hold of you? I don't have an address.'

She shook her head and, after giving me a pitying stare, she shook my hand away and was gone. She'd been slow before, trudging up the hill with her dirty old rucksack, but now she vanished into a side street at the speed of light.

Leaving me to return to the bus stop and home.

Steven was already there and looked happy. 'Thought we might wander down to the pub,' he said, 'then come back and watch a film? You might want to wear this.'

He handed me a dress, watching me speculatively as I examined it. It was what you might call frumpy. Pale blue, knee-length, made of slippery polyester, the sort of frock not even a middle-aged or elderly person would consider flattering. No price label this time. But I showered in the pink bath behind the plastic shower curtain, slipped it on and stood in front of the mirror, regarding myself. *Jennifer Lomax, what are you turning into? Who are you turning into?*

As we were regulars, the couple who ran the pub, Rosy and Sunny, were getting to know us and greeted us like old friends.

'I'll get the drinks and pick up a couple of menus.'

'Thank you.' Steven lounged back in his chair. 'It's nice to be waited on.'

I leaned across the bar, my back to him. Sunny was Indian; his family had arrived here three generations ago. He was a plump, happy guy and also an incorrigible gossip, which suited my purpose.

'A beer for my husband and a glass of white wine for me.'

He didn't need to ask which beer Steven would want. Steven was a man of regular habits. Simply pulling at the pump, turning around while the foam settled to pour my wine, he gave me an opportunity to start my investigation. 'You must have known the previous Mrs Taverner?'

'Not really.'

Rosy had bustled over and must have heard my question. She gave her husband a sharp glance before elaborating on Sunny's comment. 'He tended to come on his own.'

Even though my back was to him, I was aware that, curious what the conversation was about, Steven was watching from the corner table.

Rosy continued but I sensed she was reluctant to focus on this subject. 'I think she was ill when they came here. He never brought her down.'

'When did he move here?'

I didn't need to turn around to know that he was right behind me, listening in.

'We've only been here for eight years. He was here then, weren't you, Steven?' She was drawing him into the conversation.

He didn't answer but looked at me speculatively. He knew I'd been asking questions and he didn't like it.

We ate in silence. I didn't enjoy it. I could feel his suspicion surround me like dust, clogging my eyes and nose and coating my tongue.

He paid at the bar and I caught a waft of his terse conversation with them. 'I prefer you don't discuss my private life with my wife.'

That shut down one avenue of enquiry.

And so we returned home, walking the couple of hundred yards in silence before settling down to watch a film, a story about a woman who escapes an abusive marriage, only to have her husband find her; the film didn't disappoint with its dramatic denouement. We snuggled up together on the sofa, the dress material slippery and with a scent all of its own. The Light Blue hadn't impregnated the material.

'I like the beginning,' he said when I'd switched the TV off. 'Not too sure about the end though.'

I responded weakly but with honesty. 'I think I like it better when she's broken free.'

He leaned back to study me and pulled his arm away. He hadn't expected that. He thought of me as compliant. Not a rebel.

I knew the drill now when I went to bed. I lay still as a corpse bride. No, I wasn't thinking of England. I was wondering what would happen if I moved.

Try it and see.

That demon voice goading me to challenge.

I didn't. As he thrust inside me he pinched my breasts. 'Don't move,' he warned, 'or I'll stop.' I didn't. But deep inside me I could feel rebellion rising above the pleasure. I knew exactly what I was doing. I was playing his game, getting sucked into it as possibly Margaret had been. Before my experiences with various weirdos, I might have continued playing it on his terms. But now I had experience. I'd lived a bit. Suffered a bit. Life's knocks make us stronger. I would play his game for now. But the worm would turn one day. While my body remained still, my mind was busy, busy, busy, making plans.

When I went to work the next day, Scarlet was full of it. She and Andy were going on a cruise to the Caribbean. She looked so happy and so excited. 'You'll be all right on your own?'

I smiled. 'Course I will.' I felt quite excited. I was responsible for the entire place, in charge. I felt important and empowered.

For the entire ten days that Scarlet and Andy were away I was too happy to challenge the status quo. Steven seemed different and I told myself that his strange ways were at an end. We were entering a new chapter in both our lives. I constantly lectured myself. He'd lost his wife. He'd grieved. He'd not disposed of her belongings. But now, I thought. Now that he had me, he would let all that go.

Boy, could I fool myself.

THIRTY-EIGHT

A round that time, just as spring was starting to pretend it was arriving, with lighter, longer days and the promise of flowers poking their way through the soil, I started to notice a change in him.

Initially he seemed even more distant, preoccupied. His eyes seemed to slide away from mine and he would sit for periods, wrapped up in himself. Sometimes apparently talking. His lips would move and he would seem to lean in, as though listening intently. It was as though he was arguing within himself, a constant, internal argument which made him abstracted and distant. Hard to reach. Sometimes I'd find it hard to connect with him at all. And Margaret's eyes watched us from the wall of our sitting room.

That night in late February was typical. 'Steven?'

He didn't turn to look at me but sat, frowning, peering around him, searching for the speaker. 'Steven,' I said again, keeping my tone gentle because he seemed unnerved, alarmed and vulnerable, his eyes wide open with what looked like fear. Then he dropped his head into his hands. 'I should have told you,' he said.

I knelt by his side. 'Told me what?'

He was licking dry lips, still looking around him. 'I shouldn't have . . .'

'Shouldn't have what?' I was afraid of what he'd been about to say.

I shouldn't have married you.

'Steven?'

He didn't respond but sat, rocking gently, backwards and forwards. His next word chilled me more than frightened me. 'Margaret,' he said, then put his hands either side of my face and drew me to him. 'Margaret,' he said again and kissed me very gently on the lips. 'I so love you,' he said.

And now I was confused. Who was he talking to? Whom did he love? His dead wife? Me? Did he know I even existed?

I felt angry then worried and tried, mistakenly, to force out an answer.

'Steven, it's Jennifer. Jenny.' I was trying to break down a barrier, one I could neither see nor understand. As invisible as an electrical field. He was smiling at me now and looked almost back to normal. But I mistrusted this 'normality'.

I sat in the dark that evening for a long time, trying to work out what was going on and what I should do. In the end I decided to try to contact his parents.

I knew his father's name because it was on our marriage certificate. And he was alive. I knew they lived in Macclesfield, a mill town to the north of The Potteries.

I was aware that they might not welcome a visit from their new daughter-in-law. But what the hell?

I'd never met them. They'd never met me, and didn't appear to acknowledge my existence. They hadn't come to the wedding, which I had interpreted as disapproval for their son's remarriage. Selfish, in my opinion. Why shouldn't he when he'd experienced such tragedy? But they hadn't even sent us a card. Maybe they didn't know their son had married for the second time. Steven had lied. He hadn't told them. I found their telephone number on the internet, even dialling it a few times. It usually went to answerphone. I left no message. Once or twice I heard a voice answering and I put the phone down, my heart pounding. Why? What was I frightened of? Rejection? I was prepared to encounter hostility. What else did I think I would unearth?

I tried to think of an alternative, of contacting Margaret's family, but I didn't even know her maiden name. I believed she was Welsh. That was it.

In the end, call me a coward, I plumped for an alternative.

Steven had once mentioned that he had a sister, Francine, who was a lecturer at Keele University, and on an off chance I searched her too on the internet and found out she lived in Stone, not far from here. I'd picked up a landline number.

I thought an approach to her might be easier than his parents. I knew nothing about her beyond her name. He hadn't said whether they got on or not. I suspected not, or I would have met her before, and maybe she would have been the family member to attend the wedding.

To be honest I was nervous about meeting his parents. I had the feeling that their version of his first marriage would be nearest the truth and that whatever they said about their son remarrying I wasn't going to like it. It would be hostile. There was a reason why he was as he was and I believed I would find that reason embedded in his first marriage and I would find the answer unpalatable.

I waited for a quiet moment at work when the grey screens were empty of their ghost people and there were no vehicles in the yard. Then I picked up the phone and dialled the number.

She answered and I managed to speak, the words pouring out like grain from a holed sack.

'You don't know me. My name is Jennifer. I'm married to your brother.' Even over the phone line I sensed shock. The silence was as heavy as the atmosphere just before a thunderstorm breaks.

'Sorry?' Her voice was soft and not unkind. I repeated my statement and waited.

'Steve is married?' She couldn't hide her shock.

But I was missing a word. *Again.* The query should have been: Steve is *married again?*

'Yes. We married last month.' My voice was prim, through tight lips. 'You didn't know?'

'No.' Then, hoarsely, 'Do my parents know?'

'I assume so. Steven assured me he'd . . .' The words died away as the truth seeped into my brain.

'You've been to visit them?' Now I heard disbelief. 'Were they at the wedding?'

'No.'

'Goodness.' A long pause before her voice curled round. 'Why are you ringing me, Jennifer?'

'Because . . .' The truth? I didn't know why.

There was another long pause before she followed that up with, 'What do you want of me?'

'Nothing. Nothing. I promise you. I just thought you might want to know.' The words were lame, like my voice.

I could almost feel her shaking her head, tossing me off as a dog does the rain. But her next sentence surprised even me. 'What do you expect me to do about it?'

'Do about it? Nothing. Nothing.' I was puzzled by her question. But not as puzzled as I was by her next sentence. 'I'm sorry.'

I was stunned. She was *sorry*? Sorry? What was she apologizing for? Or more pertinently, who was she apologizing to?

There was only one possible response. If I dared ask it.

'Why?'

Silence.

I repeated my question. 'Why are you sorry, Francine? Is it something to do with what happened to Margaret?'

'Margaret?' Her shock was compounding.

'I know that she was ill and died,' I said, speaking defensively.

'Jesus.' I got the feeling this was a plea for help rather than blasphemy.

The silence this time was awkward and prolonged. 'Jennifer,' she said finally. 'Leave my parents out of this. They've had enough worry . . .'

Didn't she mean grief?

'Promise me,' she followed that up with, 'that you won't try to get in touch with them.'

'But they're my . . .' My dream was blowing away, a feather in the wind. I had thought my in-laws would provide the happy healthy family background where my parents had failed me. I felt cheated, and disappointment made me silent.

'Just don't contact them.'

'Can we meet?' I could hear my voice close to begging.

The silence this time was thin as gauze. I could hear her breathing through it. 'Let me think about it. I don't . . . I don't know. I'll get back to you.'

And she put the phone down.

Outside The Green Banana was springing into life. I heard the sound of engines roaring into the yard followed by two cars, Serena's pink Fiesta and Stanley paying yet another pilgrimage to his mother's shrine, A7. As Serena flounced in I promised her I would speak to Steven about emptying the container. She gave me a sideways look and held her finger up (index finger, a long-shaped nail bright with yellow gel). 'Promise?'

I pretended to spit on my finger. 'Hope to die.'

Stanley wanted to talk, mumbling little stories about his mum. This time the one how she liked her chocolates hard. 'If her finger went in them,' he said, laughing, showing irregular teeth stained by years of cups of tea and cigarettes, 'she wouldn't eat them.' He laughed so hard some spittle landed on the desk. I tried to ignore it. 'But of course no one else could eat them either. Not with ruddy great holes in them.'

I laughed too. I liked Stan. He was a sad man whose life had been defined by his mother – who sounded a character.

'The other thing she liked,' he said, still laughing, 'was orange peel. Just the peel. She'd leave the orange on the shelf.'

I'd heard the stories before. All of them, but they were funny. And it didn't take much effort to laugh with him.

It was almost five when the yard finally quietened, the screens showing no sign of life. I was ready to leave when Steven's car entered the yard. Large and white as a ghost, silently slipping into my view. I watched as he opened the door, climbed out, locked it. Steven was always careful with his belongings. He looked around him, checking no one was there and then he stepped out of my view and into the office.

'Hello.'

I felt suddenly glad to see him. He looked reassuringly normal. 'Hi,' I returned.

'Are you ready to leave?'

'Two minutes.'

He was my husband. My protector. And I knew I was growing really fond of him.

THIRTY-NINE

But unpleasantness cannot simply be swept under the carpet. The lumps and bumps were underneath. Some things cannot be ignored. I knew it was there and one day I would be forced to confront it, whatever 'it' was. I also knew I would keep digging.

I waited for a couple of days until I was on my own in The Green Banana.

And this time I was a little more oblique and cunning.

First I rang The Lobster Pot and after a chat about our lovely honeymoon, instead of asking a direct question about the wife they'd never met, I substituted another one.

'I came across a Welsh word,' I said, 'and wondered what it meant.'

'Go on then,' Gwen encouraged. 'Noah and me both speak Welsh – when the occasion calls for it.'

I spelt it out because I wasn't sure how to pronounce it. Y-R-A-R-C-H.'

Gwen was laughing. 'Now why would you want to know the meaning of that?'

'Because it's the name of our house.'

'Oh.' That stopped her short. And now she didn't know what to say.

'So what does it mean?'

She tried to prevaricate. 'Maybe it's not Welsh after all.'

'I believe it is and I believe you know the meaning but you don't want to tell me.'

She still tried to avoid answering. 'Maybe it's got another meaning in the north of Wales. Lots of words do.'

I persisted. 'What does it mean?'

There was another long silence. This is why I hate the phone. If you are sitting opposite someone, you can read their faces through a silence. Watch each process until they reach a resolution. With a phone call you have nothing. No clues; no hints.

'In the south,' she said finally, 'it's a word that can be used for a coffin.'

I nearly dropped the phone.

As though to further shift me in a direction I did not want to take, Ruby waltzed in, singing the first line of 'Living Doll' over and over again and looking pleased with herself.

'Ruby?'

'Met him on a dating site. Gary Flacks.'

'Not another . . .?'

'No, someone more my age and a widower.' She looked at me sharply then. 'Just like your Steven.' She tacked on, 'So he says.'

'Yeah.' There must have been doubt in my response because she looked at me sharply. 'You all right there, Jenny?'

'Yeah.' Then some of the truth leaked out. 'You know you said when you're young a man wants to get inside your knickers.'

She laughed. 'And when you're older.'

'Your bank account,' I supplied.

'Not Gary,' she said warningly. 'He just wants company.'

That hadn't been what I was about to ask. 'Which sort do you think "my Steven" is?'

She came round the desk then and put her arm around me. 'Not sure there, Jenny,' she said, her voice sober for once. 'Something funny. I haven't quite worked him out yet, love.' Some of her natural buoyancy returned. 'I'll tell you when I do. Anyway . . .' She waltzed back to the other side of the desk. 'I don't think I'll be needing to rent your lovely storage facility much longer. My new man has a bungalow in Fenton.' She gave me a wicked grin. 'I've always fancied living in sin.'

And she was gone.

Two days later I asked Scarlet if I could have a day off to go 'shopping'. She looked a bit bemused but agreed. After all, these days I was holding the fort of The Green Banana most of the time. She was having an easy life.

Since the phone call with Francine, I had felt constantly fidgety and on edge, and Steven had noticed. He didn't say anything but I caught him looking at me, bemused. I worried Francine had got in touch with him and told him about the phone call. It would make him suspicious and mistrustful towards me but I couldn't confide in him without risking his trust. Like a child in a darkened bedroom, I was aware that monsters were crawling out of the wardrobe. Surely, I reasoned, surely to know – whatever – could not be worse than this dread of the unknown?

Something else puzzled me. Our wedding certificate.

The day before, Steven had nipped out to the corner shop so I had been alone in the house and had opened his desk where he kept it.

On a wedding certificate there is a space under Condition where it described the bridegroom's status: Bachelor, Widower, Divorced. By his name it should have read, Steven Taverner. Condition: Widower. But it didn't. It read Bachelor. And I couldn't understand it.

The night before, as I had lain beside Steven in bed, I had puzzled over his strange predilections and the name he – or Margaret more likely – had given the house. Had I been wrong about him? Had they not actually been married? Was there, I wondered, another meaning for the house name as Gwen had tried to suggest? Had the house name been meant as a subtle irony suggested by Margaret? Steven might not even have known what the name meant.

But now I wondered. Had she been laughing when she had had the house name painted on the plaque and nailed to the front door? Had it been her idea of humour? What had really happened to her? I had only Steven's word for it that she had been ill, died of cancer. All I knew was that she was dead. I did not want to share her fate, and neither did I want to spend the rest of my life playing corpse bride. It would, in the end, kill me, as it had killed her. And it was that final thought pushing into my mind that had decided me. When Steven had left for work (always bang on 8.29 a.m. – my husband was a creature of habit as well as a creature of habits), I had pretended I too was going to work. But I had the day off.

It was impolite and a bit of a risk to simply turn up to Steven's parents without warning. But I believed that if I'd rung and asked to meet them, they would have refused. And so I decided to go on the off chance that I would find them in.

Getting to Macclesfield meant catching two buses, one into Leek and another through to Macclesfield town. It was a blustery day, with rain pouring down the bus windscreen and an evil wind blowing wheelie bins along the street, trees waving branches. It was cold too for May, but that could be helpful. Steven's parents were probably in their late sixties, maybe early seventies. I judged they would be unlikely to venture out in this weather. No one who didn't have to would leave home today.

I found their house easily, a 1940s' semi-detached which looked a bit sad and neglected, old green paint on the window frames and weeds growing through the paving slabs of the drive. An eight-year-old Citroën stood outside. It looked as though it was rarely used. Mud, leaves and dust coated it. I closed the gate behind me and approached the front door along a path made of concrete slabs. There was one bay window to the side draped with a net curtain. Beyond that I could see no sign of life. As I knocked on the door, I regretted my rashness. It felt rude to land myself on his parents unannounced. Not a good introduction to their new daughter-in-law.

Maybe, I thought, they would be out. I could tell myself I'd followed the lead but they'd been out. Maybe better that way. While I waited for the door to be opened, I told myself that – once it opened and I spoke to Steven's parents – life would return to normal.

But hey, I lectured myself, these are your in-laws. And they should have been at your wedding. The door opened and I pasted a smile on my face.

FORTY

Steven's father was an elderly gentleman with thin hair, white and wispy. He looked older than I'd expected. He was taller than his son, dressed in an open-necked shirt and casual trousers. His feet were in slippers. 'If you're selling something, even if it's just religion,' he said, the hint of a smile softening his words, 'you're wasting your time. We're heathens here and we don't need to buy anything. Not double glazing or life insurance or even a funeral plan.'

He was still smiling.

On the bus I'd tried out the words all the way here. 'I'm your daughter-in-law, Mr Taverner. I'm married to Steven. I'm . . .' The right words simply didn't exist; I sensed I'd wait a long time to be welcomed with open arms.

He just stared at me.

'Mr Taverner.'

'Yes.' His eyebrows were thick, bushy and white. He was waiting.

'I'm married to your son, Steven.'

I knew straight away I'd dropped a bombshell. He staggered back. 'What?'

'I'm Steven's wife. Your daughter-in-law.'

I knew then that Steven had not told his parents we were married. His father looked too shocked. They knew nothing about me. Obviously Francine had not told them of our conversation.

From inside the house I heard a woman calling. 'Scott. Scott. Who is it?' Steven's mother.

Without a word Mr Taverner stepped aside, but not before I had seen some terrible apprehension freeze his face.

God, what were these family's secrets?

A woman emerged from a door on the right.

'Who are you?'

She was small and tired-looking, but with Steven's lovely hazel eyes, long lashes, the whites very white, contrasting with the light brown, and I swear the identical pattern of gold flecks in them. I stared at her.

'I'm Steven's wife.'

She slumped against the wall and I felt as though a hand had reached into my chest and was squeezing my heart.

Steven's mother looked at her husband and leaned into him for support. She was as pale as death. 'You're married to Steven?'

I looked from one to the other. I couldn't understand this response. I had been prepared for stiffness, resentment, even hostility, but not this outright shock. Incredulity. I could have made some sarcastic remark that, as I was Steven's wife, it followed that of course we were married. Maybe I should have brought the faulty marriage certificate with me to prove it.

I was still standing on the doorstep.

'When?' His father barked out the question.

I summoned up some dignity to respond.

'We were married at Hanley registry office on the twelfth of January,' I said formally, as though giving evidence in a court of law. I felt compelled to add. 'I understood Steven had invited you.'

Both parents shook their heads.

'But you declined to come because, I suppose . . .' I looked from one to the other, blundering my way through the forest of words, 'out of some loyalty for Margaret.' I started babbling then. 'Maybe you thought it was too soon to remarry? Maybe you didn't like the sound of me. Maybe you thought I was . . .' My voice trailed away as I looked from one to the other. That was not it.

I tried another theory. 'Perhaps he thought you might disapprove?'

That wasn't it either. That couldn't account for the shock and sheer horror on their faces.

Then Steven's mother put out a hand. 'You'd better come in.'

She led the way, Steven's father trailing behind. Both seemed shrunken and shocked, stumbling the few steps into a small sitting room, a gas fire burning in the grate. It felt stuffy after the blustery weather outside.

'Sit down.' Steven's father's voice was still weak but this was unmistakably an order.

He softened it with an introduction. 'My name is Scott. My wife is Diana.'

I tried a smile but did not hold out a hand that I sensed would not be shaken. 'Jennifer.'

It was Diana who spoke, in a quiet voice she was struggling to control. 'Why did you come, Jennifer?' There was real fear behind the question.

That was a tricky one. I could have done with a little more time to evolve a story. They hadn't even done the usual delaying tactic of asking me if I wanted a cup of tea. They'd just flopped down on the sofa and now stared at me, waiting. And I sensed it was with some trepidation.

I cleared my throat and began with the usual irrelevancies. 'I work at a storage facility where Steven is storing a few of his wife's belongings. Late wife,' I corrected. 'That's where we met.' I tried a smile but they weren't buying.

They nodded like a pair of mandarin dolls. Glassy-eyed robots. I wasn't sure they were taking this in.

I pushed on. 'Are you angry that Steven's married again?'

'Angry – no.' It was his father who spoke after a swift glance at his wife. 'Not angry. Of course not.'

Diana butted in in her soft voice. 'Is something wrong, Jennifer?'

Now it was my turn to look confused. 'Wrong? No . . .' *And that was a lie.* 'Why *should* something be wrong? We've only been married . . .' The words died on my lips.

I wished I could erase the look they exchanged. Conspiratorial but also frightened.

'Why?' I repeated.

Neither of them seemed to have an answer but sat, clinging on to one another.

I wasn't sure how to phrase this but tried. 'What happened to Margaret?'

That shook them. 'Margaret?'

'Steven's first wife. What happened to her?'

They looked at one another.

'I know she died.'

'You know she died?'

Why the confusion?

Steven's father did his best to find some order, logic.

'My dear . . .' He was stumbling over the words. 'Congratulations. We're pleased that you and Steven are married and happy.' But his tone had risen, as though there was a question mark on the end of the statement.

I tried again to extrude some facts out of them. And tried with a placatory: 'We *are* happy. I was just a bit concerned that you might not be pleased about his remarriage.'

Diana managed a smile. But it was unconvincing.

'I expect you were fond of Margaret.'

No one could have missed the shudder that rippled down both of them and then neatly they turned the tables on me.

'What has Steven said about Margaret?'

I kept my response guarded. 'Not much. He doesn't seem to want to talk about her.'

'That's good,' Steven's dad said heartily. 'That's how it should be.'

But his wife still looked concerned.

'You're still living at . . .' *Did they know the meaning of the house name?*

But I sensed we were on safer ground here. 'Yes. It's a lovely bungalow. Wants a bit of attention.'

'Yes. Yes.' Both were enthusiastic over Yr Arch.

'Redecorating mainly.'

'Ye–es. I expect you'll enjoy doing that.' Maybe the enthusiasm was a bit overdone?

'Yeah, we will.'

When were they last there?

'It's a bit dated,' I added, still trying to get a handle on these two.

Scott tried his best. 'And I expect your tastes are more contemporary.' Like his wife's words they were a bit over-hearty.

I wanted to ask a hundred thousand questions but couldn't seem to find the right tone. We were all acting a part.

'So, do you still work there, at this storage facility?' The conversation was getting more limp.

'Yes. I work six days a week.'

'Gosh.'

I felt so awkward I stood up. 'I'd better go,' I said, lying. 'I'm at work this afternoon.'

'Ri–ight.' Scott had sprung to his feet. They couldn't wait for me to leave.

'Well, we're glad you dropped in on us,' Steven's mother lied.

'Probably . . . probably it's best if you don't mention to Steven that I visited you.'

Did they even have any communication with their son?

'All right,' Diana said brightly.

'And we hope you'll come and visit us?'

'Of course.' Again, the forced heartiness was testimony to the lie.

They saw me to the door and I sensed their relief when it closed behind me. I wondered how the conversation would run and was aware I had learned nothing from my visit.

So where next?

FORTY-ONE

caught the bus back to Stanley and climbed the hill, trying to puzzle it out. I was home early, but if Steven was there I had my excuse, tucked up my sleeve. Lame but there if I needed it.

I had a headache.

His car was in the drive.

I had a headache, I insisted to myself.

He met me in the hall.

'I had a headache,' I said, before it registered he hadn't even asked.

That was the exact point at which the worm turned, the viper bit. His eyes narrowed with suspicion. 'Where have you been, Jennifer?' His tone sounded menacing.

It presented me with a quandary. If he didn't know I'd seen his parents, under the circumstances, it was better that he remained in ignorance. On the other hand, if they'd rung and told him, it was better that I gave him the truth.

I searched his face for a clue. And in the end plumped for a duck dive. 'I could murder a cup of tea.'

Automatically we both turned towards the kitchen door and I breathed a sigh of relief, convincing myself the moment was passed. As if!

Instead of sitting at the kitchen table, I led the way into the sitting room and sat, cup of tea in hand, studying the picture, while Steven kept his eyes on me from the doorway.

Who are you? Where are you? What happened to you?

She held all the answers.

I stood up to peer more closely. It was little more than a rough sketch of a woman with blue eyes, dark hair in a bob cut, lips, nose, chin portrayed only sketchily. There was nothing to distinguish it except for a small signature in the corner. My eyesight is good but I could hardly read it. It looked like *Eleri Dale 2015.*

So Margaret must have already been ill when this picture had been drawn. And had died sometime soon after.

But it gave me something to work on. No one, Steven included, seemed to want to talk about Margaret and I did not know her family. Not even her surname. I was beginning to realize just how patchy my knowledge was of my predecessor. Maybe this Eleri artist would remember something about her subject. I looked at it again and thought this had been run off pretty quickly. She must do loads of these in a day throughout the summer season. The chances of her remembering this one particular woman were remote. But what else did I have? Steven's family weren't exactly welcoming or forthcoming. If anything, they seemed shocked, or appalled at us marrying, their manner bordering on hostile. Whether it was through loyalty to his dead first wife or simply a dislike of me, I couldn't work out. But they were never going to draw me into the bosom of their family; there would never be a close bond between us.

The next day was a Thursday and our grumpy pair of solicitors, Nash & Broughton, were moving out, saying they couldn't afford our extortionate prices. *As if,* I thought, taking in their expensive pinstriped suits and brogue shoes. I noticed they did none of the carrying themselves but had hired a pair of tattooed jerks. Nash & Broughton directed proceedings from their cars, bollocking the guys when they dropped a couple of files.

I was glad when they'd gone but it was too late now to track down Eleri.

I'd run a search on her: 'Eleri' plus 'Artist' plus 'Southwest Wales' and had seen some of her work. Not outstanding, though she was good with her sketches of eyes which seemed her particular talent. They were good. I looked at lots – large and blue, big and dark, small, mean, piggy eyes on a couple of girls who, in spite of their giggling faces, looked set up for a hard life. Not like me, I laughed inwardly, and then wondered who was laughing at whom?

But the last entry on Eleri's website was two years ago and there was no way of contacting her except . . .

I rang The Lobster Pot again and connected with Gwen who, if anything, seemed even more irritated by this call. I had to remind her again who I was and initially her response was guarded. But she unwound when I mentioned the name.

'Eleri? Oh, yes. I remember her. Art student she was. Lovely girl. Earned some money through the summer doing sketches of the tourists. Mind you . . .' her voice was confiding now, '. . . I didn't think they were that good. A bit rough round the edges, if you know what I mean. But she could knock 'em out in ten, twenty minutes. Quite lucrative.'

'How much did she charge?'

'Ten pounds, I think.' She chuckled. 'Spent it all in here. Could drink most of the men under the table.'

'What university was she at?'

'Swansea.'

'Was she from there?'

'I don't really know, Jennifer. I can't remember. Maybe – though I have a feeling it was further East. Cardiff?'

Even though she wouldn't see it, I shrugged. Who knew?

'Why do you ask?'

Again, I didn't have an answer ready. 'Oh – I have one of her pictures here. I was just interested.'

'Of Steven's wife?'

I bristled at the word yet again. *I* was Steven's wife.

'Can you remember her surname?'

'It won't help you track her down, love.' Gwen was really laughing now. 'It was Jones. Eleri Jones.'

She was right. Every other person in Wales is called Jones.

'Do you know what happened to her? Where she is now?'

'Not a clue, although Emrys might know.'

Who the fuck was Emrys?

'They had a bit of a thing going on.'

'Do you have a number for Emrys?'

'Hang on a minute . . .'

I suddenly realized that Eleri was important. She had actually sketched the invisible woman, the woman whom the landlord of the local pub had never seen. Margaret had stayed out of view the entire time they had holidayed in Dale. Steven had spent evenings drinking at The Lobster Pot but alone; Colin, supposedly Steven's best friend, had never seen her either, and neither had Kara, his wife. Gwen came back on the line and gave me a mobile number. 'Try this,' she said, kinder now. 'He's a local lad. Does a bit of fishing.'

I thanked her then sent a text to Emrys that I was trying to get in touch with Eleri and wondered if he had contact details for her. I saw by the double tick that it had gone through. So now all I could do was wait.

Of course, I did have one other option.

FORTY-TWO

A week later I still hadn't done it. I'd stood outside, even taken the skeleton key from the drawer. I hid it in my bag and hoped she wouldn't miss it. And yet if I had come clean and confided in her, I knew she'd have helped me out as she had before. But it would mean siding with her against my husband. She'd even quizzed me one day. 'Is anything wrong, Spinning Jenny?'

I was instantly defensive. 'What do you mean?'

'I don't know . . .' She was chewing gum slowly, thoughtfully. 'It's just you don't seem quite yourself.' She draped an arm around me. 'Married life not suiting you, darling?'

I got close to confiding in her then, telling her how Steven's eyes these days were clouded in suspicion, that he watched me in a way that made my skin crawl with a thousand ants, that his strange lovemaking combined with the name of our house made me afraid, apprehensive, as though something was about to happen. As something had happened to Margaret. I didn't believe for a minute she'd died of cancer. And where was she buried? Where was her headstone? Where was her death registered? I felt doubt rising to a crescendo, but to what end I didn't know except I feared it.

I had always considered myself a brave person, not frightened of ghosts or ghouls, of imaginary witches and spells. Not even of spiders or snakes. My fears had always been of real things, of being assaulted on the street when the street was my home, of blows from Scary I, of being tied up in a confined space by Scary II. I had faced up to poverty and prejudice, had been hungry, friendless and homeless. The life I had now with a peaceful, kind, decent man to whom I was married would, at one time, have been my Shangri-La. And yet it frightened me more than all those perceived terrors mixed together into a paste and smeared across my face.

'I'm all right, Scarlet,' I said. 'Just getting used to my married state.'

But Scarlet was perceptive. She'd been on the sharp end of life for most of her days, also the victim of prejudice and blind hostility. And she, too, had found someone decent in Andy. There was no pulling the wool over her eyes. She took the gum out of her mouth and chucked it in the bin then came back, put her hands on my shoulders, facing me and shaking her head slowly. 'It's more than that, Jenny. You look . . .' She spent some time searching for the word, coming up with one that was very appropriate. 'Haunted.'

I was on the verge of confiding in her then. I so wanted someone to be able to unravel the knots inside me.

'You've lost weight,' she said. 'Something *is* worrying you, isn't it?'

I would have told her but wraiths are hard to describe, too insubstantial to see properly. They have no form or solid colour to hang a description on. I opened my mouth to try.

And then my phone rang and it was a number I did not recognize.

'Hello, is that Jennifer Taverner?' The lilt was unmistakable.

'Yes.'

'It's Emrys. You rang about Eleri.' He laughed. He was finding something funny. 'I do have some contact details for her but if you're wanting her to paint your portrait she doesn't really do that any more. She's based in London in the head office of one of the big markets.' He was still laughing. 'HR, would you believe.'

'You have a number for her?'

Scarlet was *still* watching me, her eyes narrowed and suspicious as Steven's had become. When had I begun to provoke such mistrust? Even asking myself the question made me sad because the answer was, since I had hooked up with Steven. That had been when the seeds of doubt had been sown all around me. And everything that had happened had fed and watered them.

Emrys was still speaking. 'Just a mobile. I don't see much of her these days. Bit of a high-flyer. Got herself a flat in London. Who'd have thought it?'

There was only one response to this. 'Indeed.'

'I'll text her number through to you.'

I thanked him and ended the call.

The ping of a message arrived soon after and now I had the number of one of the few people – apart from Steven – who had not only seen Margaret but had drawn her. Surely as an artist she would have noted her manner, her attitude, be able to describe her persona. Perhaps confirm the fact that her subject had been terminally ill. It was a long shot but worth the effort.

Scarlet was still watching me but I knew the time for confiding in her had passed.

After a few minutes fussing around the office she left, muttering something about getting food in for the weekend.

The weekend. These days, I dreaded them. Forty-eight hours in his company, skirting round the suspicion, evading direct questions, trying to squeeze solid facts from his sketchy responses to any of my direct questions. I was tiptoeing across an ice floe that could melt or drift or sink at any time and I had no authority over its direction. I could spend my weekends cleaning up an already tidy bungalow which needed redecorating. Perhaps if we had cleared rooms and ordered colour charts, got stuck into a shared project, the tension might have eased. But Steven seemed reluctant to change anything in the bungalow. He had got into the habit of watching me, from doorways or sitting in a chair, saying nothing, his eyes following every movement. Sometimes he made a comment. 'Why are you . . .?' or 'Do you really need to do that?' Apart from that our conversation was desultory.

When I turned into the drive and saw his car already parked, that hand reached in again to my chest cavity and found my heart. When he opened the door to me, when we sat, eating a meal and the kitchen fell silent, that silence itself felt threatening. What were his thoughts? I didn't know but at some point I would.

In the evenings we tended to eat in, me practising my rudimentary cookery skills with cottage pie or chops, or we went to The

Traveller's Rest or The Plough for something to eat. But I was finding the atmosphere at home increasingly unreal. I was waiting for the storm to break and, as we welcome a dreaded event, I simply wanted it to be over.

At last it was Monday and, after the usual cluster of customers had come and gone, there was a lull at lunchtime. I locked the door and tried the number I had for Eleri, expecting to connect with an answerphone. But instead I had a bright, chirpy voice with a marked Welsh accent. 'Hello?'

'Hi. You don't know me but I have one of your sketches.'

'Oh?'

'One of the ones you must have done in Dale three years ago.'

'Ri–ight?' She was bemused and I didn't blame her.

'You see,' I grabbed at a lie, 'she was my sister.'

'Was?'

'Yes. I'm afraid she died . . . not that long after you drew her portrait.' I added, 'Actually.'

There was a pause. 'So, what do you want from me?'

'I just wondered what you remembered of her.'

She laughed then apologized. 'I'm sorry, but I did hundreds of these portraits. Kept me going right through the summer. I'm almost certain I won't remember a thing about her.'

'Please.'

'We–ell. Tell you what. You send me a picture of this drawing and I'll see if I do. But don't hold your breath, love. I'm sorry about your sister but I do so many . . .'

I already had a picture on my phone. I forwarded it to her.

And then I locked the office and went to D5. I was sick of questions with no answers, sick of evading everything. From now on I was going to head into the wind. And if the storm broke I would ride it out, I hoped.

FORTY-THREE

Neatness would always be something I would associate with Steven. Neatness and order. That and his eyes, which I had noticed from the beginning.

There they stood, the three boxes, one on top of each other, perfectly square, and the suitcase, standing by their side. The scent of Light Blue was beginning to fade. I sniffed the air, pursuing it, but it was elusive now, having been strong when he had first placed them in here. It was dingy inside, the only light source beaming in from the corridor. The top box was half empty. I was already wearing most of the clothes. All had their labels still attached. It was the same with the second and third box. Good quality, brand-new clothes. I turned my attention to the suitcase. And there I was frustrated. It was a medium-sized case in brown canvas and it was locked. I picked it up and this time knew it was not full of clothes because when I shook it, it rattled.

Well, at least it wasn't body parts, I thought, putting it back. But neither was it full of clothes.

So what was in it?

I didn't dare force the lock. But I hadn't noticed a key to it either. Not on Steven's bunch of keys – house, car, office – or so far anywhere in the house. The keys to suitcases tend to be small, light, flimsy. I stood back. Whatever the answer was, this suitcase held a clue.

I returned to the office and my phone which registered a missed call from a number I didn't recognize. I redialled the number. And got through to Eleri's bubbly voice.

'Well, it's a bit of a coincidence, see. I've been thinking about it. I do remember the picture, see, but I don't remember much about the lady.'

Someone else who didn't remember Margaret?

'So what *do* you remember?'

'As far as I can work out, it was one of the pictures that the customer . . .' she spoke the word with a tinge of sarcasm, '. . . wasn't satisfied with. Said it didn't look like her at all and she didn't want it. It did happen every now and again. The customer refused to pay. In which case I would have thrown it away.' A little tinkle of a laugh followed. 'I mean, what would I want with a picture of someone I don't even know?'

The balloon of hope was slowly deflating. 'So you don't remember her?'

'Sorry, apart from someone who had a strop on her – no.'

'And what did you do with the finished portrait?'

She laughed again. 'That's a nice way of describing it. I would have chucked it in the bin.'

'And then what?'

'Who knows? I don't know how you got it. She must have fished it out. Maybe she didn't hate it as much as she said or else she just didn't want to pay for it. I don't know how you got hold of it or why you want to follow this up?'

Because. Because it hangs on my sitting-room wall. I face it every evening and it is the only portrait of this invisible wife. My predecessor. My husband's dead spouse. Or so I thought. Now it appears it might not even be that. He could have simply plucked it from a bin.

'I'm sorry I can't be of more help.' She hesitated. 'I really am.'

There was nothing but to thank her.

Another blind alley. More unanswered questions.

This elusive Margaret was beginning to annoy me. I wasn't frightened or jealous of her any more. She was simply annoying.

When I went home late that afternoon, the drive was empty, which gave me an opportunity to search for the key to the suitcase. Nothing. But I did come across our wedding certificate and checked it again. There was no doubt about it. Steven was listed as a bachelor.

I was beginning to wonder now whether Margaret had ever existed.

I decided to try and speak again to Francine. She hadn't exactly been helpful before, but I was wary about approaching Steven's parents. His father in particular had seemed old and I worried about springing something on him which might prove stressful. Whatever the truth was about Margaret, I decided it would be kinder and less traumatic to speak to Francine.

I still had her number.

Maybe she'd forgotten me; initially she was vague when I asked if we could meet up. She still seemed confused at my name. 'Steven's wife,' I reminded her.

And then she remembered. And with her recovered memory came hostility. 'Jennifer,' she said firmly, 'I don't know what you want from me.'

'Just tell me about Margaret.'

'Nothing to tell,' she said far too quickly. Then, 'What do you want to know?'

'On our wedding certificate,' I said slowly, 'Steven is described as a bachelor.'

Silence.

'Was he married to Margaret?'

'What is he saying?' She too was skirting around the subject.

'I haven't asked him directly.'

A pause then. 'Why not?' This time her voice was softer.

'I suppose I think . . .' I was choosing my words very, very carefully. 'I think it might upset him.'

'I think it would.'

But I knew what game she was playing. She was trying to brush my curiosity under the carpet. Using her brother's . . . *frailty* was the word that popped into my mind. I knew then I was coming close to the true story. And if Francine wouldn't provide it, I would speak to his parents. But I didn't use this as a threat.

'Jennifer,' she said, some sympathy softening her voice. 'If I were you, I would let sleeping dogs lie.'

So that was what Margaret was reduced to. *A sleeping dog.*

Was that what I was supposed to do? Let a sleeping dog lie?

I would get nothing from her. Which left me no choice.

The next day I confided in Scarlet. 'I think there was something about Steven's first marriage that was unusual.'

'Right.'

This was something I loved about her. She didn't question me or challenge my statement. She didn't suggest I might be imagining something, or try to divert me by suggesting that when a woman marries a widower, strange questions invariably emerge.

All she said was, 'So what are you going to do about it, Spinning Jenny?'

'I'm going to speak to his parents.'

She lifted one eyebrow (quite a skill!) and that was her way of saying, *Really?*

This was something else I loved about Scarlet. She didn't wrap an opinion in flowery words, disguise advice. And yet her friendship was as stout as Minnie Ha-Ha's. In return I could be honest with her.

'You think that's the best way forward?'

'Yes,' I said.

But she didn't smile. 'Jenny,' she said, 'Spinning Jenny, why don't you ask Steven?'

And this was a question I didn't even dare ask myself. All I imagined were half-formed, embryonic responses which I knew would upset his equilibrium. And something deep inside me was worried about doing this.

To Scarlet, I simply shook my head slowly but quite firmly, 'No.'

She put a hand on my arm. 'Have you any reason to be worried about asking him?'

'No,' I said again but less firmly. For authenticity, I added, 'I just think it will upset him.'

How could I tell her the truth – that it would be a step into a dark and secret place where nothing was defined? All were strange shapes. And that is our primordial fear, the one that dwarfs all the others. A step into the unknown. Off the edge.

'Tomorrow,' I said. 'I'll go tomorrow.'

'Keep your phone on.'

'I won't be in any danger.'

'Let me know how you get on.'

I hugged her then. She was mother, friend, employer and more. One of the few people who had always been kind to me and never let me down.

'I'll do that,' I promised.

That evening was one of our quiet ones. I heated a pizza and chopped up some salad. While we ate I was aware of Steven watching me. He reached out and touched my hand, smiling. And I felt glad. 'You float away from me sometimes.'

He raised his eyes. 'What do you mean?'

'I mean that you seem distant, as though you're somewhere else. Thinking of some*thing* else.'

I looked into his eyes. I had always thought them pretty, brown with their gold flecks that looked as though the irises were peppered with gold leaf. And behind them I recognized something I hadn't noted before. A sort of bewilderment, a little like the inmates of The Stephanie Wright Care Home.

I stared at them until he smiled. 'Didn't your mother ever tell you it's rude to stare?' He sounded almost childlike.

I shook my head. 'I don't think she ever did.'

He smiled then. 'Sorry, Jennifer. I'm so sorry.'

I felt a real tenderness for him then. He seemed vulnerable. 'For what?' There was something in his tone that I couldn't identify.

He shook his head, apparently confused, while I waited. Was he about to confide in me? Maybe I wouldn't need to go to his parents. He would tell me. Tonight. I waited.

And waited.

And Steven ate his salad.

The next morning I returned to the tired house in Macclesfield.

FORTY-FOUR

T his time I didn't need to introduce myself. Steven's father opened the door with a snort of tired resignation. 'I thought you'd be back,' he said, his shoulders drooping. And when he led me into the lounge, his wife didn't call out to ask who it was.

They'd both known I would return.

I began by being polite. 'I'm sorry to trouble you. Again.'

They sat on the sofa, clinging on to one another as tightly as they would to a life raft, looking at each other in that way long-married couples do, exchanging thoughts, ideas, emotions, hardly blinking, without speaking a single word. Steven's father's shoulders sagged and he gave a sigh. It sounded like the wind sighing through a badly fitting window. And it was at the same time a sigh of resignation. He started with a weak defence.

'We didn't know anything about your getting married.'

I didn't bother with any preamble. 'Tell me about Margaret.'

Neither seemed to know what to say but looked at each other for their cue.

Then Diana Taverner spoke, her voice quiet and dignified. 'How much do you know, Jennifer?'

I shrugged.

'How much do you want to know?'

'Does she even exist?'

'She did.' Diana still spoke in that calm, tightly controlled voice. While Steven's father dropped his head to let his wife continue.

'When Steven was about fourteen, he had a girlfriend called Margaret.'

I could have interrupted, demanded they tell me the whole truth immediately, but I felt that this was a story they should unravel at an unhurried pace if I was to learn every small detail.

'He was obsessed with her.'

'In love,' her husband inserted.

Diana looked at him, shaking her head. 'It was more than that. For a while they . . .' She smiled and I could see that Steven's mother must once have been a very pretty girl. 'I think the Americans would say they "hung out" together.'

She swallowed and her mouth became tight and unhappy looking. She leaned forward, speaking harshly. 'His bedroom was papered with photographs of her. He'd follow her around, always with his camera, snapping away. The pictures . . .' she swallowed, '. . . even papered the ceiling.' She looked at her husband and nodded. Scott took up the narrative. 'The girl complained,' he said. 'This was in the nineties and there wasn't really a charge of stalking.'

'But she did go to the police,' Diana continued. 'They came round and had a word with Steven said he could be charged with harassment. I didn't dare let them see his bedroom. We kept them to the sitting room.' She looked around as though she could still see the ghosts of them, as could I – burly policemen speaking to a shrunken, timid teenager. I could see Steven as he would have been then. There were still traces of a frightened teenager.

Diana's smile went. 'Needless to say, she moved on. Wanted nothing to do with Steven. She found another boyfriend and Steven became increasingly morose. He kept to his bedroom with all those pictures of her, laughing, pursing her lips. Margaret dressed for going out in the evening. Some of them had been cut. You could still see her new boyfriend's arm or hand. Or another friend. Then he started to say that, when he was at school, she was talking about him with his friends. Laughing at him.'

'Not surprising. Teenage girl breaks up with boyfriend. Of course she'd gossip about him. We didn't attach too much importance to it.'

Her husband continued the story. 'But then he started saying things that couldn't be true. That she'd been trying to ring him but was prevented by her parents, her sister, her new boyfriend. He said they'd tied her up and threatened to kill her if she so much as looked in his direction. Then he started saying that she was watching him through his bedroom window. He wouldn't open his bedroom curtains. He didn't go to school even though he was bright and tipped for university. Then he started asking me to taste his food because she would try to poison him. He said she'd sent a balloon up in the sky and he tried to stop us leaving the house because he said the balloon would burst and it was filled with toxic gas. If we so much as took one step outside the door, we would die.' He covered his face with his hands. 'We knew then that something was very wrong.'

Diana met my eyes, perhaps searching for sympathy, understanding, but I was too shocked.

'When he took up the carpet in his bedroom to look under the floorboards for the bugs she'd put there, we realized things had gone too far. We took him to the GP who arranged for him to be seen by a psychiatrist – urgently. He was diagnosed with acute paranoid schizophrenia and hospitalized for a brief period while they steadied him up with medication. And then they discharged him.'

'So what happened to . . .?' I wanted the end of the story.

'He followed her one day and when she challenged him he strangled her. They were both sixteen years old.'

I'd known this was coming, seen it striding towards me, with heavy stamping steps in black jackboots. But it was still a shock.

'He was admitted to a secure mental institution.'

'They told us there was no cure, but this was a condition which could be safely managed with medication.'

'Which reassured us,' Diana said.

Her husband looked at her with pity. 'To some extent,' he said carefully, the words spoken with slow clarity.

I was truly alarmed now. 'What do you mean?'

'When they discharged him under license he went to college. He was very bright. We thought things had settled down. He was taking his medication regularly, seeing the psychiatrist. But he came home one day and said he and Margaret were engaged.'

They looked at one another, sharing this moment they must have dreaded. 'Maybe we handled it all wrong, but the psychiatrist had advised us that it was better not to flatly contradict his statements but to acquiesce.'

'And that's what we did. We kept quiet and acquiesced. Steven did well in his exams and went to university, got a good job with the council. He led a normal life,' she insisted.

They were both looking at me now for affirmation.

'He was buying clothes for her.'

They were quick to deny. 'We didn't know.'

'He found a discarded picture that he convinced himself was of her. He had it framed. It hangs on our sitting-room wall.'

'The psychiatrist said,' Scott Taverner affirmed stoutly, 'that he is capable of a perfectly normal existence. That his mental state had been exacerbated due to an abandonment issue. He's fine . . .'

His wife finished the sentence. 'Provided he takes his medication regularly.'

'You were happy for him to leave home?'

'He seemed to be doing so well.'

'We didn't know he'd married,' Scott said again.

'What would you have done if you had known?'

'Perhaps . . .' Diana's voice was weak now, '. . . maybe . . . warned you?'

Both were watching me now, the same question on all our lips. *What would I have done?*

Something inside me was laughing hysterically. My quiet husband was right up there with Scary I, Scary II, the wanker, the cheat, the married man, and the man so mean I don't think he paid for a drink in the months we had been going out. I'd been too blind to realize. I'd air-brushed all the stories, all the signs of strangeness. Because I had wanted my dream so much I had tried to push them away. So now I had Steven right up there in the pound seats.

Steven who murdered a girl, Steven who was a paranoid schizophrenic.

'He isn't dangerous.'

'Provided he takes his medication.'

I stood up. 'Can you give me the contact details for his psychiatrist?'

'Of course.' Diana left the room, moving quickly, anxious for me to have what I wanted and go.

She returned with a photocopy of a letter with the local hospital heading and, underneath, Steven's name.

'So he didn't go to prison after he'd killed Margaret?'

Both shook their heads vigorously. 'He was admitted to a secure psychiatric unit. They stabilized his condition. And then he came home.'

When I stood up I felt a little dizzy, as though I'd drunk too much wine. It was too much to take in. Margaret was dead, he'd killed her. They never were married. The sketch was of some unknown woman, the picture discarded because its subject hadn't liked her portrayal. Nothing was as it seemed. Even the rings on my fingers. They never had been hers. One thing was for sure – they were not to blame. Except . . .

They hadn't kept an eye on their son. We'd been married for only a couple of months and already things were falling apart.

'You don't see much of him?'

'He rings us, sometimes, from work. He's sounded good.'

'Happy,' her husband finished. 'We believed he had achieved some stability in life.'

'Which turns out to be you.'

I had a lot to think about. But . . . I sat down again. 'There's something you're not telling me.'

That challenge hit them hard. They clutched at each other again. Diana seemed to shrink. It was Scott who, bravely, spoke. 'We didn't give you all the details.'

Diana found her voice. 'We wanted to spare you this.'

Back to her husband. 'He murdered Margaret in her own home. Followed her after school. Her parents were both at work so the house was empty. The police found him in bed with her, trying to . . .' He couldn't go on. He didn't need to. I could fill in the detail.

I left then in a daze. It wasn't until I was halfway home that I realized something. I hadn't asked them to keep my visit a secret.

What if they told him they had met his bride? Congratulated him on his marriage?

FORTY-FIVE

I was dazed all the way home. Dazed, and worried too. My husband was a killer. All right, it wasn't that he was a psychopath or evil. Nothing deliberate. He was sick. And now he was on medication. So there was nothing to worry about, was there?'

I ordered myself to tough this one out.

He was fine, I told myself. His parents weren't worried. And then I remembered the note of shock in Francine's voice and my thought altered to, *I don't suppose Margaret was worried either, by the strange behaviour of her 'ex-boyfriend'*. Not until he put his hands round her neck. Maybe not even then. She might have laughed it off.

Until . . .

As the bus pulled into Leek, my thoughts focused on my changing attitude towards Margaret. Initially it had been curiosity which had quickly morphed into jealousy. After we were married and I'd moved into Yr Arch, I had felt haunted by her. Now I realized she'd never even been there. He'd bought the house long after her murder. For some time, I'd believed that Steven was trying to turn me into her. Now that was the thought that chilled me. She was dead. How far would he go in his desire to recreate her?

I wondered where she was buried, whether he visited her grave. And where exactly I fitted in to all this? What was my role? What would happen to me? Was I frightened of him? My gentle, quiet, kind husband? And then I remembered the sound the suitcase had made when I shook it. I knew what rattled inside. And his parents' words. They stabilized him on medication. But what if he didn't take it? What then?

It was just past lunchtime, almost two o'clock. Still hours before my usual home time. Instead of waiting for a bus to take me from Leek into Stanley, I decided to walk. I needed fresh air and time to think. I used the country lanes instead of scrambling over the grass verge which lined the main A53. While the countryside walk steadied my nerves, I managed to convince myself that all would be well. If I could just persuade Steven that he needed to stay on his medication, it would be OK.

Until I turned into the edge of the village and stopped. My heart was pounding as each step took me nearer. I reached the bottom of the drive and felt sick. His car was there, parked neatly as usual. I walked slowly up the drive, my steps dragging, my feet heavier and heavier with each step, hardly lifting from the floor. And then I realized why. He was standing in the doorway, watching me, waiting for me to reach him. He didn't say anything but I could see suspicion in his eyes. Uncertainty.

Abandonment issues . . .

The closer I drew, the more I could read in his eyes. Doubt, unhappiness, suspicion. Oh God, I thought. I so wanted things to be normal.

'Jennifer?' Even his voice seemed different. He seemed vulnerable. 'Where have you been?'

I sucked in a deep breath. Where would I begin? How could I explain? Should I explain? Or lie?

'I went to see your parents.'

He half closed his eyes, his lids drooping. 'I know,' he said. 'They congratulated me.'

I couldn't find the right response.

Still keeping his eyes on me, he stood back to let me enter, and I did.

FORTY-SIX

Now I had the backstory, I could read his emotions, his state of mind, his suspicions.

'Why?' he repeated.

'Because I was curious.'

'About what?' His voice was velvet smooth, controlled, and all the more dangerous for that. He was not a madman uncontrolled. This was Steven, at his most restrained. And he seemed a stranger.

'Margaret.'

'You wanted to know about Margaret?'

I could have interpreted his voice as simply curious, but there was a warning in the silky tone. 'Why go to my parents, Jennifer? Why didn't you simply *ask* me?'

I had the answers up my sleeve but checked them before they tumbled out.

Because you refused to talk about her. I had to learn the truth inch by inch.

Where to start?

We were in the sitting room, the picture staring down at us. I glanced up at it. 'This isn't even her,' I said, angry now at his deception.

'You . . .' I didn't dare say it. His face was calm but confused. Maybe I'd been trying to get him to face up to the fantasy too quickly. It was a step too far.

'She had another boyfriend, you know.' He was confiding in me. 'I saw them together. I watched them and I waited. I knew that I would separate them . . .' He was quiet for a moment, then, 'Jennifer,' he said, his face pleading with me, 'you won't ever leave me, will you?'

'I . . .'

I wanted a return to normality. To get back to where we had been. I wished I hadn't been to see his parents. I wished I didn't know.

I wanted to ask him about his medication – whether he'd been taking it or hoarding it in a suitcase and stashing it in D5. But I sensed it was the wrong moment.

'Let's just have a cup of tea.'

He followed me into the kitchen. He was behind me and his nearness unnerved me.

'What did they tell you?'

'That you need to take some medication. Have you been taking it?'

His eyes were troubled. 'They don't understand,' he said, his voice steady. 'I don't always need it. Sometimes Margaret suggests I leave it off.'

I didn't know what to say, how to handle this. No one had taught me the right way to approach this situation, what words to use, what phrases to avoid. I didn't know.

'I can see things more clearly without the tablets.' He was speaking slowly, his words deliberate and laboured. He was trying to convince me.

And I tried my best. 'What things, Steven?'

'I need to know who is on my side,' he said, 'and who is against me.'

I didn't like the way he was looking at me. 'I am on your side.'

'Not always.' And then he did that thing, that tilting of his head, listening to something – or someone. And now I knew who it was. Particularly when he turned his head a little further, smiling. 'I think you're right.' He was not talking to me.

The feeling overwhelmed me. I had to get away. The back door was behind me, locked and bolted. I fumbled for the key and turned it. I broke eye contact to look down. The bottom bolt was open. I turned around, shot back the top bolt and was outside, the steps in front of me. But however quick I was, Steven was just as quick.

'Steven,' I appealed, and heard terror in my voice. Our biggest fear is of the unknown and this was an adversary I could not understand.

Steven was slightly built but I felt menaced by him and afraid. 'Steven,' I appealed again, trying to find the real him. He was shaking his head.

'Oh, Jennifer,' he said, 'you were going to leave me.'

I shook my head.

He was too close, his hands outstretched towards my neck. I was cornered. Margaret was suddenly close. In that moment, I knew exactly how she'd felt, but I wasn't going to suffer the same fate. We were balanced at the top of the steps. I pushed him.

And heard his head crack on the paving slabs.

My hopes, desires, aspirations. I watched them bleed away.

Drip, drip, drip.

FORTY-SEVEN

They told me he took over an hour to die. Did I stand there, watching the pool of blood expand, drip down the step, slowly oozing? They told me that, had I rung for an ambulance straight away, they might have saved him.

It was this delay which they used against me in court, that I stood and watched my husband who had a previous psychiatric diagnosis die. That was why they charged me with manslaughter.

The pathologist said in court that Steven was thin-skulled. At which point I'd laughed. I'd heard of thin-skinned. But not thin-skulled. And this counted against me too.

My council mounted a vigorous defence, that I had feared for my life, that my husband's unstable mental condition had resulted in a young woman's death, but I heard the verdict. Guilty of manslaughter. I saw the judge's face, sympathetic towards the husband I had callously watch die, yet nothing for me, the woman who would have been his second victim. And the jury's too, disgusted at my treatment of a sick man. But the one face I remember, together with the reproach, was Miss McCormick, who was watching from the gallery. She'd spoken the words years before but they applied just as well today.

'I had hoped for so much better from you.'

Me too, Miss McCormick. Me too.

And so. 'For the court, would you please state your name.'